**Praise for John Gilstrap
and His Thrillers**

BLUE FIRE

"Engrossing. . . . Fans of doomsday military thrillers
will delight in the resilience of Gilstrap's family of
preppers and their quest for survival on their terms.
Readers will eagerly await the next installment."
—*Publishers Weekly*

"A John Gilstrap thriller, crammed with violence and
testing of the soul, might be the perfect work of fiction
to sink into in a tough time for the real world."
—*New York Journal of Books*

CRIMSON PHOENIX

"A nonstop roller coaster of suspense! *Crimson Phoenix*
ticks every box for big-book thrillerdom."
—**Jeffery Deaver**

"Don't miss this powerful new series from a master
thriller writer."
—**Jamie Freveletti**

"A single mother's smart, fierce determination to protect
her sons turns this vivid day-after-tomorrow scenario
into a gripping page-turner."
—**Taylor Stevens**

"*Crimson Phoenix* snaps with action from the very first
page. It's certain to hit the 10-ring with old and new
readers alike."
—**Marc Cameron**

"John Gilstrap is one of the finest thriller writers on the planet. *No Mercy* showcases his work at its finest—taut, action-packed, and impossible to put down!"
—**Tess Gerritsen**

"A great hero, a pulse-pounding story—and the launch of a really exciting series."
—**Joseph Finder**

"An entertaining, fast-paced tale of violence and revenge."
—***Publishers Weekly***

"No other writer is better able to combine in a single novel both rocket-paced suspense and heartfelt looks at family and the human spirit. And what a pleasure to meet Jonathan Grave, a hero for our time . . . and for all time."
—**Jeffery Deaver**

AT ALL COSTS
"Riveting . . . combines a great plot and realistic, likable characters with look-over-your-shoulder tension. A page-turner."
—***Kansas City Star***

"Gilstrap builds tension . . . until the last page, a hallmark of great thriller writers. I almost called the paramedics before I finished *At All Costs*."
—***Tulsa World***

"Gilstrap has ingeniously twisted his simple premise six ways from Sunday."
—***Kirkus Reviews***

"Not-to-be-missed."
—*Rocky Mountain News*

NATHAN'S RUN

"Gilstrap pushes every thriller button . . . a nail-biting denouement and strong characters."
—*San Francisco Chronicle*

"Gilstrap has a shot at being the next John Grisham . . . one of the best books of the year."
—*Rocky Mountain News*

"Emotionally charged . . . one of the year's best."
—*Chicago Tribune*

"Brilliantly calculated. . . . With the skill of a veteran pulp master, Gilstrap weaves a yarn that demands to be read in one sitting."
—*Publishers Weekly* (starred review)

"Like a roller coaster, the story races along on well-oiled wheels to an undeniably pulse-pounding conclusion."
—*Kirkus Reviews* (starred review)

Published by Kensington Publishing Corp.

WHITE SMOKE

JOHN GILSTRAP

PINNACLE BOOKS
Kensington Publishing Corp.
www.kensingtonbooks.com

For Joy

CHAPTER ONE

VICTORIA EMERSON HOPED THAT HER SURPRISE DIDN'T show as Althea Mountbank entered Maggie's Place and approached. "This a good time?" Althea asked.

Victoria rose from her chair and the square table that served as her desk in what used to be the dining room of Maggie's Place, a tavern that had been converted to an ersatz town hall in the aftermath of the eight-hour nuclear war that changed everything.

"Now is fine," Victoria said. From the name alone, she had not been expecting someone quite so young and attractive. "Please, have a seat."

Althea chose to sit at Victoria's nine o'clock, rather than taking the seat that would have placed her back to the door. Victoria noted it, but from the young lady's demeanor, she was not concerned.

"Mr. Barnett told me to come in and talk to you."

"I know," Victoria said. "Ben told me to expect you."

"Are you, like, the mayor or something?" Althea asked.

"Not the mayor, no. Nobody elected me to anything, but somehow, every time the music stops, I'm the only one willing to take the chair." Victoria shifted in her seat and crossed her legs. "Tell me something about yourself."

Althea started to lean back into her chair but abandoned the effort halfway. She looked nervous, and Victoria wanted to know why. "What would you like to know?"

"Anything," Victoria said. "As we try to rebuild something that will look something like a real society, and more people flood into Ortho, I think it's important that we all get to know each other. We don't have to become besties, but there's a lot of fear and loneliness out there. Start with where you're from and what you did before the war."

Althea cleared her throat and shifted again. "I'm from up near Appleton," she said. "I was a music teacher. Which is why I'm here."

"Did you come to Ortho alone? Do you have family?"

Althea cast her eyes down. "No children. My husband was killed in the days after the war."

"May I ask what happened to him?"

"It was the gangs," Althea said. "In the weeks right after the war, during the panic, it seemed that everybody was shooting everybody else."

Victoria waited for more.

Althea grew uncomfortable. "That's it."

"Tell me the circumstances surrounding your husband's death."

"Circumstances?"

Victoria hiked her shoulders and held out her hands. "How did it happen? Was he trying to defend you? The house?"

Althea's gaze shifted to the floor.

Victoria pressed harder. "Or was he maybe threatening someone else who defended *themselves*?"

"We were hungry," Althea said.

"Everybody was hungry," Victoria said. "Did he kill?"

Althea's head snapped up and her eyes were hot. "What difference does that make? He's dead himself now."

"Where were you when he was killed? Were you with him?"

Althea lost some of her attitude. "I tried to stop him."

"What was your husband's name?" Victoria asked.

"Jamie. He was a good man, I swear he was."

"How many people did Jamie kill?"

Althea shook her head aggressively. "No one. I swear."

"Okay, then how many people did he threaten?"

The eye contact disconnected again. "He was just trying to provide for his family."

"By stealing from other families." Victoria took a deep, noisy breath. "Look at me, Althea."

The young teacher rocked her gaze up to meet Victoria's.

"We can't allow that." Victoria kept her tone even. "You need to understand that here in Ortho, we expect people to earn what they have."

"That's what I want to do."

"Here in Ortho," Victoria continued, as if she hadn't been interrupted, "we punish thieves severely. You can tell a thief from the rest of the community by the *T* that's been carved in their foreheads. Men, women, children, it doesn't matter. You need to understand that."

"But I didn't steal anything," Althea said.

"I don't care about the past, Althea. But I do care about the future. I'm sure you noticed the burned structures down the street in Shanty Town?"

Althea nodded.

"Do you know who set those fires?"

"No."

"They came from up your way. From Appleton. They attacked Ortho." Victoria leaned into the table and made sure she had Althea's full attention when she said, "Every one of those attackers are dead. Those who survived the battle were tried and executed."

"But I've heard people call this place Eden," Althea said. She seemed genuinely confused.

"Perhaps it's because we still believe in justice here," Victoria explained. "Ben Barnett gave you your first week's rations and supplies, right?"

Althea bobbed her head. She seemed grateful to be talking about something else. "And he told me about the currency system here." In Ortho, ammunition doubled as money. It had inherent value—unlike the green pieces of paper that meant so much before Hell Day. "Thing is, I don't have a gun."

"Nor will you before you prove yourself to be trustworthy. What committee did you choose to participate in?"

"Education," Althea said. "That's why we're talking, as I understand it."

"That's one of the reasons," Victoria confirmed. "You want to teach music lessons as a means to support yourself."

"Exactly. Is that a problem?"

"Not as far as I'm concerned," Victoria said. "But I think you might want to think it through. Winter is marching straight at us. You'll have a tent for shelter until your cabin is built—and it will only be built with you as one of the construction workers. You've got provisions for a week. Maybe two if you don't mind being hungry, but after that, you're on your own."

"What are you suggesting?"

"I'm suggesting that in the short term, you might want to focus on the committees that the town will pay you to be a part of. Those include the construction committee and the security committee, but without a firearm, the security slot doesn't do much for you. Or for Ortho."

"I don't know anything about construction," Althea said.

"Most newcomers don't," Victoria said with a smile.

Althea seemed more confused than ever.

"You're going to have to get your hands dirty, Althea. You're going to have to perform physical labor before you can fulfill your entrepreneurial urges."

The young teacher wanted to say something, but it seemed that the words wouldn't come.

Victoria stood, ending the meeting. "Of course, you can always choose to move on down the road, leaving those provisions here, of course."

The front door opened, revealing the familiar silhouette of Joe McCrea, the Army major who had accompanied every second of Victoria's Hell Day nightmare. "Excuse me, Vicky," he said. "There's something you've got to attend to here." An M4 rifle hung from its sling across his chest. Pretty much everyone who was old enough to carry a weapon did so as a form of citizen militia—which had proven its worth more than once.

"We're finished here," Victoria said. She offered a handshake. "Welcome to Ortho."

Althea hesitated, then accepted the gesture.

"Remember everything we talked about," Victoria said. "On reflection in the coming hours and days, if there's any element of what you discussed with me that you wish to backtrack on or change, I invite you to do so." She tightened her grip just enough to make sure the young teacher was listening. "Just do it before I hear from others that you lied to me."

A bit of color drained from Althea's cheeks. "I—I didn't lie."

"Then you have nothing to worry about." Victoria let go of her hand and watched as she pressed past McCrea to walk back outside.

"What the hell was that?" McCrea asked.

"I'm seventy percent sure that she was part of the gangs in Appleton," Victoria said.

"And?"

"And I told her that the past was the past. That last part was a not-so-subtle warning that witnesses to her past are likely here." Victoria walked toward the door. "What's so urgent outside?"

"Stay where you are," McCrea said. "I'll bring him in."

Victoria didn't like these kinds of buildups to a surprise.

Thirty seconds later, McCrea returned with an emaciated young man in a tattered uniform that looked like a product from a war long in the past. "Vicky," McCrea said, "allow me to introduce you to Jerry Cameron."

Victoria wondered if this guy was going to live till morning. He looked awful. She offered her hand. "Pleased to meet you. And please sit down." She looked to McCrea, "Get him something to eat, please."

"On it already," McCrea said. "I asked Joey Abbott to get him some food and drink."

"I don't have time for a meal, ma'am," Cameron said. "You're Mrs. Emerson, right?"

"Victoria. Yes. Now sit. We're not talking until your butt is in a chair."

Cameron seemed annoyed, but he sat in the chair that Althea Mountbank had just vacated. "*Congresswoman* Victoria Emerson?"

"Not anymore. It's just Victoria now." She and McCrea both took chairs at the same table. "Vicky, if you prefer."

"Yes, ma'am, but you *were*—"

"Yes, what is this about?" Victoria had a bad feeling. A glance at McCrea's body language didn't make her feel any better.

"Okay, ma'am," the young man said. "Well, here's the thing." Then he seemed to get lost inside his head.

"Sometimes, it's easier if you just spit out the words," Victoria said with a soft smile.

"Yes, ma'am. As your friend said, my name is Jerry

Cameron. I used to work at the Annex. A bunker that was used to house—"

Victoria's gut tumbled. "I'm familiar with the Annex, Jerry. The Government Relocation Center." Located about forty miles east of Ortho, the Annex was an elaborate bunker complex built into the bedrock beneath the lavish vacation resort that called itself Hilltop Manor. It was to that very facility that Army Major Joseph McCrea and First Sergeant Paul Copley had been escorting Victoria on the night before Hell Day. She refused to enter, however, when the managers of the place—Cameron's coworkers, apparently— wouldn't allow her children to accompany her.

"Why do you look like you're going to have a heart attack?" Victoria asked. Even as the words left her throat, she knew she didn't want to hear the answer.

"Well, ma'am, here's the thing. The president of the United States and the leadership of the House and Senate have all been arrested and charged with treason. The president has asked me to find you and ask if you would preside over the trial."

The words consumed the oxygen out of the air. She understood their meaning, but the implications seemed impossible.

"Wait," she said. "What?"

"There was an uprising around the Annex. Around the whole hotel complex. A lot of people were killed."

Victoria asked, "So, were you with the security firm that oversaw the Annex?"

"Yes, ma'am. Solara. Most of us didn't make it. The civilians up there are furious that the government took care of itself but ignored the people. They're looking for blood."

Victoria tried to make the pieces fit in her head. "You said that the president was in custody?"

"Yes, ma'am."

"You're lying," she said. "The president is at a different facility. She would not be at the Annex."

Cameron looked hurt. "I'm not lying, ma'am." Then his face showed an *a-ha* moment. "Oh, I get it. I see the confusion. President Blanton and Vice President Jenkins were both killed in the attacks. The office slipped to the Speaker of the House."

"Penn Glendale?"

"Yes, ma'am." Cameron shrugged out of his backpack and reached into a side pocket. He extracted an envelope and handed it to Victoria. "The president asked me to give this to you. He asked for you personally."

McCrea spoke up. "Are you telling us that the government of the United States has been overthrown?"

The question seemed to startle the young man. "I guess so, yes. Roger Parsons has charged Mr. Glendale with treason. Like I said, they've charged everybody with treason."

"And Parsons is the leader of the uprising?" Victoria asked.

"Right."

"I'm confused," McCrea said. "You said that the president sent you, yet this Parsons guy is in charge?"

"Yes, sir. The president himself asked me. I don't think Parsons knows that he did it, though."

McCrea asked, "If the president is under arrest, how did he contact you? And how is he being held?"

"There are jail cells inside the Annex," Cameron explained. "The designers of the place anticipated people going a little stir crazy being cooped up for months. To my eye, some of them did, but Mr. Johnson never did anything about it. He was my boss before the uprising. He was also one of the first ones killed."

Victoria leaned into the conversation. "If Penn Glendale is in a jail cell, and you're not, how did he communicate with you?"

Cameron's shoulders sagged as he organized his thoughts. "It's like this," he said. "Parsons' gang is just that. They're pushy assholes who somehow found each other after the attacks and they bullied people into submission. He only feeds his cronies, and he leaves everyone else to fend for themselves."

"Are you avoiding my question?" McCrea pressed.

Anger flashed in Cameron's eyes. "I don't have a lot of time for bullshit questions," he said. "I'm not avoiding anything. I'm setting the scene for you. Arresting the president of the United States scares the shit out of people. You know what I mean? That's not something you can take back and say, *ah, I was just kidding*. Even some of the guards know that the ice is really thin for them. The president was able to talk one of them into letting me in to visit."

"How long have you been on the road?" Victoria asked. She wanted to cool the commentary down a little.

"Three days, ma'am. It was a long ride. A tough ride, too. It's brutal out there."

"Brutal how?" McCrea asked.

"Gangs. Warlords, really. Lots of suffering. Lots of awfulness. I think a lot of them work for Parsons somehow."

"How close to here?" Victoria asked. "To Ortho?"

"The awfulness? Quite a ways. Five, maybe seven miles."

"What are these gangs doing?" Victoria asked. "Are they organized? Are they on the march?"

Cameron considered the question. "Let's say sort of organized. There's one semi-permanent camp that I came through that's only a day outside Hilltop Manor. I think that one's run by a Parsons minion. I was never in Parsons' inner sanctum, so I don't know anything for sure, but my guess is that they're afraid of the people who come to Hilltop Manor."

"Afraid of what?" Victoria asked.

"The same thing as Tsar Nicholas should have been afraid of. People are not happy. But there are other gangs, too. And . . . I guess you'd call them refugees. Some are just wandering, like they're in a daze. A lot of them become victims of the ones who have found each other and formed up gangs. I saw a lot of bodies along the road. Pretty much all of them had been stripped naked."

"Had they been murdered?" Victoria asked.

"Clearly, some of them had," Cameron said. "Others, I don't know. I didn't stop and look all that closely. I tried to get through them as fast as I could. I needed to get to you. And I need to get you back to Hilltop."

"Did you *walk* all the way from Hilltop?" McCrea asked.

"No, sir, I have a horse. He's grazing in the field across the street."

The door to Maggie's opened and Joey Abbott stepped in from the chill, balancing a plate of food in his right hand. The ever-present AR15 was slung behind his back. "Here's some scrambled eggs and venison sausage," he said as he walked in. He handed the plate to Cameron. "You look like you could use this." The proprietor of Joey's Pawn Shop in the years before Hell Day, Joey had stepped up to be one of the town's leaders.

As Cameron dug into the food, McCrea asked, "Do you have any reason to believe that there'll actually be a trial, or are they just going to hang the president from a tree?"

"Holy shit!" Joey exclaimed. "What president? *Our* president?"

Victoria took thirty seconds to catch Joey up.

"I don't know if there'll be a trial or not," Cameron said. "All I know is that everybody was arrested, and the president asked me to come and get you."

"How does he even know I'm here?"

"I don't have an answer for that, ma'am," Cameron said. "It's probably because everyone knows you're here."

Victoria looked to McCrea for clarity but got a shrug instead.

"A lot of the people I passed on the way here from Hilltop said they were on their way to Eden," Cameron said.

"That's here?" Victoria asked.

"Yes, ma'am. Turns out the rumor mill survived Armageddon."

It was too much. Victoria stood to end the meeting, though prepared to leave the room so Cameron could continue eating. "Thank you, Mr. Cameron," Victoria said. "I'll have an answer for you in the next day or two."

Cameron stood, too. "Um, ma'am? We don't have a

day or two. Roger Parsons is a scary dude. He's champing at the bit to hang the lot of them."

"I'll give you my decision in a day or two," Victoria repeated. "Take your time in here. Finish your meal. Do you need a place to shelter for the night?"

"No, ma'am. With you or without you, I need to get back to Hilltop."

"Why?" McCrea asked.

Cameron glared. "You were an Army officer, right?"

"Major," McCrea said.

"If you'd left a bunch of your comrades in danger, wouldn't you want to get back to them?"

McCrea knitted his brow, looked at Victoria, and then patted the young man's shoulder. "Yes, I would," he said. "But do you and me both the favor of resting for the rest of the day and we'll find shelter for you. Start fresh tomorrow. If we end up going, we'll want you along. Any extra hands we can get."

"Sorry, Major, but I can't do that." Cameron wiped his mouth and stood. "Thanks for the grub." He stuffed what remained on his plate into the towel that served as his napkin and shoved it all into a patch pocket on his trousers. "I hope you can make it, ma'am," he said. He looked to McCrea. "Major."

And then he was gone.

"Gotta admire his loyalty," Victoria said.

"Or suspect that he's setting a trap," McCrea countered. "You know, draw you out so that this Parsons guy can take you out, too."

"Why would he do that? What have *I* done?"

"Nothing makes petty men more nervous than a successful woman," Joey said.

Victoria rolled her eyes. "I thought we were past virtue signaling."

"It's not about virtue," McCrea said. "It's about power. Those who want it are always angry at those who have it. You need to be careful."

"Also," Joey added, "you were a member of the House. Wouldn't that put you on the extended hit list?"

Victoria sighed and sat back down in her chair. "Clearly, we need to discuss this. Joey, could you find George Simmons and ask him to join us?"

"What about your boys?" McCrea asked.

"Yeah, them, too."

CHAPTER TWO

*W*ithin fifteen minutes, Victoria's family had all gathered in the main room of Maggie's Place. Adam was the oldest at eighteen, and his girlfriend, Emma, was pregnant, though not yet showing. At sixteen, Caleb had grown two inches in the past two months. He spent his days helping Doc Rory Stevenson, working on patients and learning cowboy medicine as a trade. Luke would turn fifteen soon, and his work in Lavinia Sloan's blacksmith shop had broadened his shoulders and blackened his hands without darkening his outlook. Just like his father had been, Luke was an unapologetic optimist in all things. Thanks to a lifetime of training, all her boys were expert marksmen.

First Sergeant Paul Copley was there, too, along with George Simmons and Joey Abbott. George, like Joey, was a lifelong resident of Ortho and its environs, and through them, Victoria avoided some of the social landmines that were so common in small towns. They knew the personalities, and friendships. More importantly, they knew the lifelong enmities that existed between some.

The letter was real. There was no forging the elaborate scrawl that was Penn Glendale's handwriting. Written on the reverse side of the stationery for the House of Representatives, on which the logo on the front had been marked out with heavy black ink, the letter explained much of what young Mr. Cameron had told her. Penn's was a personal plea for assistance.

As she read the letter aloud, her voice choked at the concluding paragraphs.

> *"Vicky, I ask you to do this thing—to preside over our trial—not to avoid punishment or to evade responsibility for the mess that the war has wrought. I ask so that some semblance of sanity might reign over this last gasp of government as we once knew it.*
>
> *"If my colleagues and I are to be executed, let it be done mercifully and in a lawful manner. Decades from now, long after the government has fallen, the United States of America will remain as a population of citizens who are striving to thrive in the wilderness, much as our ancestors did. What succeeds the present must be built upon principles of freedom and the rule of law.*
>
> *"I believe that you are uniquely suited to the task of leading the way. No matter what you choose to do, know that I am grateful for your consideration, and stand in admiration of what you have achieved while so many have foundered.*
>
> *"Your obedient servant, Pennington Glendale, President of the United States of America."*

Victoria folded the letter and wiped her eyes with her palms.

"So, it's all gone," Joey Abbott said, his voice barely a whisper. "The government is gone."

"How the hell did everything go so wrong?" George Simmons wondered aloud.

"The government is *not* gone," Victoria said. Under the circumstances, the strength of her voice surprised her. "We are the government. The *people* are the government. All that's gone are the trappings of power."

"And electricity," Luke said, drawing a laugh

"Tell me you're not thinking about doing this," McCrea said. "The letter was very moving, but if we believe Cameron—and I have no reason not to—President . . . What's his name?"

"Penn Glendale," Victoria reminded him. "He was—"

"Speaker of the House, yeah. I remember now. If we're to believe Cameron, this new guy—Parsons, right?"

He got nods from Victoria and Joey.

"Parsons doesn't even know about the note."

Victoria stopped him. "That's not what he said. He said he wasn't sure whether or not Parsons was aware."

"We have to make some assumptions," Joey said. "Why would he approve that?"

"I don't know," Victoria admitted. "But it's important to be precise when talking about what we *know* versus what we *think*."

"Still," McCrea said, "Penn Glendale is the prisoner, not the warden. There's not a chance in hell that they haven't already done to him whatever they're going to do."

"So, we do nothing?" Adam asked. "Is that what you're suggesting?"

"We're talking about the overthrow of the United States," George said.

"Think about it, Vicky," McCrea pushed. "Why would they keep him alive?"

For Victoria, the answer seemed obvious. "Because killing him would be a stupid thing to do. Precisely *because* it would be the overthrow of the government. It would be a putsch. That's a tough line to walk back from."

First Sergeant Copley said, "They arrested them for treason, right? Isn't that what you said? Well, that's a capital offense. They wouldn't have filed the charges that way if they weren't prepared to execute the guy."

"Maybe they didn't know that," Adam said. "Maybe it was just the first thing they thought of to charge him with."

"Dangerous assumption," McCrea said. "The kind that can get your mom killed."

Victoria said, "I think Adam might be right. The events that Mr. Cameron described seemed more like a temper tantrum than a serious effort at justice."

"You think that's better?" McCrea asked. "A tantrum is the very definition of irrational action. If they're pissed enough, what's to stop them? And if they're pissed enough to execute him, what are you going to be walking into?"

"People act in their own best interest," Victoria said. It had long been a governing principle of her life. "Executing the president outright makes no sense. Murdering a man for spite? The president of the United States, no less?"

"Very little of what's happened in the past few months makes any damn sense at all," George said.

Joey agreed. "Who's to say they haven't already tried him? Guilty or innocent, alive or dead, this whole thing is probably over."

"Cameron said he'd been on the road three days to get here," George said. "That's plenty of time to have some kind of a trial."

"By the time we can get to him, that'll be three more days, for a total of six," McCrea said. "Plenty of time for trial, verdict, sentencing and execution."

"Suppose saner heads prevail," Victoria said. "Suppose the president and this Parsons guy had a conversation that Cameron didn't know about. Suppose they're waiting there for me to arrive."

"You have no cause to make such an assumption," McCrea said.

"And you have no cause to assume the worst," Victoria fired back.

"What about Ortho?" Emma asked.

Victoria understood that her grandchild was in Emma's belly but bristled at her entry into the conversation. "What about Ortho?"

"All the good work you've done here," Emma said. "These people depend on you."

"No," George said, his tone louder than he probably wanted it to be. "There's no need to feel guilty about leaving us. I don't want that to be a factor in your decision about doing something crazy like hiking up to the Hilltop Manor on a suicide mission. I get what you're wrestling with, Vicky, and we can carry on what you've started. You make the call based on what you think is *right*, not on what you think makes things easiest for us." He looked to Joey for agreement.

"Absolutely," Joey said. "We'll miss you if you go, and you'll always have a home here."

"A home that looks a lot like the corner of a church," Luke said with a smile.

"I'm happy to play the guilt card," McCrea said. "You've got to be reasonable, Vicky. You've just re-united with your boys, and now you're going to risk all of that by walking into a buzz saw?"

"If she goes, she won't be alone," Adam said. "I'll be there, too."

"Me and Luke, too," Caleb said.

Victoria noted the look of surprise in Luke's face when his brother volunteered him, but he didn't object. In fact, he nodded and stood. "We're not splitting up again," Luke said.

"With me, that makes four," Emma said. "If Adam goes, I go."

"Me and the major, too," Copley said. "Right, Major?"

"Of course," McCrea said. "But the smart course—"

"You've made your point, Joe," Victoria said. "I'll even stipulate that you're probably right, that this is a fool's errand. But in a moment of crisis, you don't say no to the president of the United States."

"We're going to need more people," Copley said. He still had the angular features of a longtime soldier, but in the weeks since the war, he, like everyone else, had lost a lot of weight. It showed in the hollows of his cheeks. His neck girth had shrunk to the proportions of a mere human. "Between the gangs that your man Cameron talked about and whatever we're going to find on the far end at the Hilltop Manor, more guns and ammo is better than less guns and ammo."

Victoria waved the suggestion away, as if shooing a fly. "No, we can't do that," she said. "We can't strip down the Ortho militia. That would be too dangerous. If the gangs and marauders attack here—"

"We'll hold our own," George said.

"I won't allow it," Victoria said.

The others all chuckled at once.

"What?" Victoria didn't see the joke.

"You ain't in charge of everything, Vicky," George said. "Nor are you in charge of every*body*."

Victoria didn't want to back down. "George, I'm serious."

"I know you are," he said, the grin still prominent.

McCrea seethed. His face was red, and his lips were pressed into a tight line. Victoria watched as he wrangled himself together. His shoulders relaxed and his facial muscles loosened up.

"Are you okay, Joe?" Victoria asked.

"My thoughts about this are on the record," he said. "But I know when to pivot from defeat to planning." He walked to the front wall, planted his fists on his hips and looked out the window. "We need a strategy," he said.

Joey stood. "While you strategize, I'll spread the word that we need a force of fifteen or twenty people to go with you to the Hilltop Manor to rescue the leader of the Free World. That should fire people up a little."

"Or maybe not," Luke said. "I'm kind of on the side of the people who want to try the president for getting us into whatever happened and for getting everybody killed."

"And that's exactly what will happen if I have anything to say about it," Victoria said. "He'll get a trial. A fair one. But for that to happen, I have to get to Hilltop Manor."

"I've got a question," Luke said. "Why would this Parsons guy even allow you to be judge? Y'all are convinced that he's not going to allow a fair trial because his mind is already made up. How are you going to convince anybody that yours isn't already made up, too?"

The question stopped conversation.

"He's right," Caleb said. "If they're as pissed as this messenger guy told you, and you somehow convince Parsons that you can deliver a fair verdict, what happens if you find people not guilty? They'll never believe that you didn't cheat."

"And then they'll come at *you* with torches and pitchforks," McCrea said. "No matter how this ends, they're coming at you with torches and pitchforks."

Victoria knew what was coming and she held out her hands to stop it. "Look, Joe, I appreciate your concern. There are all kinds of things that can go wrong here, and none of us knows the future. All I'm saying—and I'm saying it for the last time—is that I have a duty to perform, and I'm going to perform it. Could I possibly be clearer?"

The heat of his glare told her how badly he wanted to reopen the argument, but in the end, he backed down.

"We're going to need provisions," Copley said. "Food, water, medical supplies." He paused as an idea bloomed. "Do you think Doc Rory might be interested in coming along? He's got Jayne Young and Leroy Robinson to help him now."

All eyes turned to Caleb.

"What?" he said. "I work with him, but I don't make up his mind for him."

"Don't be a dick," Adam said. "You know him better than the rest of us. Is this something you think he might be interested in doing?"

"I think he might be," Caleb said. "We can always ask."

CHAPTER THREE

*T*HE NEXT MORNING DAWNED CHILLY BUT NOT AS COLD as the previous few. Victoria never considered herself to be a predictor of the weather—or any other element of the future, for that matter—but she sensed that this autumn day may feel a lot like summer by the time this trip was over. It was the nature of the West Virginia climate to be fickle when the seasons changed.

First Sergeant Paul Copley had overseen the logistics of the journey. Each member of the caravan was responsible for their own clothing and shelter—two people per tent—while food and ammunition were combined and carried among the cargo that had been distributed between two rubber-tired farm wagons that had been retrofitted to be pulled by horses. The wagons also carried medical gear, spare batteries for flashlights as well as kerosene for lanterns.

Victoria had requested the extra supplies on the theory that once they arrived at Hilltop Manor, if things were as bad as Cameron had described them, new provisions might go a long way to help change some hearts and minds.

As the expedition gathered at the intersection of Kanawha Road and Mountain Road—the default town square—Victoria counted fourteen people, including herself, her three boys, Emma, McCrea, and Copley. Teenage twins Kyle and Caine Foster had signed on as well, triggering a long discussion between Victoria, George Simmons and the twins.

"I appreciate your desire to help," Victoria said to one of the Fosters. Honestly, they looked so much alike she could never tell one from the other. "But you two provide too valuable a service to just cut it off."

"We bury bodies," one brother said with an ostentatious roll of his eyes.

"It's not a skilled job," said the other.

"The hell it's not," Victoria said. "Not only is there skill in handling bodies with respect and dealing with grieving families, but there's the basic willingness to do the job in the first place."

"That's not as important as rescuing the president of the United States," the first brother said.

"I'm sorry," Victoria said. "Which Foster are you?"

The young man blushed and smiled. "Kyle."

Caine added, "And while we're talking about basic willingness to do the job, I think you need our guns on your adventure to save the Free World, and Kyle and me are both willing to do that job."

Victoria caught the accusatory glare the teen shot at George Simmons, who puffed up at the implication of cowardice as the reason George was hanging back in Ortho.

"You'd best watch your mouth," George said.

Victoria jumped in quickly. "George and Joey are staying on my insistence. We've built a good community here in Ortho, but it's as fragile as the first serious blunder. George and Joey are the two men who have the best feel for the pulse of the town."

"I'd be there in a heartbeat if I could," Joey added. Victoria didn't realize that he was as close to the conversation as he was.

"Okay, then you two have an excuse," Kyle said. "There must be a couple hundred people in this town by now."

"And they need to stay to defend it," Victoria said. She felt anger rising.

"You're getting mad at us," Caine said. "Don't. My only point is that of the couple hundred people staying behind, *somebody* ought to be able to step up and care for the dead. It's not like you can hurt the clients, if you know what I mean."

"I do know what you mean," Victoria said. This was one of her concerns when the inner circle pressed her into bringing others along. There was enough pain and angst going around without introducing an element of who's-braver-than-whom?

"You're free to do what you want," George said. "I think maybe I just wanted you to know that your efforts here will be missed. We'll figure something out."

From down near the boat launch, Major McCrea's voice rose above the din of the mingling crowd. "Listen up, everybody!" he yelled. It took two more attempts and a two-fingered whistle to settle everybody down.

Victoria pressed closer but stayed near the back of

the human horseshoe. This part of the get-together was all on McCrea.

"Ladies and gentlemen," McCrea said, "we have every reason to believe that it's a tough road between here and there. People, we're told, are desperate and crazy. Gangs are forming up, and lots of people are falling victim to them. There'll be bodies along the road—"

"We made a few of them ourselves," Victoria heard Caleb say to his brother Adam.

"That's not funny," Luke said.

"Luke's right," Adam admonished.

Caleb looked hurt.

Victoria dialed back into McCrea's speech. "Vicky and her boys, First Sergeant Copley and I traveled the route we'll be taking during the night and morning after Hell Day. We did most of it by car before the electromagnetic pulse knocked everything out and we had to walk the rest of the way. I know a number of you probably walked some or all of it if you came into Ortho via Mountain Road. Lots of steep hills and switch-backs—"

"Welcome to West Virginia, Major," someone called from the crowd, sparking a laugh from everyone, including McCrea.

"Okay, yeah," he said. "My point is that we need to take the road slowly and not push the horses too hard. We tried to limit the load on the wagons, but those beasts are going to work their asses off on some of the uphill portions. This poses some tactical concerns. . . ."

McCrea told the expedition that slow-moving groups pose enticing targets for bad guys. Those long, uphill segments should trigger extra vigilance on everyone's part.

"When you look at a switchback on a map, what you'll see if you squint the right way, is that they are peninsulas of land that allow a small group of shooters in the woods to have a continuing opportunity to wreak havoc."

Victoria felt her stomach churn. She hadn't considered that bit of tactical detail.

"I know it sounds counterintuitive," McCrea went on, "but those periods of greatest exposure are the periods when we need to be farthest apart. I don't know if we're going to come under fire at all, but we have to assume the worst. And the worst for me is the hand grenade."

That sparked a murmur through the crowd. "Who's got access to hand grenades?" asked Greg Gonzales. He and his wife Mary were recent arrivals in Ortho, having walked the route from the very place they were headed. Victoria was shocked when they volunteered to go back. Greg said he wanted to bring justice to Parsons for the misery he caused to the people in the hotel.

"Maybe nobody," McCrea said. "*Probably* nobody. But a modern hand grenade has a fifty-foot kill radius. If we bunch up, one grenade would wipe out many. If we stay at least fifty feet apart, we're a much less tempting target."

McCrea paused for questions, but no one had any.

"Finally," he said, "my rules of engagement are tough. Everybody and his Aunt Maude is going to be armed out there. You can't shoot someone just because they have a gun or a crossbow. But if they point that weapon at you or anyone else in this expedition, drop them right away. No challenge, no questions."

Marius Miller, the always-cranky purveyor of a local body shop, asked, "Suppose they didn't mean any harm?"

"Then they shouldn't have pointed a weapon at us," McCrea said. "Bullets travel at two thousand feet per second. Your shouted warning tops out at around half that. These are tough times requiring tough decisions with little warning." He shifted his stance, moving his M4 rifle off to the side and planting his fists on his hips. "And we'd all be wise to remember that every-body out there—even the ones who mean no harm—are going to be scared shitless, and they're likely to have rules similar to ours."

He let the words hang in the air for a second or two. "If you point a weapon at someone, you'd best squeeze the trigger. By contrast, if you don't want to have a gunfight, keep your muzzles pointed down. Any questions now?"

As Victoria scanned the faces around her, everyone looked as if they harbored questions but were hesitant to ask.

"Yeah, I got one," Marius said. "Are we going to ac-tually mount up at some point, or are we just gonna jawbone the morning away?"

"I've got one more thing to add," Victoria said, eas-ing her way to the front of the crowd. With her back to the river, she looked out on the people who had gath-ered along the boat ramp.

"Not until I go first," George Simmons said. He stuck his hand out so she couldn't get past him.

Victoria took a step back.

George raised his voice, presumably to be more easily heard by the crowd. "You stay right up here with me, Vicky." Joey Abbott and Ben Barnett came in from the side and joined them.

"Vicky Emerson," George said, "you are one special lady. On the day you walked into this town and kept me from killing the Foster boys—which I woulda done, but you already know that—I hated your guts."

Now there's a tribute, Victoria thought.

"I thought, who the hell does this bitch think she is to threaten to shoot me in my own town? Pardon my French. The whole world was coming apart, everything was broken, everybody was scared shitless, and there you were tellin' me and Joey that we were bad people for tryin' to punish a couple of thieves."

Kyle and Caine Foster's faces had turned red, but Victoria couldn't tell if it was from anger or embarrassment. In the aftermath of that incident—

"And within a couple of hours I knew that I was wrong, and that you'd prevented me from becomin' a murderer."

"There's somethin' special in you, Vicky," said Ben Barnett, the purveyor of a grocery store back before the world changed.

Joey added, "People follow you. Not because you ask them to, but despite the fact that you ask them *not* to. There aren't many people in the world who are like that."

Victoria felt a presence behind her and turned to see that McCrea had joined her. He hugged her from behind. "Do you have anything to do with this?" she whispered.

"Seeing and hearing it for the first time," McCrea said.

Victoria wanted them to stop. She wanted to explain that they were wrong, that she had no special skill or leadership quality. She just said what was on her mind, and people listened. If someone else had said the same things, they would have listened to that person, too. But this seemed important to the three men in front of her, so she stayed silent.

"This trip you're going on," George said. "This mission you're on to somehow rescue the president and save the United States of America is pure Vicky. If you ask me, there's not a chance in hell of success, so therefore I am confident that you will somehow make it happen."

Laughter rippled through the crowd. The friendly kind, not the derisive kind.

"And I wish I could be there to help keep you out of trouble," George said.

"We all do," Joey added.

"Not me," Ben said. "My horse-ridin' days are way behind me."

More laughter.

George said, "As you're about to set off on this crazy thing, I want you to know that every person here is thankful for what you've done. We have a strong security force because of you, a food and clothing bank, and the means to build shelters for new folks as they come in. That's all on you."

Victoria raised her hand. "I've got to stop you there," she said. "Y'all did those things yourself. If Ortho were a train line—"

"It would be stalled and unusable." This from her Luke. Ever the jokester, even if his sense of timing sucked.

"If Ortho were a train—be quiet, Luke—y'all are the ones who laid the tracks, built the engine and made it move. You—all of you—are the security committee. You are the food and clothing banks. You are all of those things. All I did was make some suggestions."

That was a big laugh line for the crowd.

"You go ahead and think that if you want, Vicky, but we know the truth. And we want to thank you for it."

The assembled townsfolk broke into applause, and Victoria felt tears pressing behind her eyes. McCrea's embrace tightened.

"This will always be home for you, whether you're here or not," Joey said. "We'll do our best not to let you down."

Victoria smiled. She hugged each of them, one at a time. When she got to Ben Barnett, he cupped her face in his hands. They felt like sandpaper. "You're a winner, Vicky," he said. "You're gonna make this thing happen."

"I hope so," she said, and her voice caught in her throat.

"There's no thinkin' in it," Ben said. "It's who you are." He folded her into a hug, then pushed her away. "You're burnin' daylight. Now git."

Victoria wanted to say her own thanks, make her own speech, to tell the people of Ortho that in the awfulness that followed Hell Day, their friendship and support were what made life seem nearly normal—or as normal as life could be under the circumstances.

Instead, she pulled away from Ben and turned to McCrea. "He's right," she said. "It's time for us to hit the road."

CHAPTER FOUR

*I*T HAD BEEN A COUPLE OF MONTHS SINCE CALEB EMER-son took a bullet through his left ass cheek. The round hadn't hit any bone and left most of the muscle un-touched, and when he volunteered for this horse ride, he thought he'd be able to handle the wide straddle of the saddle, but less than two miles into the trip, he began to regret his decision. Every time the horse took a step—he'd named the gelding Tom—the rise of the cantle worked at the scar. He tried to adjust himself in the seat, but there was only so much room to move. At least they were all riding western saddles. That tiny bit of extra padding had to be helping some.

He'd make it, that was for certain. No way was he going to be separated from his family. If there was a fight and his mom or one of his brothers got hurt, he wouldn't be able to live with himself if he hadn't been there to help them out. Yeah, there were lots of other people in the caravan, but they weren't family. They weren't part of Caleb's innermost circle, and the Emersons weren't in the innermost circle of anyone else. Even Major McCrea and First Sergeant Copley, while nearly like family, weren't *real* family.

"You ride like you've got hemorrhoids," Luke called from behind.

Without turning around to look, Caleb raised his right arm straight up until his elbow locked and brought his middle finger to full extension.

"Not everyone's proud that their IQ is one," Luke poked. "It's good you're happy with who you are."

Caleb mirrored the gesture with his left arm. "Why don't you come kiss my ass and see if you can make it better?"

"Oh, hell no. Nobody knows where it's been."

"Really, boys?" Victoria called back. She'd turned in her saddle.

First Sergeant Copley's voice boomed, "I sure hope we can continue to make lots of noise as we try to move quietly!"

Caleb cringed at the volume and the tenor of the voice. He'd never heard that from Paul before. As intimidating as it was, he thought the objection was overkill. They were barely past the town limits. Cameron had told them that the trouble didn't start for miles past here.

It occurred to Caleb that if the world hadn't turned upside down, he'd be driving by now. He'd gotten his license the day after his sixteenth birthday—two months before Hell Day—but his mom had insisted that he drive only with another adult in the car for the next three months. It had pissed him off at the time. And let's be honest: He was still pissed off about it. In the before times, when Mom was in full Madam Representative mode, she was really difficult to be around. He swore that she sometimes did things specifically designed to make him mad.

And that was one thing she was really good at.

Caleb didn't like this business of being separated by fifty feet. If the trip took two or three days like Jerry Cameron said it would, that was a long time to go without talking to anyone. He understood the strategic part of keeping your distance, but it was a shitty way to travel.

He was fifth in line as they moved north and east. Major McCrea was in the lead, with Mom in the number two slot. Then came Adam, followed by Emma, and then Caleb. Luke was in the sixth slot, and First Sergeant Copley nine slots back, in the very rear. Like everyone else he could see, Caleb rode with his M4 rifle slung over his shoulder, but with the weight of the weapon supported by his thighs.

The coat he wore was probably two sizes too big, but the extra girth allowed him to bulk up with extra sweaters if it got really cold. Plus, the oversized pockets allowed him to carry two extra 30-round magazines in addition to the four that he'd stuffed into a chest rig, plus the one in the mag well. He rode with a round in the chamber, with the safety on. If something bad happened, he needed only to thumb the safety off and go to work.

He'd done it before, and to good effect. For as long as he could remember his mom—and his dad before he was killed—obsessed about teaching him and his brothers the finer points of shooting, along with the essentials of surviving off the land if somehow modern society stopped working. He and his brothers all turned out to be natural shooters with long guns. Pistols were harder, of course, but the Emerson boys could hold their own with those, too.

With iron sights, Caleb had dropped a deer from 150 yards. With optics, he could reach out as far as he wanted. Their dad had been a Special Forces operator until he was killed in the line of duty in the Middle East, and he'd taught all of them how to read the sight picture for wind, and how to correct for it. Because he was oldest, Adam was the one who got the most training, and he'd done a good job of passing that knowledge along to his brothers.

Growing up as an Emerson was an experience in weirdness. All the time at the range, the hand-to-hand training sessions and all the survival bullshit had led other kids to label them as weirdos and future active shooter nutjobs. By being largely shunned by his high school peers, Caleb had found himself drawn more frequently to the shooting range, where he found people who understood the importance of being able to protect yourself and the people you care about.

While he enjoyed the training more than he hated it, there wasn't a single day of it that he didn't think they were totally bullshit exercises. Why did he have to know how to turn humidity into drinkable water when he had two liters of bottled water in his backpack? He loved venison, so the deer hunting was great, but squirrels and moles and voles? Really? They all tasted like crap, didn't have enough meat on them to count as a real meal. He didn't understand how any of that could be useful to him.

Then came Hell Day and everything made sense. No, that wasn't true. *Nothing* made sense in a way that he would have expected it to in the past, but the focus of all that training became obvious. It was as if his crazy parents had been able to see the future.

What surprised Caleb most of all—shocked him, really—was how easy it was to kill people. He didn't enjoy it, of course, but it didn't bother him like he thought it would. Once the bombs fell and all the infrastructure was fried by the electromagnetic pulse, a shocking number of people reverted to their animal instincts. Too many became murderous.

If you had stuff they wanted, they felt free to take it and kill you in the process. Now that he thought about it, even when the world was "normal"—if anything in the past ten years had been anything approaching that—stealing stuff and burning things had been decriminalized and relabeled as peaceful protest. Mayors of big cities were actually telling people that by driving expensive cars or wearing jewelry, they should expect to be mugged because muggers weren't being prosecuted anymore.

For some, maybe the lawless elements after Hell Day weren't as shocking as they were for Caleb.

Every person Caleb had killed would have done the same for him if he wasn't a better shot. Or, in one case, wasn't better with a knife. That one—the one that ended with him jamming a knife into a guy's gut—was the one that haunted him most.

As for the ones he shot, well, they just fell down and it was done. Caleb thought for a while that his mom was upset that he wasn't more bothered, but now he thought that maybe she got it.

She'd taken out her fair share of attackers, too, after

all. So had Luke and Adam and Emma and everybody else it seemed. That was just the way of the world now.

As the value of life diminished, the importance of keeping those personal circles tight became more and more important.

After an hour or so, the slope of the road started to rise. He recognized exactly where they were because up ahead lay the spot where he'd killed a person for the first time. It was a woman who was lying in wait for him and some others from Ortho and he'd shot her in the ear.

"She would have shot me if I hadn't have shot her," he mumbled to Tom-the horse, who didn't seem to care at all. But that wasn't true, not really. She wasn't going to shoot Caleb, but rather she was going to shoot at others from their group. That was the same, right? Defending someone on your side was the same as self-defense. That's what he told himself, anyway.

You couldn't let this stuff get under your skin. It'd mess up your thinking. Made you hesitate in the moment when quick action meant the difference between survival and the forever dirt nap. These days, you didn't even get a marker at your head. Just a board across your chest with your name carved into it with a hot poker.

The slope of the road wasn't all that steep, Caleb didn't think, but he remembered from when they were first approaching the town from the other direction, he thought it would never end. A glance behind, beyond Luke, showed that the horses pulling the wagons were beginning to look tired. Their heads hung low and they snorted a lot.

"Hey, big brother," Luke said from behind. "Look up on the hill. We're being watched."

Caleb jerked his head up and to the left. The roadway had been cut out of the mountain, leaving steep hills on either side, too shallow to be called cliffs, but too steep and rocky to want to climb. He had to squint and train his mind to ignore all the brightly colored foliage, but he eventually saw a guy with a rifle standing beside a tree, watching as they passed. There was no effort to hide.

"Do you think he wants us to see him?" Caleb asked.

"There's another one on the right," Luke said. "They're not trying to hide, that's for sure."

"Hey, Adam," Caleb said.

"I see them," Adam said. "Watch their hands, and if you can see them, watch their eyes."

"Pass the word up to Mom and the major," Caleb said.

"I already did."

Caleb didn't hear him do that. How could he have missed it? For now, the men on the hill were just watching. The muzzles of their rifles posed no threat—the guy on the left had his pointing toward the ground, the one on the right toward the sky. Caleb kept his rifle slung across his lap, but he thumbed the safety off.

Victoria didn't like the way the situation was unfolding. The fact that people were watching them meant that they were approaching a group that was lying in wait for something. Was it an ambush possibly, or did they merely want to be forewarned of any potential hazard that might be coming their way?

On the positive side, the watchers weren't hiding themselves. Could that be a gesture of friendliness, or one of intimidation? Victoria's caravan was not the right group to try and intimidate, but the people up on the hill couldn't know that.

On the roads leading to Ortho, Victoria had likewise deployed watchers—they called themselves tree frogs—to alert the townsfolk to the approach of strangers. They used whistle signals to communicate. Victoria didn't see any overt effort by these watchers to communicate what they saw.

She was fully aware of what lay beyond the next curve—or, what used to lie there. A gang led by a thug named Grubbs had killed a tractor trailer driver named Ryan Hamilton in hopes of stealing his cargo and profiting from it. The murder was tragic enough—denying a young Ortho family of their husband and father—but was somehow made even worse by the irony that the cargo contained only electronic equipment that was rendered useless by the Hell Day EMP.

Up ahead, Joe McCrea started into the long curve that would define a wide switchback. She saw his back stiffen, and she disengaged the safety on her M4. This didn't have to get ugly, but if it did, it would happen quickly. That's the way violence always happened.

McCrea's back straightened and he shifted in his saddle. She read the body language as a danger signal.

"Be alert, boys," Victoria said.

"But don't pick the fight," Adam added.

All her boys had changed since Hell Day, but none as dramatically as Adam. Rebellious enough as a teenager to earn himself a transfer to military school to get his act together, he'd now become a man. A responsible adult. With a baby on the way. He acted less like a brother to his siblings than he did a surrogate father.

As Victoria rounded the curve, she kept her face passive as she took everything in. A lot of people milled about in the road and along the sides. More than a dozen, fewer than two dozen. Some had apparently turned the remains of Ryan Hamilton's trailer into a form of shelter, others appeared to be doing nothing. Most were armed. Equal numbers of men and women, give or take, no children that she could see—though some of the men and women looked awfully young.

Something about their positioning bothered Victoria. People didn't seem to be in the midst of doing anything. They weren't chatting, they weren't sewing or praying or reading. They were just . . . there. And they didn't seem surprised to see the caravan.

It was almost as if someone had posed them.

McCrea led the line at a slow walk through the gathered people.

Victoria made eye contact with a wispy-faced young man whose beard needed another couple of years to look right. "Hello," she said.

The young man looked away.

"Well, hello!" A booming voice came from behind and on her left.

Victoria placed one hand on the saddle horn and her other on the cantle so she could turn and see who was approaching her. A man of about thirty strode up past Caleb and Emma, on his way to her. He looked healthier than most, and better dressed. He had the smile of a banker. None of those things made her feel any more comfortable.

"You're Victoria Emerson, aren't you?" the man

said. "I recognize you from the news programs, back before the shit hit the fan." His smile wasn't right. Neither were his questions. The people around him looked drawn. All of them undernourished to her eye, and maybe a few of them were sick.

The man approached without hesitation, his hand extended. "Allow me to shake your hand, ma'am."

"Stand where you are," Victoria said.

The man took an extra step, and McCrea said, "Do you want to die today? Please do as the lady asks and keep your distance."

The man looked hurt. "That's hardly a friendly way to greet someone."

"These aren't friendly times," McCrea said.

Victoria tried a softer tone when she said, "Let's start with your name."

"Baggins," he said. "Josh Baggins. I've got a Hobbit's last name." He laughed too hard at his own joke.

"What's going on here?" Victoria asked. In her peripheral vision, she saw movement, but she didn't look away from the man who called himself Josh.

"We've got people with guns," Adam said. "Moving closer."

"Don't worry about them," Josh said. "They're just paranoid. Like we're all paranoid these days." He smiled again.

"Mr. Baggins," Victoria said, "you seem to be selling me something—or to be on the edge of selling me something, and I have to tell you I'm not in the mood for buying." She righted herself in her saddle and nodded to McCrea. "Let's go, Major."

"I just want to talk for a minute," Baggins said. "A young man came through here twice yesterday, once down the mountain and once back up. He told us that there would be a supply train coming through here today. I guess you're it. He said you wasn't gonna want to share with us, but I told him that I could be persuasive."

"Is that a fact?" Victoria knew it was a mistake to engage like this, but to disengage meant turning away.

Baggins made his move. He leaped forward and grabbed Victoria by her belt and pulled her sideways out of the saddle. She was airborne for what seemed like a couple of seconds, and then she hit the pavement hard. She heard shouting and then gunshots, but she kept her focus on breaking her attacker's grasp.

She punched his forearm, but the angle was wrong, and she couldn't get a full swing. His grip didn't weaken a bit.

Victoria's scalp pulled tight as Baggins used his other hand to lift her by a handful of hair.

All around her, the shooting and the shouting continued.

Victoria's hand found the Glock 19 on her belt, and she drew it.

"No!" Baggins yelled. He let go of her hair and went for her weapon. His palm covered the muzzle and she pulled the trigger. Fingers flew like wood chips.

Baggins yelled. As he took a step back and cradled his hand, Victoria worked the slide to clear the stovepipe jam Baggins caused when he grabbed her pistol, then blew a hole through his head, from the tip of his nose through his brain stem.

* * *

Caleb jumped in his saddle when the guy lunged at his mom and pulled her down to the ground.

"It's an ambush!" someone called from behind. He thought it was First Sergeant Copley, but he couldn't be sure. "Keep your eyes on your targets!"

All around him, rifles were being brought to shoulders. Without thinking, Caleb swung his leg over his horse's mane and slid to the ground, dropping to his right knee. Above and behind him, he heard someone shooting, and ahead of him, someone fell.

Caleb raised his rifle, settled the crosshairs of his 4-power scope on the throat of some guy with a lever action rifle and pressed the trigger. His scope was zeroed at a hundred yards, so it was no surprise when the other shooter's head blew apart.

Crouching lower and sitting on his right heel for a steadier shot, he scanned for more targets. He saw a ton of people lying low and hugging the ground to stay out of the crossfire, but he didn't see any more shooters.

He pivoted to face the other way, and realized for the first time that his horse, Tom, had bolted and disappeared, leaving him an unobstructed view of the other side of the battlefield. Scanning like this, it was hard to tell the difference between the dead and the cowering, but he supposed it didn't matter as long as the shooting had stopped. About fifty yards out, a wounded lady was crawling across the rocks to retrieve a dropped rifle.

Caleb rose to his feet for a better angle and yelled, "You! Stay where you are! Don't reach for that gun!"

She either didn't hear him or didn't care. He yelled

one more time. She placed her hand on the rifle, lifted it, and he shot her in the head, too.

"All you people stay down!" Copley yelled. "If you have a weapon, keep your hands away from it!"

Caleb looked back toward his mom. She seemed to be okay, but the man who attacked her was definitely *not* okay.

"Any of our people hurt?" Mom called out.

"Doc Rory!" That came from one of the Foster twins. Caleb never could tell them apart. "He's been hit! Caleb! Come help!"

"Oh, shit." Caleb felt panic rising in his chest. He was qualified to help out in the clinic, but he wasn't a doctor. He knew how to stitch people up and how to stop bleeding, but not something like this.

Adam barked, "Caleb! Go!" As he spoke, Adam dismounted his horse.

Then everyone dismounted and headed back toward Rory's spot in the line.

"Keep your positions!" Copley yelled. "This isn't over yet. There might be other shooters. Keep your eyes where they belong. Adam and Luke, you cover the sectors that belong to your brother. Caleb, get your ass in gear."

Slinging his rifle to the rear, Caleb jogged the two hundred feet to where Doc Rory lay on the ground on his left side, having fallen off his horse. The man's left arm showed an angulated fracture of the ulna and radius, and for an instant, Caleb felt hope. He knew how to handle broken bones.

Then he saw the blood. It leaked out from under Rory's farm coat and spread onto the pavement. His color was awful, his skin pale, his lips gray on the way to blue.

"Is it as bad as it looks?" Rory asked. His teeth were wet with blood.

"I don't know yet," Caleb said. It was true that he didn't *know* because he hadn't yet seen the wound, but he knew it was awful.

A dimple in the fabric of the doctor's coat showed where the bullet had entered—high belly, low chest. As Caleb's hands worked the buttons, he saw that they were trembling.

"Don't look so scared," Rory said, forcing a smile.

"You've got this," First Sergeant Copley said. He stood above and behind Caleb, his eyes constantly scanning the horizon.

Caleb undid the buttons on Rory's coat and pulled it open. The volume of blood was worse than he'd feared. The garment's lining shimmered wet with blood, and his shirt was soaked.

"Doesn't look good at all," Rory said. "What's been hit?"

Caleb found himself staring, unable to find the words.

"Caleb, you can't freeze. We've talked about that." Doc Rory rolled onto his back, stared up at the sky. His eyes weren't right. "Upper right quadrant. What's there? What's not . . ." He seemed to lose the strength to speak.

"It's liver," Caleb said. "Not the spleen because the spleen is on the left."

But Doc Rory wasn't there anymore.

Caleb's vision clouded.

"It's not your fault," Copley said softly.

"Who shot him?" Caleb asked.

"One of the bad guys."

"Which one?"

"I don't know. Does it matter?"

"It matters to me."

"As far as I can tell, they're all dead. Everyone who shot. Come on, Caleb, get back with the program."

"Are we going to bury him?"

"That's not my call to make," Copley said. "It's not yours to make, either." He paused. "Now, man up and go to work."

Something boiled in Caleb's gut. "Doc Rory was my friend."

"He was my friend, too. He was everybody's friend. Now he's dead. Welcome to war." Copley turned away and retook his spot at the end of the line.

CHAPTER FIVE

"*E*VERYBODY ELSE, FACE DOWN ON THE GROUND!" McCrea yelled.

Victoria kept her rifle up and ready as she scanned for more threats. From what she could see, everyone complied with McCrea's command with the exception of one young man in his twenties. He lowered himself to his knees and held his hands high, but he did not complete the move to kiss the dirt.

"Don't press me, young man!" McCrea yelled.

"We didn't do anything wrong," the man said. "Those guys you just killed were road pirates."

"You don't want me to shoot you!" McCrea ordered.

The man brought his hands down quickly, slapping his thighs with them. Damn lucky he didn't get drilled. "Then do it!" the man said. He stood.

"Don't!" McCrea yelled.

"Don't what? Goddammit, if you're going to shoot

unarmed, innocent people, then you need to get to it."
He was angry, but not threatening. He made no move
to advance, but his arm gesticulations were broad. "I,
for one, am sick to death of people with guns telling
me what the hell to do. So, now I'm telling you: If
you're going to shoot, shoot. Otherwise, what do you
say we have a talk?"

Victoria let her rifle drop against its sling and she
took a step forward. "Talk about what?"

The young man pivoted away and looked down at a
young lady in a flannel shirt and jeans that looked too
big for her. "Stand up, Amy," he said. "We're not grov-
eling anymore."

Amy said something that Victoria couldn't hear.

"What difference does it make?" the man said. "Anybody can shoot us anytime they'd like. The difference
is all in the dignity. Let's have some."

McCrea said, "Young man, I am not telling you
again—"

Victoria held out her hand for silence. "Don't," she
said.

Hesitantly, Amy rose first to her knees and then she
stood the rest of the way up, with the help of the man's
hand. When she was on her feet, the man shifted his
grip to one of a husband. "My name is Alex Kramer,"
he said. "And this is my wife, Amy. We're from Pittsburgh. We were on our way to visit friends in Arkansas
when the war happened."

Victoria had so many questions, so much she wanted
to know. "Tell me what—"

"No," Alex said. "These people are all my friends. I
had no idea who they were until the shit happened, but
now they're my friends. I think they should be allowed

to sit, stand, lie on their backs or do any damn thing they want."

"You ambushed us," Luke said.

"I didn't ambush anybody, kid. You don't know a goddamn thing."

It was hard to hear such harsh words directed at her son, but he'd started it with his challenge.

"Not until we're convinced—"

Victoria interrupted McCrea. "Fine," she said. Then, louder, "You all can sit however you'd like."

"Make no threatening moves," Adam said.

"We're not suicidal," Alex replied. "Just tired of being beaten up. And I'm sorry about what they did to your friend."

From his words, Victoria thought he was talking about Doc Rory. But the way he tossed his head in a different direction, she thought maybe she was wrong. "Which friend?"

"The one last night," Alex said. "This Baggins guy you just killed took his time bleeding information out of Jerry Cameron."

"They *tortured* him?"

"Yes, ma'am, and he made us watch. He told us that he thought you would be coming this way. For what it's worth, he didn't want to, but there's only so much a man can endure. It's when they cut—"

"Stop," Victoria said. "I don't need to know the rest. I have the gist of it. I presume he's dead?"

"Finally. That was hard to watch."

"It was beyond awful," Amy said.

"Where is his body?" Victoria asked.

Alex pointed vaguely to a spot in the woods. "They dumped him in there someplace."

Greg Gonzales started to dismount his horse. "I'll go find him."

Victoria thought it was a fruitless endeavor but nodded anyway. Sometimes in difficult circumstances, people just needed something to do.

"Tell me about Baggins," Victoria said.

"If we're going to be here for a while, I'm going to establish a secure perimeter," McCrea said.

"I think that's a good idea." Victoria walked toward Alex Kramer, her hand extended. "I'm Victoria Emerson," she said. "I'd apologize for the way we had to meet, but it's almost seeming to feel natural these days." She'd meant it as a joke, but it fell flat.

"I told you about Baggins," Alex said. "He was a pirate."

A voice called from some distance away. "Excuse me, ma'am?"

Victoria turned to see a woman in tattered hiking clothes. She could have been thirty or she could have been sixty. She was that drawn.

"Are you really Victoria Emerson? I mean, really? They say you're the mayor of Eden. Is that right?"

Victoria heard Luke scoff at the question, but she ignored him. "I'm not the mayor of anything," she said.

"But I heard—"

"She's the leader of a town a few miles from here," McCrea said.

"Is it true that there are shelters for people? And food and water?"

Despite the death of all technology and modern communications mechanisms, somehow the rumor mill had survived Armageddon.

"Yes, that's true," Victoria said. "But it all has to be earned."

Another man in his thirties approached with what might have been his wife or his sister. "And there are laws there, right? It's not like out here?"

Victoria objected to the form of the question. It presumed that somewhere along the way, laws had been suspended, when the reality was nothing like that. People had chosen to go feral. "We do our best to keep the peace," she said.

"How?" the man asked. "The gangs and pirates are everywhere."

Victoria didn't know what to say to that, so she went for the platitude. "Even wild animals can be trained. They need to be treated well—treated fairly and the rest will follow. You know, you're only a few hours from being there. Mountain Road runs straight down to the river, and you'll be in Ortho."

Alex said, "Some of our people can't make the trip, even that far. We're stopped here waiting for them to . . . well, you know."

"Are they injured?" Victoria asked. "Sick?"

"They're Mr. and Mrs. Stannis," Amy said. "They're in the seventies, and I think they needed medications that no one has."

"How close to the end are they?" Luke asked. Right away, he seemed to be appalled by his own tone.

"None of us can know that, can we?" Amy said.

First Sergeant Copley called from the rear, "The longer we sit here, the better target we become."

The lady who was so wowed to be in the presence of Victoria's greatness said, "Mr. Cameron said that you were going to put the president on trial for all that has happened."

Victoria walked closer to her. "What's your name, ma'am?"

"Monica James," she said. "I'm from Fairfax, Virginia, but we were camping out here when the war happened."

"We?"

"My husband and I." She cast her eyes at the ground.

"Where is your husband now, Monica?"

"He, uh, he didn't make it."

"You mean he's dead?" Victoria asked.

Monica nodded.

"May I ask what happened?"

"They killed him."

"Who?"

"I don't know. The human animals. The people with the guns who enjoy shooting good, decent people."

"How long ago did that happen?"

"Why does it matter?"

"Because it does," Victoria said. She felt no need to explain that sooner or later she and her family were likely to confront the same monsters and she wanted to have some feel for how long they had.

"Maybe two weeks ago?"

"Are you asking me or telling me?" Victoria pressed.

"I'm telling you." Monica was beginning to show some emotion—something more than downtrodden sadness. "Sixteen days, to be exact."

"And what have you been doing for the past sixteen days?"

Caleb called from behind, "Mom! What are we going to do with Doc Rory's body?"

"I've got it," Adam said. He walked back to help his brother.

Victoria kept her gaze on Monica. "We were talking about the last sixteen days," she reminded.

"I don't understand the question," Monica said. Her confusion seemed real. "I've been . . . surviving."

Alex said, "She's been with us for the past week or so. That's how this group formed. Twos and threes and fours just wandering up on each other."

"None of you were armed?" Victoria asked.

"I was in the beginning," Alex said. "I'm a hunter, so I was able to keep us alive."

"So, you had a gun in the car as you were driving from Pittsburgh."

"No. I took it off a body." Something in his eyes dared Victoria to ask for more details.

"Body means dead guy," Victoria said. "How did he become dead?"

"I made him that way," Alex said. "He attacked us, and we won. Lucky swing of a car jack. I make no apologies."

"I didn't ask for one," Victoria said. "These are difficult times. So, where is that gun now?"

"Underneath the body of the guy you just shot. In fact, I'd like it back."

"In good time," Victoria promised. She found herself liking this guy. She appreciated his direct delivery, and the way he stuck up for the people he was with. "So, how many are there in your group now?"

"About a dozen, I guess. Give or take. Twice that many have come in and then wandered off."

"I'm not sure I understand," Victoria said. "Wandered off to where?"

Alex looked confused—concerned, maybe—that he needed to explain this. "Have you not even left your town since all this started? There are hundreds of people like us—maybe thousands, I don't know—just wandering. I want to say that it's like the stuff you'd see on the news about the Texas border or Ukraine back in the before times, but it's more than that. Worse than that. Those people on the news were all trying to get someplace. They had a goal. Out here, people just wander. They don't know where they're going or what they'll be doing twenty minutes from now. They're dazed. Adrift. Rudderless."

"But people find each other," Monica said, as if continuing Alex's thoughts. "Alex and Amy had already hooked up with the Stannis family over there."

"It was sad," Amy said. "They really couldn't care for themselves. Pirates took over their house and told them they had to leave. Poor things."

Monica brought the conversation back on point. "We almost literally ran into the Kramers in the woods. They had a gun, and I was scared, and they agreed to let me join them."

Amy said, "That's how it happens out here. It's terrible. People are killing themselves, and who can blame them?"

Alex continued with his story. "We'd heard about this place people called Eden, and we'd heard that this is the road to it. I guess we were right—at least that's what I think I just heard you say."

Alex lowered his voice. "Mr. and Mrs. Stannis both have heart issues, and he has a stomach thing that makes it so he can't eat. When we wandered up on this wrecked truck, we decided this was as good a place as any to try to set up camp. That was a week ago, and two days ago, that Baggins asshole wandered in with his friends, making threats."

"Did you confront them?" Victoria asked.

"I didn't see the point," Alex said. "There are a few others in our group with guns and stuff, but everybody's just so tired. I figured if I took a strong stand, I'd find myself alone, and if they took me out, Amy would be all alone."

Victoria pivoted to look at the rest of the vista that surrounded her. Down past the first wagon, McCrea and her boys were stripping off Doc Rory's clothes and shoes. As times got tighter, naked burial had become the norm. Clothes and shoes were too valuable a commodity.

"Tell you what," Victoria said, returning her attention to Alex. "You look able-bodied to me. I'd like you to assist my family over there in burying our doctor's body."

"How?" Alex said. "It's all rock."

"Burial is a relative thing," Victoria said. "It may be just finding a low spot and covering it with rocks, but it's something."

Alex seemed appalled by the idea, but he had the good sense not to say anything. "What about this guy?" he asked, indicating the mostly headless Baggins carcass.

"Strip him of his clothes, put them in the wagon. Take back your weapon and leave the body there to rot. Same for all the others. Give the vultures something to snack on."

Alex hesitated. Gave Victoria an odd look.

"If you've got something on your mind, say it," Victoria said.

"These people aren't the first to be killed in a shootout around here, are they?"

"Again, I urge you to say what's on your mind."

Alex clearly had more, but ended with, "Nah, I'm okay."

CHAPTER SIX

PENN GLENDALE, PRESIDENT OF THE UNITED STATES of America, heard footsteps on the concrete floor as they approached the door of his jail cell, so he stood from his cot and dressed. As was the case every time people came to his cell, he again expected to be taken to his execution.

He plucked his olive-drab shirt from its hanging spot at the end of the cot, shrugged into it and, before buttoning it, stepped into the matching olive-drab trousers. These were the sartorial selections of the geniuses who designed the United States Government Relocation Center—the Annex—and carved it out of the West Virginia bedrock. Next came the generic black tennis shoes, and bingo! He looked like every other resident, and all of them looked like they'd flown in from Castro's Cuba.

He'd worn the shoes enough that he no longer needed to deal with the laces when taking them off or putting them back on. He was on his feet by the time his visitor reached his wall of bars. It was a new face. A graying man in his fifties who'd shrunk away from his filthy casual business attire, the man appeared to be unarmed, but he was accompanied by another man—a much younger one—who was armed with an AR15 rifle. The man with the rifle was a guard named Jason, and he seemed primed to shoot pretty much anyone who crossed him.

"Glendale, you have a visitor," Jason said.

"That's Mr. President to you," Penn replied. They'd had this very exchange at least three times a day since the time of the putsch that resulted in Roger Parsons—a forgotten professional wrestler—conquering the government of the United States.

Penn waited for the man to introduce himself. "How do you do, Mr. President?" the man said, extending his hand. "My name is Taylor Barnes. I am your attorney."

Penn stared at the hand. He'd gotten used to being treated like shit by the new regime. Friendliness made him nervous.

Barnes turned to Jason. "I'd like to speak to my client alone and in his cell, please."

"Ain't gonna happen," Jason said.

Barnes barely blinked. "Very well, then," he said. "I'm sorry, Mr. President. I'll be back right after I speak with Mr. Parsons." He pushed past Jason, who stuck out his arm as if it were the gate at a toll booth.

"You don't have to do that," Jason said.

"I believe Mr. Parsons told you to show me *every courtesy*. Those were his words."

Jason blushed. "I remember."

"That would mean that you comply with my very reasonable request to be alone."

The younger man looked to be both pissed and embarrassed as he fished a giant, old-school key out of his pocket and slid it into the lock of the cell door. As he pulled it open, Barnes slipped past and entered the cell.

Penn thought the move to be forward and rude, but he liked seeing Jason get put in his place.

"Leave the door open," Barnes said.

Penn noticed that his attorney never turned back to the jailer, but rather assumed that the man would leave. He was right.

Barnes extended his hand again. "Let's start over. Taylor Barnes, attorney-at-law."

"Penn Glendale, president of the United States of America." He gestured to the bottom half of the cot. "Have a seat."

Barnes lowered himself carefully onto the thin mattress, as if he wasn't sure whether the structure was strong enough to hold him. "I'll stipulate that you are in fact the president, despite what others say, but might I ask how that came to be? The last time I heard the news or read the paper, you were Speaker of the House of Representatives."

"That put me third in line for the Oval Office," Penn said. "When the president and vice president both disappeared—we presumed they were dead—I inherited the job."

Barnes scowled. "That's really sucky timing."

"Now, there's a word I've never heard from a lawyer. I guess I should ask. Are you *really* a lawyer?"

"I was, last time I wrote myself a paycheck. My name was on the front of the building and everything. Barnes, Connolly and Tate. We had offices in DC, New York, Chicago and Los Angeles. My wife and I were staying here at the Hilltop Manor for a couple of days when the war happened." His head tilted as a thought occurred to him. "There *was* a war, right? That's what all of this misery is about? I mean, that's what everyone assumes, but since I'm talking to the guy who would really know . . ."

Penn liked this guy. He liked his manner and his directness. And now that he got a closer look, he saw that the suit that no longer fit the man was of very high quality. "I know that there was a war, and that it lasted about eight hours," Penn explained. "What I *don't* know is who won, as if that's an option in the wake of a nuclear holocaust."

"Not to pile on," Barnes said, "but how can you not know? The military reports to you."

"And not to be obtuse, the military didn't report to me, per se. They reported to the president. When the missiles started flying, that wasn't my gig."

Barnes seemed to grow concerned. "Please don't use that as part of your defense—that it wasn't your butt in the seat."

"Mr. Barnes, I don't even know what I'm defending myself against. In Mr. Parsons' world, arraignment isn't really a thing."

Barnes scoffed. "First of all, please call me Taylor. Tay is even better. And second, Mr. Parsons is a dickhead. I don't know what his inner circle is telling him, but the buzz among the common folk is ugly. A different conversation. Can I ask *why* we went to war? Did it have anything to do with Iran developing their nukes?"

"It had everything to do with that."

"I knew it." Barnes slapped his knee.

"On the night of the war, Israel was going to use a couple of tactical nukes on the Iranian launch and storage sites. The press leaked the plan, Iran shot first. Israel launched, the Russians got spooked and released their birds, and we released ours because we had to. Within only a couple of minutes, the stratosphere was filled with hundreds of warheads. And here we are."

"Indeed."

"And for what it's worth, the last thing I told President Blanton was that I thought the entire plan was a bad idea, but she wouldn't listen to me."

"Oh, to travel back in time." Barnes's tone was dismissive, and Penn understood. If ever there was a time when past mistakes could not be undone, it was when the world was in smoldering ruins. "So, this place we're sitting in," Barnes continued. "Tell me about it."

"Shouldn't you be taking notes or something?"

"I want to listen for a while first, and then the note taking can start later. I know that you call this place the Annex, and that its official designation is the United States Government Relocation Center, so you don't have to go into that. Am I correct to assume that the facility is in fact an emergency Situation Room?"

Penn found himself smiling at the irony. "Do you want the theoretical version, or the reality?"

"Theory first."

"Okay, sure. The war planners planned big. Everybody knows that life gets tough after a nuclear exchange, but governments need to continue to function. The theory was that if the balloon went up, as they say, the House and the Senate would relocate to this bunker where we would be sheltered from all but a direct hit, and from here, we would keep the train of government on its tracks. The executive branch would go to a different location, and the judiciary to still another."

"How could anyone possibly have that much forewarning?" Barnes asked.

"That's a very good question," the president replied. "And it's one that no one asked. We politicians have spent generations trying to get Americans to trust themselves less and trust the government more. And we were very successful. Hell, we barely hold—*held*—Americans accountable for their own debt anymore. The truth that they would be on their own in the event of a nuclear exchange was the last thing we could say to the American public."

"Your cynicism surprises me, Mr. President."

"Cynicism and reality can be close cousins," Penn said. "Which brings us to the reality of this place. We had time to get here because our ally was planning a first strike and Crimson Phoenix was called as an abundance of caution."

Barnes raised his hand. "Crimson Phoenix?"

"That was the code phrase for imminent threat of nuclear war. It's the phrase that honor bound us politicians to come to the bunker. No one thought Israel's strike would spin out of control, but it was always a possibility. That's the hubris of Washington. They game stuff out and then assume that our enemies will react in the way that is most advantageous to us and give the war planners a warm feeling."

Barnes raised his hand again. "You're venting now, sir. Could we—"

"Goddamn right I'm venting, and now that I'm on a roll, I'm not going to stop for a little bit. That was my counsel to the president, but she had no interest in listening. She assumed—as all of Washington assumed twenty-four/seven in the final years—that my cautions were politically motivated. An attempt to make her look indecisive."

Penn stopped and pumped the air with his hands in an attempt to settle himself. "You're right," he said. "Reliving the past accomplishes nothing. What do you need to know?"

Barnes's scowl deepened. "So, what did you all do? I mean, as unlikely as it might have been to get the engine started on the Annex, you did. You got it up and running. Things are still very shitty out there. What did you put in place for the people while you were drinking clean water, sleeping on sheets and eating three squares a day? The people out there are pretty pissed off. It would help if we could show them that you actually accomplished something."

Penn recoiled from the words. When you'd spent as many years in politics at the level he'd achieved, people were rarely so blunt.

Barnes seemed to understand. "I'm sorry, sir, but I need you to understand the reality of this. Whatever you can give me would help."

Penn allowed himself a smile. "Do you really think I have a chance at anything that looks like a fair trial?"

"Can you please answer my question? Sir?"

Penn inhaled deeply and let it go slowly as he organized his thoughts and the way he wanted to present them. "Tay, we have the most advanced communications equipment and expertise on the planet ensconced in the Annex. Or we did, before Parsons and his band of roaches shot it all up. The Solara people—the consulting firm that ran the facility itself—tested it all three times per week. I'm talking top notch stuff."

The president propped his elbows on his knees and leaned in closer. "But we couldn't talk to anyone. The EMP—electromagnetic pulse—wiped out all modern conveniences and comms in the first microseconds of the war, so all that civil defense bullshit we were supposed to be communicating to the masses couldn't make it past the end of our transmitting antennas. I have reason to believe that every military installation of note was incinerated, just as I assume that we got our missiles out of our silos."

"Excuse me, sir. You *assume*? Who would know if not you?"

"The guys who watched them exit their silos, I suppose." He sat straight again. "Tay, I am not hyperbolizing when I tell you that we have spent the weeks since the war trying to find the right button to push or string to pull to reach out to the people of the United States."

Barnes grew uncomfortable. He shifted his position and squinted as if enduring a gas pain. "Were you aware of the crowds in and around the Hilltop Manor during those weeks that you were chasing your tails? Apology for the characterization."

"You're really my lawyer, right? I'm supposed to be blunt and truthful with you?"

"That would make my job a lot easier."

Another deep breath. "I think we went out of our way to preserve plausible deniability. The Solara staff didn't share much with us about their surveillance of the area, but when I pressed hard enough, they confessed that they'd heard signs of movement and seen quite a crowd of people."

Barnes's jaw set. "So, despite knowing that people were suffering, you, as commander in chief, and the others as the entirety of the House and Senate, decided to keep the doors closed and let them suffer while you lounged in comparative luxury."

The words hit hard. "I asked if you were *my* attorney, right?"

"This is a bad time to be sensitive, Mr. President. That's the case that they're making. You politicians put your own safety and health above that of your constituents. As you've presented the facts, I don't see where they're wrong."

"You make it sound much less complicated than it was. There were procedures in place that prevented us from opening the blast doors."

"Which is another way of saying that the war planners you talk about—the *government*—had always intended to take care of its own at the expense of the people they were elected to serve."

"Jesus, Counselor."

"You're taking offense again." Barnes made a slashing gesture across his throat. "Okay, cut. Let's try a different tack. I need to prepare you for what lies ahead. Parsons and his prosecutors are going to try and paint you and yours as uncaring sons of bitches. Nothing ever has to be true for people to believe it."

No one knew the truth of that statement better than Penn Glendale. He'd been in the media's crosshairs for his entire career. It was a rare day when a mention of his name in the media wasn't followed by deliberate misrepresentations of the truth. News had given way to political narratives, and facts ceased to matter.

"When I look at it from their point of view," Penn

said, "I think they have a point. I'd be pretty damned pissed if I were them." He leaned in again. "But *treason*?"

"It's the first charge they could think of, I'm sure. So, let's turn to the topic of your defense."

"How about we start with the elements of the law?" Penn said. "You know that treason is the only crime that is specifically defined by the Constitution? And I quote: *Treason against the United States shall consist only in levying War against them, or in adhering to their Enemies, giving them Aid and Comfort. No Person shall be convicted of Treason unless on the Testimony of two Witnesses to the same overt Act, or on Confession in open Court.* By that definition, Parsons is the traitor."

Barnes smiled as if addressing a confused child. "And Benjamin Franklin is credited with saying that treason is a charge invented by winners as an excuse for hanging the losers. You're talking about words, sir, and words—even the ones that are rooted in the Constitution—are no match for emotions."

Penn stood and wandered two steps to his wall of bars. He rested his wrists on a crossbar and looked out into the dimly lit battleship-gray hallway beyond. "You know, Tay, you're sounding more and more like you're here to measure my neck for a noose. What happened to the rule of law?"

Barnes coughed out a laugh. "Oh, my God, you *have* been out of touch, haven't you? The rule of law is a convenience born of trustworthy governments. We don't have one of those anymore."

Penn turned around again and faced his visitor. "So, I'm doomed?"

Barnes stood, too. "I can't say that your future looks

terribly bright, Mr. President, but I won't give up if you don't. This is why we need to craft a defense to keep you away from that short drop from a high platform."

The attorney's glibness pissed Penn off. "What's the best outcome you can predict?"

Barnes said nothing for more than ten seconds. He sat back down. "You're a worldly guy, Mr. President. It makes no sense whatsoever to try to predict the future. All we can do is our best."

Penn sat back down, too. "So, how does this go? When is this monkey trial set to start?"

"Stop showing that level of disrespect, sir," Barnes snapped. "You don't have to respect the *people who are determining your future*, but you'd better by-God respect what they've been through. Whether you made the decision to end the world, or you opposed it, you were the one with the knife in your hand when the music stopped." He paused and smiled. "Good Lord, that was a lot of metaphors all in one sentence."

Penn smiled back. "So, how long do I have?"

"Hard to tell," Barnes confessed. "A while, I imagine. You know that Parsons used to be a professional wrestler, right?"

"So I've heard. As sports go, that was not one I kept up with."

"I understand. It's less than, shall we say, spontaneous. But it is well choreographed and those guys know how to put on a good show. And I predict that's exactly what Parsons will be thinking about when he comes for you and yours."

"A good show? What, is he going to dance?"

"Um, no. But he is going to put on a show. I don't

know exactly how many trials there are going to be, but I'm confident that yours will be the last one. You know, build to the climax."

"How many trials can there be?"

"How many of you were able to make it to the Annex before they had to button it up for the unexpected war?"

"A few over two hundred," Penn said. As he heard his words, he felt terrible that he didn't know the exact number.

"That's your trial docket, then. Though I don't expect it will be nearly that many. I imagine they'll do the president of the Senate first, and then the Speaker of the House, but they could conceivably go one at a time. Then it will be your turn."

"Do I have a week?" Penn asked.

Barnes's scowl seemed to absorb his whole face. "Is there something special about a week? That seems very specific."

Penn tried to read the attorney's face. The glib banter and annoying casualness clearly masked a lot of smarts.

"You're not telling me something," Barnes said. "Is it something I need to know?"

Penn didn't want to trust anyone with the news of the emissary he'd launched in the form of Jerry Cameron, but since the young man had left, Penn had been troubled by the possible outcomes. Maybe having another person inside the wire, as it were, aware of the plan, could play to his benefit. He decided to roll the dice.

"I need for you to stall for as much time as you can," Penn said. He told of the note he'd sent.

"Does this have anything to do with that Eden nonsense that's been making the rounds? Nicki Somebody?"

"Vicky," Penn corrected. "Victoria Emerson. She was a colleague of mine in the House, and she resigned her seat at the front door of the Annex when she found out she couldn't bring her kids with her. Even in this box, I've heard the rumors about Eden, and if there's anyone who could accomplish those kinds of leadership goals, it would be she."

"What makes you think she would leave there to come here?"

"I don't think it's in her character to say no," Penn said.

"Okay," Barnes countered. "What makes you think that Roger Parsons would want to give up the stage to an outsider who's making far less of a mess of things than he is?"

"That's the part that's been bothering me since I sent for her," Penn confessed. "I've been trying to think of a way to presell Parsons on the idea, but until you showed up, I never had a handle to pull."

"I'm not sure you have the handle even now," Barnes said. "Even if Parsons would talk to me, I don't have magic words. I'm not even sure what you would want me to say."

Penn was ready for this. The idea had been swirling between his ears for days. "It all comes down to his legacy," he said. "You quoted Benjamin Franklin before. Well, old Ben wondered in a letter to Thomas Jefferson whether, two hundred years later, they would be seen as heroes or as traitors to future generations. If you can work on Parsons' sense of pride—his vision for the future—maybe you can get him to see the need for these proceedings to be performed in a way that seems fair and just."

"Why isn't he going to just see this as a way for you to bring in a friend to find you not guilty and let you go? That is, after all, what you're trying to do, isn't it?"

Penn was ready for that question, and he responded from his heart. "No, actually that's not what I'm trying to do. I know that my colleagues and I made a mess of things here. It doesn't matter that we meant well when the results were so horrifying. But no matter what happens to me, I do love the United States. I love the *idea* of the United States. Two hundred years from now, if we still have historians, I want the record to show that the idea of justice was important, even at the end. Even as America's leaders let everybody down."

Penn's voice cracked at that last part, so he stopped talking. Barnes seemed to be looking *through* him, all the way past his brain and beyond. He clearly was weighing the president's words, and the sincerity behind them.

"I think you'd have made a good president if you'd had the chance to lead," Barnes said. "Personally, I think that you overrate Parsons' capacity for introspection, but I will give it a try."

They stood together and shook hands.

CHAPTER SEVEN

*D*OC RORY HAD BEEN KEY TO STABILIZING ORTHO. Beyond his role as sole physician for the first weeks, he was also the one who approved the location of outhouses and other sanitation facilities in the town. Victoria had grown quite close to him, and she was grateful for the way he took Caleb under his wing to teach him as much medicine as the new Stone Age allowed. Rory's term for it was *cowboy medicine*, and he approached it with Caleb as an apprenticeship.

The Foster brothers handled the physical aspect of Doc's burial, but Caleb stayed close to the action. It seemed important to him to oversee the interment. As Victoria had predicted, there'd been no hole dug because of the unforgiving terrain, but by the time the rocks had been arranged around the body, Doc Rory was completely covered.

"How long do you think before animals get him?" Caleb asked no one in particular after placing the last rock on the top of the burial pile.

Victoria placed a hand on his shoulder, but he jerked away from it.

"Screw it," he said. "Everybody dies anyway, right?" Then he walked away toward his horse.

Victoria looked to Adam.

"I'll talk to him," Adam said, and he walked off.

"He's hurting," McCrea said. "I guess we all are. He'll be okay."

"None of us will be okay again," Victoria said. Then she squeezed McCrea's hand and forced a smile. "I guess maybe we need to think up a new standard for *okay*."

"Something closer to *not awful*, maybe."

First Sergeant Copley approached with purpose— long strides. As he closed the distance, he slowed. "Excuse me, Major, but we really need to get moving. Sitting still doesn't get us where we need to be, and it exposes us as stationary targets."

"I get it," Victoria said. "Tell everybody to mount up and get ready to move."

"What do we do with the refugees?" Copley asked.

"Nothing. We leave them alone, send them on their way, I suppose."

"Excuse me, Mrs. Emerson?" It was Alex Kramer. His wife, Amy, stood next to him.

Victoria waited for it.

"Amy and I want to come along with you." Amy nodded as her husband spoke.

"Do you know where we're going?"

"I think so. You're going to bring the fight back to the head guy at the Hilltop Manor, right?"

Victoria and McCrea exchanged looks. "What do you know about that?" she asked.

"Just what I've heard. That guy last night. Baggins. The one you killed? Last night he was popping off that some guy named Roger had taken over as king or some such, and that he was headquartered in that big hotel, the Hilltop Manor."

"It's not our intent to bring a fight to anyone," Victoria said. "Our intent is to bring justice for one man. There doesn't have to be violence." As she listened to her own words, she knew she was probably lying. It was hard to conceive of a scenario where there wouldn't have to be a fight, but if there was a way to avoid it, that was what she would do.

Alex wasn't done. "Baggins said that Parsons wanted it all. That's what he said."

"What does that mean?" Victoria asked. "Wanting it all?"

"I didn't spend a lot of time talking with him. In fact, I tried to avoid him. But from the way they started by taking away guns and ammunition, and then they turned to everybody's stuff, I take him literally. He *wants it all.*"

McCrea asked, "Do you get the sense that Baggins and Parsons were somehow affiliated? Working with each other?"

"I can't say for sure. I mean, Baggins could have been lying out of his ass, but he seemed to know Parsons. The goal of getting everything—whatever that means—kinda goes with the rest of the buzz. People you pass on the road. Everybody's afraid of the Mauler. That's what they say he calls himself. Anyway, he sends out these gangs to flex his muscle and take their stuff. Guns and ammo in particular."

First Sergeant Copley asked, "Why would you want

to go back to all that? You're just a few hours from Ortho, and it's pretty safe there. Why would you walk back into danger?"

Alex looked to Amy, who nodded to him, as if to give him permission to speak. "It's not complicated," Alex said. "I've already told you that I'm tired of running. I'm tired of hiding and being a victim. Those people have no right to do the kinds of things they're doing to other people, and I like the idea of fighting back. They've always been organized, and we've been one-offs and we get our asses handed to us. I want to change that."

Victoria loved the words, and her assessment of his eyes told her that he was speaking from his heart.

"Be pleased to have you along," Victoria said. "You'll follow the orders given to you by First Sergeant Copley here and by Major McCrea. And also from pretty much everybody else, at least until we know more about you."

"Thank you, ma'am," Amy said. "This life is hard enough without feeling ashamed all the time."

Victoria cocked her head. "Ashamed? Of what?"

"Cowering. Hiding. Begging for mercy from monsters."

"There's no shame in doing what you have to do to survive," McCrea said.

"When was the last time you cowered, Major?" Then she turned to Copley. "How about you?"

Copley wanted none of that. He looked back at the rest of the idle caravan.

"I want to go, too," Monica said. "This is like dying in slow motion. I want a vote in my future again."

"What about the old couple?" McCrea asked.

"We'll give them a choice," Victoria said. "They can stay, or we can clear a spot for them in one of the wagons. They'll have to move forward, though. We won't go back to Ortho."

"What about the food rations?" Copley asked.

"Adjust as necessary," Victoria said. "Nobody's going to gain weight on this trip, but no one's going to starve, either."

"And their weapons?" Copley asked.

"If they've got them, they keep them."

McCrea shifted his stance uncomfortably. He clearly didn't like the part about them keeping their weapons.

"Our rules of engagement don't change, Major," Victoria said. "If they shoot at us, we'll shoot back, but we have to start trusting people." She looked at Alex. "You're not going to shoot us, are you?"

"I'll try not to, ma'am."

"Try hard," Victoria said.

"You've got your orders, First Sergeant," McCrea said. "Round 'em up and move 'em out."

Copley spun on his heel. "All right, everybody listen up!"

In the end, the elder Stannises decided to stay behind at the trailer. "We're comin' up on a moment Mother and I have trained for our whole lives," the old man said. "We've lived good and we've prayed hard. In a day or two, we'll have a forever of happiness spread out before us in Heaven. I actually feel sorry for you young folks. Looks like there's a lot of sufferin' looming ahead for you between now and eternal rest."

McCrea held back while Victoria and the Kramers

comforted the couple. He admired anyone who could summon that level of certainty in an afterlife. Reasonably sure that his wife and daughters had crossed that plane on Hell Day, he hoped that Heaven existed, and that it was as wonderful as the Stannises expected it to be.

Alex took over Doc Rory's horse, and Amy took a spot in Kyle Foster's wagon. Monica rode one of the spare horses bareback and looked comfortable doing it. She refused a gun, though, stating her belief that she couldn't pull the trigger on another human being.

McCrea couldn't wrap his head around that, especially since Monica's husband had been killed by roadside thieves. In his heart, he had no doubt that she would change her mind if the time came when people were shooting at her and she couldn't shoot back.

McCrea figured their traveling speed to be about two miles per hour uphill, and maybe twice that on the flat ground. A few more hours into the journey, he saw a flash of red paint at the bottom of the hill that fell away from the road surface. He knew without approaching that the paint belonged to a Toyota sedan and that the front seat held two corpses. A man and a woman had crashed the vehicle as the bombs were dropping in the distance. The man died on impact, but the woman was suffering terribly with broken legs and other injuries.

As an act of mercy, McCrea had had to shoot her.

"Mom!" Luke called from behind. "Look to the left! That's the car!"

"I see it," Victoria called back. More quietly, McCrea heard her add, "And I wish I didn't."

As far as McCrea was concerned, just a few hours

into this journey, they'd already paid too high a price. He thought it had to be soul stealing for the Emersons to pass by all the past carnage, and he thought it was foolish—sinful, perhaps—to turn away from all the hard work and accomplishments they'd made back in Ortho, all for the purpose of protecting some elusive goal of being seen in a good light by next century's historians.

But he'd committed to her that he would stay by her side, and he'd committed to the others to make this sojourn as safe as it could be.

At least from this point on, the family wouldn't have to confront the remains of old conflicts.

No, from here on, all the conflicts would be brand new.

The number of strangers—refugees—wandering along the road did, in fact, number into the dozens, but so far, they all seemed docile, and none had formed into groups of more than five or six people. Certainly, none had posed an overt threat, but McCrea knew how fast violence could happen. Most had a dazed quality about their eyes that made him wonder if they were even aware that they were walking.

The overall vibe reminded him of a television show he used to watch back in normal times that featured wandering zombies.

Up ahead, a group of six people stretched across the road—two adult women and four children, aged probably thirteen to eighteen, two boys, two girls. They looked tired, beaten. Blood stained the flannel shirt and denim jeans of the woman on the left. The youngest of the children, a little girl, held her left arm in her right, and listed to the hurt side.

"Spread out!" McCrea commanded from his horse. After the ambush that killed Doc Rory, they'd decided to change their tactics. Once a threat was recognized, the team would spread out in a kind of skirmish line.

McCrea opened up space between his horse and Victoria's, turning it sideway across the roadway to allow for a lane of fire that did not include the horse's head.

"Please move out of the way," McCrea said. "We need to pass by."

"You don't want to go that way," the bloody lady said. "Not if you don't want a big fight."

"Gangs?" Victoria asked.

"I guess you could call it that," the lady said. "More like a roadblock. They're sociopaths." She tossed a nod toward the injured girl. "I think they broke Brenda's arm."

Victoria stood in her stirrup and dismounted. "Caleb!" she called. "Can you come up, please?"

"Vicky, please don't do that."

"They need help. That girl is hurt."

"Goddammit. Point to someone who's not hurt somewhere." McCrea spun his horse to face backward, toward the column behind him. "Dismount! Hobble your horses, set up a perimeter." This was the problem of dealing with tactical threats with people who didn't have a feel for tactics. "First Sergeant Copley, please check their positions."

"I don't need help with my position," Caleb said as he passed with a heavy medical kit hanging from his right arm.

This situation of a wounded family in the middle of the street could have been lifted from a jihadi textbook, a scenario he'd seen far too many times during his tours in the Sandbox. Bad guys saw compassion and pity as weaknesses, and that's exactly what they were in a war zone.

When would he learn, he chided himself, that Victoria didn't consider what was left of the world to be an evolving war zone. She saw it as a population of people who needed help. That worldview was fine—admirable, even—during the convenience of peaceful times, but it was nothing but liability when the fabric of the world had been reduced to shredded strands of thread.

He wondered sometimes if Vicky's refusal to see the world as he saw it wasn't one of the things about her that he loved most. Her optimism and trust of strangers—however cautious—could be infectious. It was one of the qualities that made her a great leader.

But when the stakes were as high as they'd been since Hell Day, she was also a fierce warrior when warfare was necessary.

"Hey!" someone called from behind. It was Alex, the stray they'd picked up in the last fight. "What do you want us to do?"

"First Sergeant Copley!"

"I'm on it, Major."

As Copley arranged the entourage along the sides of the road in a way to give them the greatest defensive advantage if this turned out to be a trap, McCrea dismounted his horse and walked up to join Victoria.

Caleb had taken a knee in front of the injured girl and was negotiating for a chance to take a look at her arm. Apparently, it hurt a lot, and she didn't welcome someone else handling it.

"I promise I won't hurt you," Caleb said.

Bad choice of words, McCrea thought, but he kept it to himself. Dealing with a broken bone *always* hurt, and kids were literalists. He'd have been better off telling her that he'd do his best not to hurt her.

McCrea dialed into Victoria's conversation while it was already underway. ". . . so they just hit her and took it away. What kind of monster would steal a little girl's Buddy Bear? She hasn't been apart from that toy for years. And since the bombs, it . . ." The lady's voice trailed away into tears.

"What's your name, honey?" Victoria asked the woman.

"Marney. Marney Bates."

"Where did the blood come from?" McCrea asked. The color hadn't dulled to copper yet. That meant it was fairly fresh.

"She tried to help my husband," the second woman said. For the first time, McCrea noticed bruises around the woman's eyes, and maybe on her neck. "They shot him."

"You didn't help your husband?" McCrea asked. As soon as the question left his throat, he knew it was a mistake.

"I was busy being raped," the woman said.

McCrea didn't have words.

"And what's your name?" Victoria asked.

"Simone Tyler. These are my children, Max, Tommy, Tabby and Brenda."

"They had to hold me back," said Max, the eldest. "I tried to help, but I couldn't. None of us could."

The hollowness in the young man's tone—the sadness—hurt McCrea's heart. The kid was apologizing for his own trauma.

McCrea shifted away from the emotion. "How long ago and how far?" he asked.

"How long from when it started or when it ended?" Marney asked.

No one knew how to answer that.

"It started three or four hours ago. We've only been walking again for a half hour or so."

McCrea took a step away, turned, and called for Copley to join them. When Copley arrived, McCrea took half a minute to fill him in on what they knew.

"I'm very sorry for your loss," Copley said.

"Tell me about the people," McCrea said. "How many? How are they armed?"

"I didn't take time to count," Simone said.

McCrea turned to Marney.

Max answered first. "There are fifteen of them. The guy in charge calls himself Buster. Big man, maybe two-fifty, wearing a red plaid lumberjack shirt."

Under these circumstances, McCrea had a hard time understanding how anyone could still be that size, but he took the boy at his word. "Are they armed?"

"More guns than they can carry," Max said. "They've got them propped up against trees, and all of them are carrying at least a rifle. Some have other guns, too. And knives. Lots and lots of knives."

"I'm guessing the guns were taken from other people they victimized," McCrea said. "Did you see other signs of violence? Dead bodies, wounded people?"

"They've set themselves up on a part of the road where one side—the left side looking up from here—is a cliff," Marney said. "That's where they disposed of Alan's body—Simone's husband." She looked at the ground. "They said they would throw our bodies there, too, if we didn't do what they told us to do."

"And what did they tell you to do?" McCrea asked. With a nod to Simone, he added, "Other than what we know already."

"They told me that they would choose me or one of my daughters," Simone said.

"I'm sorry that happened," McCrea said.

"Would you let your daughters be raped?" Simone was in a bad place, a place that McCrea couldn't imagine. He didn't mention that his own daughters—in fact, his entire family, in all probability, was dead.

"It was about robbery," Marney said. "And about humiliation. They said something about that slice of the road belonging to them, and if you wanted to pass through, you had to give them everything you owned. They said our dignity was part of that."

McCrea cast a glance toward the children, who likewise showed bruises. He decided that he didn't want to know the answer to the next question that occurred to him.

"When they were done, they told us that we'd earned our freedom," Simone said.

"Do you believe that?" Marney asked. "They wanted us to be grateful."

Victoria said, "Excuse us for a second." She touched McCrea's arm and pulled him back a few feet, where they turned their back on the others. "We can't allow this," she said. "We have to do something."

McCrea's gut boiled. Was it possible that the reason he resisted this sojourn was because he didn't want to confront this kind of reality? "Someone does, yes. But are you sure you want it to be us? You'd be exposing your whole family, plus a lot of friends. Is this a cause worth dying for? Remember, your mission is to guarantee justice for the president."

Victoria looked surprised. And maybe a little angry. "Are you suggesting we just ignore this?"

"I'm suggesting that I'll do whatever you want to do. And to be honest, I'd get great pleasure from killing those sons of bitches. This is a step that can't be walked back, so I just wanted to make sure you're sure."

Victoria considered it for three seconds, max. "They're in our way," she said. "On our way. Let's see how they handle a lone, lonely former congresswoman as she comes through their little roadblock."

McCrea couldn't suppress his grin. "You have a plan."

"I do, indeed."

CHAPTER EIGHT

*M*IDWAY THROUGH HIS FIFTH DECADE ON EARTH, Roger Parsons felt like a much older man. His back and knees were constant sources of discomfort, thanks to hundreds of sparring sessions and thirty-seven victories as the Mauler, against some of the largest and strongest men ever to draw a breath. Parsons understood that people derided professional wrestling as being faked, but he'd never heard those words from anyone who'd ever walked the walk. Sure, the winners and losers were picked ahead of time, and tricks and stunts kept you from getting hurt as bad as it looked, but every one of those slams was a real trip through gravity, and every throw strained muscles.

Until the war happened, Parsons got through his days on a cocktail of oxycodone, ibuprofen, and bourbon. In the weeks since the bombs dropped, the oxy had disappeared entirely, and the Vitamin I was ever harder to find. Thanks to the Hilltop Manor Resort's hospitality managers, he didn't have to fear an end to the bourbon for a long while, but that time would one day come. He'd assigned two of his men to find people who knew how to build a still and to get a production operation going.

He needed to be careful with the booze, though. Left to follow his inclinations, he would be drunk by noon, and unconscious by dinnertime. Back in normal times, when he wasn't in training, such was the nature of pretty much every day, though he wouldn't pass out until nine-thirty or ten at night. That's what happened when you didn't wake up until noon.

The situation at the Hilltop Manor didn't allow the luxury of sleeping late. It barely allowed the luxury of sleeping at all. He had too many enemies to keep his eyes closed for more than a few hours at a time. He had his team, of course—his *posse*—his training crew whom he'd worked with for God knew how many years, and he had some of the early survivors who'd declared their allegiance to Parsons, but more people flowed into this godforsaken valley every day, and while he'd been able to disarm them and send most on their way, too many saw the Hilltop Manor as what it used to be, as opposed to what it had become.

Once a grand resort for old money millionaires, now it was a homeless shelter and refugee center. So far, Parsons and his team had been successful in keeping the throngs frightened and compliant, but as the numbers grew and the unrest blossomed, it would take only one misstep for it all to come crashing in on him. When that happened, he'd be forced to fight. His enemy would be mostly unarmed and weak from the ordeal they'd lived since the day of the war, but he knew from his wrestling days that it wasn't always the strongest fighter who won the day. Sometimes, it was the luck-iest.

"We've got to feed them, Champ," said Mason Goode, Parsons' longtime friend and sparring coach. "You want to avoid a riot, you've got to feed them."

Parsons had gathered his team in the Presidential Suite, a sprawling apartment with three bedrooms, a full kitchen, dining room and music parlor. The windows on all three sides of the apartment looked out from the fifth floor onto the once opulent green lawn that had transformed into an open sewer populated by the most disgusting collection of human beings that he'd ever witnessed. Even up this high, and despite the cool air, the stench turned his stomach when the wind blew in the right direction.

"How many are out there now?" Parsons asked. He sat at the ebony-inlaid walnut dining room table. "All told, how many appetites are we talking about?"

Goode made a face. "I don't have an exact number. Two hundred, maybe?"

"With ten or fifteen more arriving every day, right?" Parsons asked.

"At least," said Winston "Stony" McGillis. Stony was pushing sixty and had been on Parsons' team since the beginning, though for the life of him, Parsons couldn't say what he did. Half father figure, half coach, Stony always had Parsons' ear. "But at least that many are dying every day, too."

"The cremation fire never stops," said Kenny DeWilde. Not yet out of his teens, DeWilde was a late arrival to the posse. He'd been so star struck when he'd found out that the Mauler was marooned at the same hotel as he and his parents, Parsons couldn't say no to him.

"Where are we going to find food for two hundred people on an ongoing basis?" Parsons asked. "We've got foragers out there, but for every bit of food and goods we take in, we're making a lot of enemies."

"There was food here for a couple *thousand* people when the war happened," Goode said.

"Most of that is spoiled now," Parsons said.

"Not the canned goods and dry goods," Stony said. "Not the frozen stuff, neither. Leastwise not until the generators run outta diesel. And, hell, I don't see that happening for months. I hate to beat that dead horse, but I done told you at the time that you'd have gone a long way toward winning hearts and minds if you'd shared the perishables from the refrigerator when we had the chance to."

"You've sung that song before, Stony," Parsons said. "Past is past."

In the hours immediately following the first bombs that dropped in the distance, Parsons read the situation for exactly what it was. He foresaw the panic and the anger and the fear, and he rallied his buddies right away.

They tracked down the general manager as he was trying to comfort his own terrified family in their quarters onsite, and Parsons had been able to persuade the guy whose name he could no longer remember to fork over the keys and combinations to all the resort's food stores.

Then he raided the gun vault in the skeet and trap range to take custody of the shotguns and ammunition, which he used to intimidate newcomers into giving up the firearms they inevitably brought with them for personal protection while wandering like nomads. Two things about those times surprised Parsons: First, there was the overwhelming number of firearms he'd collected, and second, precious few of the people who thought to arm themselves had the balls to actually use the weapons they'd brought against strangers who told them to disarm.

Most people, Parsons learned, were inherently hesitant to kill.

The bombs hit in the wee hours of the morning. By the time the sun rose through the murky, smoky atmosphere, Parsons had realized that supplies would soon be scarce, and that the rabble would raid whatever resources they wanted in order to fill their pockets and their mouths.

Parsons' initial posse consisted only of the three of them. They would need reinforcements if they were not to starve to death within the first weeks after the war. He recruited a larger posse with the offer of food and supplies and indoor shelter if they pledged to be on Parsons' side.

Another surprise for Parsons was the number of people who refused his entreaties. A shocking number of idiots decided that it was more honorable to suffer with the many than to thrive with the few. He wondered sometimes how long it took those morons to realize their mistake. He also wondered, though not in a serious way, whether the idiot morons were still alive.

"You've got another opportunity, Champ," Stony said. "If we opened those doors—"

"We'd have a riot of a different kind," Goode said. "People would swarm like locusts."

"Then, we control it," Stony said.

"How?"

"I don't know that, Champ. What's the variable we're solving for in this conversation? I thought we were trying to find a way to keep the masses out there a little calmer."

Parsons looked to Kenny DeWilde. "What do you think, Kenny?"

The young man looked shocked. "You're asking *me*?"

"You're out there on the lawn a lot. What are people saying?"

"About what?" He looked nervous.

"Don't dance around it, Ken. How angry are they out there? How scared?"

Kenny impressed Parsons as a kid who liked to have the inside scoop while remaining invisible. He clearly did not want to give an answer.

"I promise I won't be mad," Parsons said.

"Well, they're really, *really* scared. Like Mr. Stony said—"

"It's just Stony," the man corrected, not for the first time. "No *Mister* necessary."

"Like *Stony* said, a lot of people are dying every day."

"What are they dying of?" Parsons asked.

"How should I know?" Kenny said. His voice raised significantly when he was frustrated.

"I don't need a specific cause of death," Parsons said. "Are they killing each other? Is there disease out there?"

"Oh, there's definitely disease," Goode said. "And it's not pleasant. In certain clusters, the air reeks of diarrhea. It'll gag a maggot."

"So, maybe our problem solves itself," Parsons said, half joking, but half not. "Everybody just dies."

"We're part of everybody," Stony said. "That's the problem with disease. Sooner or later, everybody gets sick."

"We could make everybody wear masks," Goode said with a chuckle shared by all.

Kenny said, "The people who aren't sick are afraid of the ones who are."

"Are we talking dysentery?" Parsons asked.

"Or something like it," Goode said. "Cholera, maybe? It's the lack of sanitation. People have started shitting in the swimming pool."

"Why do they stick around?" Parsons asked. "Why don't they just leave?"

"They're scared of the gangs that everybody talks about," Kenny said.

"We *are* the gangs that everybody's talking about," Parsons scoffed. "Those are our foragers."

"Who we wouldn't need if we just shared more," Stony pressed.

"Just stop, will you?" Parsons snapped. "That food needs to last us for a long time. That's posse food. Those zombies out there, those wanderers or whatever the hell we're supposed to call them, are three-quarters dead as it is. We're not going to waste food on them, and we're not going to waste medicine on them, and they will not have access to the hotel or the bunker. So, just stop."

Parsons stood and stretched his back, then worked his knees. "What about this Eden I keep hearing about? Is that a real place, and if it's so great, why don't these assholes wander there and leave us alone?"

"That's probably a three-day walk from here, Champ," Stony said.

"I don't believe it's real," Kenny said. "They all got to live the same life we do. I mean, there's stories of food banks and, like, housing developments out there. That's just not possible."

"We'll know one way or another in a few days," Parsons said. "Remember Jerry Cameron, the posse member who sneaked away a few days ago? Well, Glendale's attorney came to me and gave me a patriotic speech about how the mayor or whatever of this Eden place—Valerie something, I think—should be the judge for Glendale's trial. Something about the rule of law and serving history. Glendale asked Cameron to deliver a note to Eden asking this chick to sit as judge. I figure if she's coming, she'll be here in a few days."

"You're not going to let her do that, are you?" Stony asked. He looked appalled by the idea.

"I don't know," Parsons said. "It was a pretty good speech Barnes gave me. I figure why not?"

"It's not Valerie something," Goode said. "It's Victoria something. Emerson, to be more specific. Victoria Emerson."

Parsons scowled. "Why do you say that like there should be a big organ chord?"

"Because she's one of them. She's a congresswoman. She and Glendale are old buddies."

"Why isn't she here, then?" Parsons asked.

DeWilde took this one. "She quit when she couldn't take her kids inside with her. That's what I've heard, anyway."

"You don't want that, Champ," Stony said. "There's talk about her being some big hero. You know, there's a whole myth building up around her and her town. You don't want her coming in here and solving your problems."

Goode raised his hand at the elbow. "I have a thought."

Parsons gave him the nod to go ahead.

"We solve a bunch of problems all at the same time. One way to get people to stop thinking about how hungry they are is to give them something different to think about. Something to feel angry about."

This clearly was Parsons' cue to ask him to go on, but he wouldn't give him the satisfaction.

"The politicos," Goode said. "Those dickheads have been a strain on all the resources anyway. They started this war in the first place and now they're still hanging out in their bunker and using flushing toilets. I say we start the trials right away. Let all those suffering people see how the politicians treated themselves while everybody else was drinking dirty water out of mud puddles."

"Be careful," Stony said. "That can work against us. We've been living pretty good in here ourselves."

"But that's not what anybody's going to talk about," Goode said. He clearly was getting a head of steam behind his own idea. "All this misery—all *their* misery—is the fault of those self-righteous assholes we've got locked up in the bunker. A little bit of revenge will make everybody happier. You were going to hang that

Glendale guy anyway, weren't you? The *president*?" He used finger quotes at the end.

"We are going to try him," Parsons said. "Among the refugees, I've found a couple of lawyers. I've put them on it."

"What's the point?" Goode asked.

"If I just wanted to kill him, I could have shot him when we first took control," Parsons said. "It didn't feel right then, and it doesn't feel right now. We need to give him a chance to explain himself, and I think we need to give him as fair a shot as we can. That's why I think it's an okay idea for this Valerie—"

"Victoria."

"I don't care. That's why I think it's not a bad idea for *Victoria* what's-her-name to sit in as judge."

"Emerson."

"Again, I don't care."

"You should care," Stony said. "If she is half the inspired leader that people say she is, they're going to follow her. That can't be good for us. Only one person can sit in the chair at the same time."

"Okay, then I won't let her run the trial."

"The trials need to be over with by the time she gets here," Goode said. "For all the reasons we've already talked about, you don't want to have any kind of power struggle with somebody who has a mythical reputation behind her."

"We make a spectacle of it," Stony said. "Like the old days. We put on a real show. Whoever you get to play the role of prosecutor, make sure he's good at the theatrics of interrogating witnesses."

Goode piled on. "We can show all those suffering

people how House and Senate members valued themselves over the common people. Not only will that get the revenge juices flowing, it'll also fire a couple of shots into the Emerson chick's bow before she gets here. She'll be damaged goods."

Parsons found himself warming to the idea. "We'll do it in the Crystal Ballroom." Of all the many ballrooms in the Hilltop Manor Resort, the Crystal Ballroom was by far the most opulent. The gilded mirror ceiling alone must have cost hundreds of thousands of dollars when it was installed.

"That room isn't all that it used to be," Goode said. "Like every other corner of the hotel, it got pretty dirty."

"Then we'll clean it," Parsons said. "We can't run vacuum cleaners, but we've got plenty of brooms, don't we? We'll use our posse."

"We'll start the trials tomorrow?" Stony asked. "The days are getting pretty short. I don't know how the sun hits that wall of windows, but there's no way we can light that big a space with candles and lamps without burning the place down."

These were all very good points.

Parsons stood again and walked back to the windows. He looked out, but he wasn't seeing the view. He was seeing the show. "We'll take the furniture out of the Boardroom," he said. "You know, that really fancy stuff, and we'll put it up on one of those riser things, like they use for the wedding party at a reception. We'll put a desk and a chair up there for me to sit on."

"Why not just use the Boardroom?" Stony asked. "That shit's heavy as hell. The Boardroom is pretty big."

"Not big enough," Parsons said. "If we're going to have a show, we're going to have a *show*. We want as many people in there to see it as we can." He turned to Mason Goode and pointed at his nose. "You, my friend, had a brilliant idea. We'll get all of these refugees so spun up and angry that we'll be lucky if they don't tear those politicians apart."

"You going to try them all one at a time?" Stony asked.

"Oh, hell no. That'd take forever." Parsons took a few seconds to think it through. "We'll try the leaders as exemplars of the rest. They all committed the same offenses, right? Try 'em as a group and pass sentence on all of them together."

"Start with Glendale?" Goode asked. "Get him out of the way?"

Parsons gave him a look that said, *Are you crazy?* "Think drama, Mason. You don't start with the climax, do you? Maybe we start with that bitch who ran the House. What's her name?"

"Angela Fortnight," Stony said.

"Right. Jesus, what a pain in the ass. I'll enjoy passing sentence on her. Then we do whoever the leader of the Senate was. Then we end with Penn Glendale." He grinned. "Now, *that's* how you plan a program."

"How are we going to choose the jury?" Goode asked.

"I'll be judge *and* jury," Parsons said.

"So, first we do every House member, and then we do every senator?"

"That's what I was thinking," Parsons said. "Do you think that will work?"

"That's a lot of bodies to deal with," Stony said.

"We'll keep the burn pit going hot all the time," Goode said. "What do you see as the method of execution?"

Parsons brought his hands to the sides of his head, inspired by an idea so brilliant that it threatened to burst through his skull. "We'll let the people decide what to do with them."

CHAPTER NINE

THE SUN HAD ALREADY BEGUN TO DIP WHEN ADAM and his brothers set out on this insane mission. Emma insisted on coming along, too, and that pissed him off. The chances she took didn't put just herself at risk. She had a baby in her belly, and he thought she should stay out of any fight that came at them.

He'd tried challenging her with that argument before, and it didn't go well. Being pregnant didn't make her incompetent. It wasn't an illness. She was perfectly capable of doing everything now that she'd always been able to do. On and on.

Disinclined to stick his face into that propeller again, he'd simply said okay when she'd announced her intent.

They had one hour to find overwatch positions over a roadblock whose location they didn't know. After they were in place, presumably after their one-hour head start, his mom and the rest of the caravan would resume their trip up the road. When they reached the obstacle, Adam's team was to keep an eye on what the bad guys did. If they went to guns, then the Emerson boys would kill them. If they let the caravan pass unobstructed, well, they actually didn't have a plan for that because no one expected this to end without violence.

Adam didn't get it. There was no doubt how the asshats at the roadblock were going to react, so why go through the charade of making them show their intentions? In his mind, all that did was expose his mom unnecessarily to danger. It'd be a lot easier just to assume ambush positions and take them out. But no. Mom wanted at least the appearance of a fair fight.

He worried that she was campaigning again. She said that she didn't want the power and responsibility of leading the people of Ortho, but her actions expressed an entirely different view. Adam believed in his heart that his mom grooved on the leadership thing, that she somehow *needed* to be in charge. That wasn't a bad thing, necessarily, but he wished she would be honest with herself and everybody else.

Hell, look at the way people just naturally followed her. That guy Alex and his wife could have wandered back to Ortho and lived in relative safety, but somehow, instead, they decided to come along. The Gonzaleses had been free and clear in Ortho, yet decided to come *back* to what they described as misery at the Hilltop Manor. That had to reflect on Victoria Emerson's natural ability to lead, didn't it?

Adam himself wasn't entirely convinced that the roadblock existed at all, but there was no denying the trauma done to that family. *Someone* did something awful, but the whole roadblock thing just seemed too easy an explanation. They'd know soon enough.

The scenario that troubled Adam was the indeterminant one. After he and his brothers got set up to see the roadblock, suppose Adam couldn't hear what the pirates were saying? If his overwatch team missed the early cues, the bad guys could cause harm before the good guys could stop it. The Emerson brothers would have to pay serious attention to nuance and body language.

Adam knew that he could trust Caleb and Luke. They were levelheaded and well-trained, but when people are spun up and nervous, even the best can misinterpret a nose rub to be a threatening gesture and jump the gun with deadly force. In normal times, that would be called murder.

Today, given the stories he'd heard from those abused families, he could live with killing them even as innocents. But it wouldn't be right.

They'd burned up about twenty minutes of their lead when Adam decided that it was time to move from the roadway up into the trees that clung to the steep hill on the right-hand side of the road.

"Everybody put on your billy goat pants," Luke said as he turned into the hill.

"Wait a second," Adam said.

Everybody paused.

"Look, you know what we're supposed to do, and we all know the risks. Here's the one thing I want us all to pledge. If one of us sees something and shoots, we all shoot."

"At who?" Caleb asked.

"Anybody with a gun," Adam said. "We have to trust each other's judgment. If Luke or Emma sees something that is enough of a threat to eliminate, then we have to take out the rest of the threats."

Luke's scowl joined his eyebrows over his nose. "Suppose they're not all—"

"They've made their choices," Adam said. "And their choices were bad. We already know that they killed that lady's husband."

"No, we don't," Emma said. "We know that's what they said."

"Please don't let's argue on this point," Adam said. "Mom and the others are going to be in the middle of stuff down there, in close proximity to God only knows what might happen. They're depending on us to keep a lid on this. If one of us shoots, we all shoot. Agreed?"

Caleb shrugged one shoulder. "Sure."

"Suppose it's an accidental discharge?" Luke asked. "Or just a flat-out mistake?"

"Keep your finger off the trigger till you're ready to press it, and don't make mistakes," Adam said. He hoped Luke heard the smile he tried to put in his tone.

Luke heaved a deep breath, and then went back to climbing up the hill.

"Luke?"

"Don't screw up. Got it. I'll go up first."

"Holy shit," Luke grunted as he advanced parallel to the road, leaning hard to his right not to go tumbling down the hill. The trees here were sparser than when they'd first started the climb, and they grew up through erupted clusters of gray rock. What little ground cover there was had been designed by Satan, sporting long tendril-like branches that sprouted thorns that were way tougher than denim. If his thighs and calves were not bleeding, he'd be surprised.

His view of the roadway below came and went depending on the thickness of the undergrowth, but so far, he'd seen nothing that looked like a person, let alone a roadblock.

As an avid and talented hunter who could drive nails with a rifle round at a hundred yards, he knew that motion and noise were the big giveaways to prey when you were stalking. Smell, too, for some prey, but not so much for humans. With each step, he took care to plant his feet in a way that would make as little noise as possible, and to move slowly and deliberately.

His dad had taught him that steady motion through the underbrush mimicked the movement of the wind and would often go unnoticed by even skittish prey. It was sudden, irregular motion that caught attention. And that *was* a trait shared by humans as well as other game.

With this steep a hill, he also needed to worry about dislodging rocks and pebbles that would be scooped up by gravity and rain down on the road below.

That was a lot to consider when you had a deadline to be someplace. He hoped that Mom and the others moved slowly when they finally started up the road.

Every ten steps or so, Luke paused to listen and smell the air. Mostly he heard his own heart pounding from the effort of the climb, and he mostly smelled his own funk. It was hard to remember the last time he had a shower. As winter closed in, he shuddered to think of what bathing in the river would be like. Of all the things he missed from the old—

He heard a voice.

Luke froze and raised a hand so that the others behind him would know that he was on point, that something was happening.

He closed his eyes and held his breath to vector all of his energy to his ears.

There it was again. Adult male. Not threatening, beyond the fact that it was there.

He had to get closer.

Leaning into a tree for balance, he took a careful step. He steadied his balance over that foot, and then stepped forward again. And again.

The next step initiated an avalanche of pebbles and he froze.

He still couldn't understand the words, but the pace of the banter hadn't changed. Either they hadn't heard the tumbling pebbles, or they didn't care.

After waiting a ten count, he started forward again.

Twelve steps later, he was close enough to hear the actual words being spoken. Something about being hungry. And then something about the look in "that dipshit's" face when they shot him.

Figuring that they must be talking about Simone's husband, Luke decided right then that yeah, if one of them started shooting, he would shoot, too. The devil on his shoulder suggested that maybe he might want to intentionally trigger an accidental discharge.

As the point man, Luke's job was to move past the roadblock and take position behind the pirates, leaving room for Caleb to look straight down on them, and then Adam and Emma—Luke assumed they would share the same spot because they *always* shared the same spot—could take aim from their front side.

For perspective, Luke leaned into another tree, this time facing downhill to see what he could see.

He saw the top of a cowboy style hat, but little else because an enormous rock blocked the line of sight. This spot was pretty much directly over the roadblock. If he were Caleb, he'd ease down to that rock to see what the view beyond it was like. It felt to Luke like pretty much the perfect sniper's nest.

Luke looked back at Caleb, pointed at the rock that his brother probably couldn't yet see, and made an okay sign with his left hand. *Perfect spot for you.*

Time to move on.

The pressure of moving so slowly was crushing. Another avalanche now, whether pebbles or rocks, would result in only bad things.

As he moved, the sounds of people chattering shifted behind him, assuring him that he was approaching the perfect spot for his overwatch position. Five more steps, he told himself, and then he would ease down the hill for a position that would allow a better view.

Something was wrong. He wasn't sure what it was, but something had changed.

The people below had stopped talking.

Just a lull in the conversation, or had they gone on alert?

Keeping his feet planted, he pivoted his body to look back at Caleb, who seemed confused. An ostentatious shrug said, *What's wrong?*

Luke pointed to his ears and shook his head.

Caleb still didn't get it.

Maybe there was nothing to get.

"I don't hear anything," someone said from down below.

"Shh," came the harsh reply.

"Oh, for God's sake, Buster. You're jumpy as shit."

All the voices were male. And wasn't Buster the name that the ladies dropped as the leader of the gang?

Luke didn't move for what must have been a whole minute. He wasn't sure he even breathed.

"How long are we going to just hang out here?" a voice asked. Another male.

"Been working pretty good for us so far. We got more stuff than we can use, so that means we got stuff to trade."

"How are we gonna carry all this shit?"

Luke decided it was time to move again. Five more steps, each thirty seconds apart.

Holding his rifle close so it wouldn't rattle against anything, he leaned left, into a tree, and then scanned left and right for something that might provide cover and concealment, plus a good view of the kill zone.

And he knew that's what it was about to be—a kill zone.

He saw a rock outcropping about ten yards down the hill. It was much smaller than the one he'd found for Caleb, but as he belly crawled, he thought it would provide the concealment he wanted.

But to go to all that effort only to find out he didn't have a good view would double the problems of making noise. Maybe he should—

Somebody screamed, and everything changed.

* * *

Adam stayed put for what felt like five minutes as he watched his brothers head off to establish their positions. Because they were ultimately going to be stretching out over sixty yards, give or take, it made no sense for them to bunch up.

He'd asked Emma to stay with him instead of taking a fourth position for herself, and she'd agreed that that made the most sense. In the days since Hell Day, she'd proven herself to be tough on more occasions than he could count, but she hadn't trained for situations like this as he and his brothers had. She'd be there for him even if it came to violence, but she said she felt more comfortable with him at her side.

Adam felt happy with that.

He waited at the bottom of the hill, on the edge of the roadway until Caleb was nearly out of sight, before he started up with Emma.

"You go first," he said. "If I fall back, I don't want to knock you down."

"And if I fall, you want to be there to catch me?" Emma asked with a knowing smile.

"What do you mean? I don't care what happens to you." The words were clearly a joke, but as they left his mouth, he wished he could take them back. "I didn't mean that, you know?"

Emma cupped his jawline with her palm. "You're funny. And very sweet." She patted her belly. "And soon, I'll outweigh you by twenty pounds."

Over the next ten minutes or so, he had to remind her a couple of times to be more careful with where she planted her feet, but otherwise, she took to the climb like a mountain goat. Or maybe an Army Ranger.

She kept her rifle pressed in close to limit noise, and she held her balance really well.

Adam wondered if he'd done the right thing telling the younger brothers to go first. He was the oldest, after all, and therefore the one with the most training, but what if he led and one of the others got hurt? How would he know? This way, if something happened to them, he'd wander up on them. They wouldn't have to shout for assistance.

The steepness of the slope made his ankles ache. He figured the slope to be nearly 60 percent. It was navigable, but it was tough, especially walking across the slope. He'd skied steeper runs, but they definitely were marked with black diamonds. The trees helped to keep from rolling down the hill, but it was still exhausting.

Up ahead, he could see Caleb again. Either they'd been moving more quickly than he, or Caleb had stopped.

"What do you think is happening?" Emma asked.

As if he'd heard the question, Caleb pointed to his ears and then pointed down the hill.

"I think they've found where we need to be," Adam said. Using broad motions, he pointed down the hill from the spot where he was standing, and then waited.

Caleb gave him a thumbs-up.

"Okay, this is where we settle in," Adam said.

"But we can't see anything."

"Okay, not *here*. We work our way down until we have eyes on the roadblock."

"And then we just wait?"

"Right. But no more talking. I'll go first now. Do what I do."

Keeping his feet perpendicular to the slope, Adam

dug the outside of his right boot as best he could into the hillside, and then stepped down, planting the inside of his left boot as firmly as it would be seated. Then he brought his right foot down and repeated the process. In his mind, he was pretending that he wore invisible skies, and that he was sidestepping down a ski slope.

After two steps, he stopped and checked Emma. She was doing fine. Then he checked to see if he could see the people at the roadblock.

Not yet.

Two more steps, and he could hear talking.

Above him, he heard a scrape and a thump.

"Oh, shit!" Emma didn't shout it really, but it was instinctive. Her eyes grew huge.

Below, the conversation stopped.

In the silence, Adam listened to the sound of pebbles as they slid down the hillside. He brought his finger to his lips and kept it there as he tried to assess just how bad their situation was.

After a long while, someone said, "Oh, for God's sake, Buster, you're jumpy as shit."

The group started talking again, but Adam didn't listen to what they were saying. The clock was ticking, and they needed to get into position.

On the next step, it was as if the top layer of the mountain sloughed away from the bedrock.

It was time to ride an avalanche.

Without warning, Adam was tumbling, rotating around his own vertical axis. Tangled in his rifle sling, he couldn't get his hands out to grab enough ground or ground cover to slow himself down.

Emma yelled again. This time, it was more like a scream.

If he could roll to his back, cross his ankles and fold his arms, he could do a lot to prevent broken bones from the twisting motion, but hitting a rock or folding in two around a tree trunk could end it all.

Looking up and behind, he saw that Emma was falling, too, but in the instant he had eyes on her, he saw her torso fold around a stout tree.

Then he hit his own tree. It nailed him hard in the shoulder and spun him to face downhill.

Then the hill was gone, replaced by a six-foot free fall that ended on the hard road surface.

He smelled blood and knew that he was hurt, but the pain hadn't found him yet.

He saw people up the hill, and they were bringing their weapons to bear. "Holy shit!" one of them yelled. "He's got a gun!"

Adam wrestled with his M4, trying to bring it up and into a shooting position, but at least two of them got shots off at him.

It felt like someone kicked him in the belly.

CHAPTER TEN

"*W*HAT THE HELL IS THAT?" SOMEONE YELLED FROM the roadblock. "I told you that I heard something."

Luke didn't know what had happened, but he knew instinctively that the shooting was about to start.

To hell with belly crawling. He sat on his butt and used his heels to pull him down the hill till he could get a clear view. The rough terrain clawed at his flesh through his jeans, but he ignored the pain of the bruises.

"Who the hell is that?" someone yelled from the roadblock.

Luke didn't know who they were talking to or who they were talking about, but it didn't matter anymore. This thing was going to shit fast.

"Holy shit, he's got a gun!"

A rifle shot split the air, followed by more.

Shit, shit, shit.

Luke finally got his heels under him and he launched upright to finish the last ten yards of the hill on his feet, though with too much forward momentum. He pitched forward in his last couple of steps, executing the kind of somersault he'd never been able to pull off in gym class.

He made a barking sound as he landed hard on his ass.

The world was pulsing with gunfire, but above the din, he heard someone shout, "Look, there's another one!"

Luke saw movement and caught a glimpse of a person with a rifle. It wasn't anyone he knew, so he fired three quick rounds without aiming. The person fell.

Above him, from high on the hill, someone pumped round after round into the group in front of Luke.

The gang tried to fire back, but they clearly didn't see who their target was.

Caleb owed him a solid for finding him such a great spot.

The group was larger than Luke was expecting—probably ten, maybe twelve men—and with the exception of the guy Luke just shot (and they didn't seem to know yet that they'd lost one of their own), they seemed focused on Caleb's position.

This was Luke's opportunity.

Just as his mom had made him practice hundreds of times even before Hell Day, he assumed a textbook sitting shooter's stance. On his butt, knees up, elbows braced against the insides of his thighs, he went to work.

His scope was zeroed to one hundred yards, so at this range, his shots would hit a little high, but that wouldn't matter. Half an inch one way or the other meant hitting the right ventricle instead of the left, or in the worst case, the liver instead of the heart. At this range, every shot was a kill shot.

Keeping both eyes open, he settled the reticle of his scope on somebody's ear and pressed the trigger. That target was still falling when Luke shifted his aim to the next guy. That target's head was bobbing around too much, so Luke took him through the lungs. Ditto the next target, who was standing in full profile.

The gang members finally alerted to Luke's presence, but as the first one pivoted to take aim, his jaw flew away from his face as Caleb shot him dead from above.

A bullet whizzed past Luke's right ear, causing him to pivot like a top and drop to his belly.

The shooting had dwindled to virtually nothing, so where did that come from?

He rose to his knees, and then to a squat, scanning every compass point with the M4's butt stock pressed firmly into his shoulder.

A flash of movement in his peripheral vision brought his gaze forward and to the right, where he saw someone running full tilt away from them, down the hill, toward the caravan.

Luke took off after the runner. Their rules of engagement had always been the same. If you drop your weapon and run, you get to live. If you drop your weapon and surrender, you get to live. If you keep your weapon and run away, you get killed.

The runner was fast and had too much of a head start for Luke to catch up, so he skidded to a halt. He lowered himself to one knee and brought his rifle to his shoulder. He guessed the head start to be around 150 yards now, so he settled his reticle at the top of the target's head, with the intent of nailing him somewhere between his shoulder blades.

His rifle barked, and the runner fell.

Luke held his aim. When the fallen man didn't get back up, he declared victory and went back to his brothers.

Through his focus on acquiring and dropping targets, he'd missed the extent of the carnage they'd created on the roadway. Blood ran in rivulets downhill from the corpses that appeared from this angle to be nearly a single dead animal. They'd fallen that close together.

"Caleb!" Luke called. "Adam! It's me! It's clear down here. Everybody's dead!"

"I'm coming down!" Caleb said. An instant later, pebbles and rocks started tumbling down the slope as he moved from behind his sniper's post.

"Adam?" Luke called.

No response. He felt a sense of dread.

"Adam? Are you there?"

He heard something, but he wasn't sure what it was. A groan, maybe?

"Adam! Shout out if you can hear me!"

Nothing.

"Oh, shit. Please, no." Luke started back up the hill, but stopped when he saw Adam on the ground at the base of the hill, one foot on the roadway, and the rest of him in the weeds.

"Caleb! Adam's hurt!"

He ran over to his brother. He lay facedown and still. Blood matted his hair and spattered the scrubby ground cover.

"Adam, are you okay?" He shook his shoulder, but

he didn't move. He fought the urge to roll him over, because that was one of the primary rules of first aid that he'd learned. A lot of people end up with serious spinal injuries when they are improperly moved by well-meaning bystanders.

"Adam, come on. Wake up."

He checked his wrist for a pulse and felt instant relief. The pulse was present, but it wasn't very strong.

So, what happened to him? The head injury was obvious, but was there something else? Had he been shot? He didn't see any obvious wounds. He pulled Adam's jacket up to his shoulder blades, and then his shirt. Another rule from basic first aid. You can't treat a wound you can't see.

There was a hole in Adam's back about the diameter of a number two pencil, and it was leaking blood.

"Oh, God, no," Luke moaned. "Adam's been shot!"

Adam moaned again. "Where's Emma?"

"I don't know," Luke said. "You've got to be still."

"Find Emma. She's up on the hill. She's hurt."

Caleb skidded to a halt next to him. "Let me see."

"Goddamnit, go find Emma!" It wasn't much of a shout, but he'd tried.

"I'll take it," Caleb said. "You find Emma."

It's not what Luke wanted to do. It wasn't that he didn't care—he really *did* care—but how could he leave Adam at a time like this?

Caleb seemed to sense his brother's hesitation. "Really, Luke. Let me see what I can do here. You see how bad Emma is."

Luke stood. Moving his rifle sling to shift the weapon out of the way of his legs, Luke started back up the slope. Figuring that Emma and Adam had stayed together for the fight, he charted a course straight up from where he lay on the roadside.

"Emma? Emma! Where are you?"

This was bad. He didn't know how bad yet, but this had to be really, really bad. Adam and Emma both hurt. Why wasn't she answering?

"Emma! Goddammit, answer up!"

He heard another moan. He thought it was human, and he wanted it to be Emma, but he dropped to his knee and brought his weapon up again, just in case. He fell silent and listened. After a few seconds of silence, he was about to talk himself into believing that he'd made it up.

Then he heard it again. It was coming from farther up the hill, slightly to the left, he thought.

Luke moved cautiously, his rifle to his shoulder, but with the safety on in case it *was* his future sister-in-law.

"Emma?"

"Over here." Emma's voice.

Luke let his rifle fall back against its sling and he ran the last ten strides up the hill.

Emma looked awful. She lay on her back, at the base of a towering tree. Clearly in pain, she seemed to be having trouble breathing.

"Jesus, what happened to you?" Luke said as he stooped to her side.

"The ground just let go under us. I fell hard. Where's Adam?"

"He fell all the way down." Luke considered telling her that Adam had been shot but decided not to. He didn't know why. "He's asking about you. How bad are you hurt?"

"Why didn't he come himself?"

Luke felt like he'd been caught in a lie. "Let's go down the hill. Ask him yourself."

"How badly is he hurt?"

Whatever his eyes showed, she saw it instantly. "Oh, God, how bad is he hurt?"

Luke looked down. "He's been shot." He choked on the words as he spoke them.

Emma closed her eyes and squeezed them tight. "Where? How bad?"

"In the back, I think. It might be through-and-through. Caleb is . . ." He couldn't finish the sentence.

Emma struggled to sit upright. "I didn't hear the shooting," she said. She held out her hand. "Help me. I've got to go to him." The effort seemed to take everything out of her.

"What hurts?" Luke asked. "Talk to me."

"I think I probably broke a couple of ribs. I'll be okay."

"You look like shit."

"How nice. Now, please give me a hand."

Luke grasped Emma's hand in a thumb grip and leaned back as a counterbalance as she attempted to heave herself up. She made it about halfway, then wrapped her other hand around her ribs and leaned back to the ground.

"Shit, that hurts." Rolling to her hands and knees, she hand-crawled up the side of the tree to get to her feet.

"You're in trouble," Luke said.

"Yeah." Using the tips of her fingers on her right hand, she gently examined the ribs on her left side. The wince was instant and severe. "I'm in *serious* trouble. Help me down the hill."

"Do you think the baby is okay?" Right away, he wished he could take the words back. She didn't need any more burden than what she already had.

"I hope it's okay," he said, trying to make things better. That sounded lame as hell.

"Just help me down the hill."

"How? You can't move."

"I can do whatever I want," Emma said. "It's only pain."

Man, that was Adam talking through her mouth. "It's broken ribs," Luke corrected. "They're an important part of breathing."

"Just don't let me fall again."

Emma's face stayed tight, her lips pressed into a thin line and her eyes crinkled nearly shut as she winced against the agony. But she didn't complain. She moved carefully, keeping her left side covered with her elbow as she inched down the hill, going from one tree to another. Twenty yards into the trip, she had to stop.

"Go ahead," she said. "Go see how Adam is. I'll be there."

"I'll get there when you get there. Caleb is taking care of him."

Emma gave a wan smile. "Not my first choice for primary care physician."

"He's got more training than we do."

Emma didn't argue. Instead, she pressed off her tree and restarted her oh-so-slow descent down toward the street. Five minutes later, they were back on level ground.

Emma headed straight toward Adam. Caleb had rolled him onto his back. He kneeled next to him bare chested, his jacket and outer shirt in a heap off to the side, and his T-shirt pressed against Adam's head. Blood had already soaked through.

"How is he?" Emma asked.

"You look terrible."

"So I'm told. How hurt is Adam?"

"I don't know. He's alive, but he's shot in the belly and took a hell of a blow to the head. You can see he's bleeding."

"Was he shot in the head, too?" Emma asked. She carefully lowered herself to her knees.

"Maybe he was grazed," Caleb said. "My guess is that he hit a rock on the way down."

"You know I'm right here, right?" Adam said. He kept his eyes closed but managed a smile.

"I figured you were faking it," Caleb said.

"How's Emma?"

"I'm right here."

Adam's eyes fluttered open. "Hi."

She stroked his hair. "You sure know how to show a girl a good time."

He closed his eyes again. "My gift. Tell me about you."

Emma explained about the fall and the impact at the end. "I think I broke a rib or two."

"This whole adventure is screwed up," Luke declared. "It's been snakebit from the very beginning. We need to stop trying to save the Union and go back to Ortho where we can do some real good."

"That's not going to happen," Adam said. His eyes stayed closed. "This isn't an adventure, first of all. It's a mission, and it's an important one."

"You can't keep going the way you are," Caleb said. "We have to take you back."

"We all know I'll be dead by morning," Adam said.

"Stop that!" Luke shouted. "Don't say shit like that." He looked to Caleb for moral support, or at least shared indignation. He didn't get what he wanted in return. "Bullshit!" Luke said, and he kicked at the ground. "We're going to be fine. *You're* going to be fine."

They were the Emersons, goddammit. They were the winners, not the losers. It wasn't possible that Adam would get shot down in some random firefight. Not after all the shit he'd been through. Not after they'd been separated for all that time and then reunited. This couldn't possibly be God's plan. This couldn't be the way things were supposed to go.

"Luke, give me your T-shirt," Caleb ordered. "Better yet, do you have a knife on you?"

"Of course I do. I always—"

"Okay, take your T-shirt off and cut it into strips."

"What are you going to do?" Adam asked. His voice was leaden with dread.

"I'm going to try and make you wrong. You're not going to die on my watch if I can help it."

Luke slid out of his rifle sling and placed the weapon on the ground. Next, he unzipped the down jacket he'd only yesterday snagged from the clothing bank, and then he slid his flannel shirt over his head without unbuttoning it. He pulled his pale green T-shirt over his head and smelled it.

"It's pretty dirty."

"Doesn't matter," Caleb said.

Luke pulled on the clip of his locking blade folder

and flicked it open. "How big do you need the strips to be?"

"Four or five inches wide, as long as you can make them."

Working in the blacksmith shop alongside Lavinia Sloan gave him all day access to a sharpening stone. His blade made quick work of the shirt. When he was done, he had six long strips, which he dangled in front of Caleb's face.

Caleb took them and draped them across Adam's naked chest. "Okay, now, Emma, pick one of his arms to sit on, and Luke, you take the other."

Adam resisted, but the pain seemed to be too much. "What are you going to do?"

"I told you I wouldn't let you die," Caleb said. "That doesn't mean you won't want to."

Luke and Emma stretched Adam's arms out, cruciform, and Luke literally sat on the forearm.

"Hey," Adam said. "Watch it. That's—"

His words transformed into a howl of agony as Caleb used a forefinger to jam the T-shirt into the bullet hole in his belly.

"Stop!" Emma commanded. "What are you doing? You're hurting him!"

Caleb gave her a stern look but didn't reply.

Luke said, "He's bleeding out inside. The cotton shirt will soak it all up."

"Wrong," Caleb said. He had to shout to be heard above the agonized screams. Adam tried to buck them off, but he didn't have the strength. "If I stuff enough fabric into the wound channel, I'm hoping to tamponade his gut and slow the bleeding."

"Oh, God," Adam yelled. "Please stop. Please, please stop!"

Emma begged for him to stop, too, but Caleb kept his focus. His hands and forearms glistened with Adam's blood.

"Talk to him," Caleb said to Emma. "Try to calm him. This hurts like shit, I'm sure, but it's got to be done. Everybody shouting at me doesn't help."

In the near distance, Luke heard the sound of approaching horses. They were at a fast trot, and then they stopped. His mom's voice yelled, "Little Boy!"

Luke yelled back, "Fat Man!" The sign and countersign were what the Manhattan Project scientists had named the first two atomic bombs. That had been First Sergeant Copley's idea of humor.

The beat of horse hooves picked up again.

"We heard the shooting," their mom said. "Is everything—"

When Caleb raised his head to look up at his mom, his eyes were red and wet.

Adam had fallen silent.

CHAPTER ELEVEN

*A*t first, Victoria saw only the blood. Corpses littered the roadway. The sign and countersign were correct, and she recognized Luke's voice, so she knew that the good guys had won, but good Lord, what a battle.

She saw Caleb and Luke on their knees along with Emma. "We heard the shooting," she said. "Is everything—"

She brought her hands to her mouth. "Oh, my God, it's Adam," she said aloud. Standing on her left stirrup, she swung her right leg over the saddle and dismounted.

Behind her, McCrea yelled, "First Sergeant Copley! Bring up the medical gear! Hustle!"

Victoria ran toward her sons but stopped when she was still ten feet away. She didn't want to interrupt what they were doing. "How badly is he wounded?" she asked.

Caleb pressed his hand over Adam's belly and

looked past her. "Major McCrea! I need the Quick Clot!" To Victoria, he said, "He's shot through-and-through. He's bleeding out and he's got a head injury. It's bad."

McCrea and Copley jogged past her, the med kit dangling from Copley's left arm.

"You can let his arms go," Caleb said. "He's out." As if he'd heard Victoria's silent panic, he shot a glance her way. "He's still alive."

"Thank God," Victoria tried to say, but her voice eluded her.

Luke rose to his feet and walked over to her. He extended his arms and she folded him into a hug. Nearly taller than her now, with broad shoulders and strong arms, he buried his face in her neck and sobbed. His whole body trembled from the effort of it.

Victoria's vision blurred with tears, and she kissed the top of his head, just as she used to do when he was a little boy.

"I don't want him to die," Luke whispered.

Victoria let the words hang. She didn't know what to say. No words would help.

McCrea's face was grim as he walked back to her. The mother-son moment clearly made him uncomfortable. His hands deep in his pockets, he looked at a spot on the roadway as he rolled a stone around with the toe of his boot.

After a minute or so, Luke settled himself and eased away from her. "I'm sorry," he said. He wiped tears with his palms and snot with his forearm. He looked back at Caleb, who'd been joined by First Sergeant Copley in stuffing Adam's wound.

"We need to get him back to Ortho," McCrea said.

"Maybe Doc Young or Doc Robinson can help him. But he's hurt bad. If we set out now, we can be back in seven or eight hours. It'll be dark, but—"

"I'm not going back," Victoria said. McCrea and Luke both looked at once startled and angry.

"Mom, he'll die if we don't."

"We'll send Adam back with Caleb and maybe First Sergeant Copley to assist. And you, too, Luke. And Emma, of course. Can we combine the contents of the two wagons into one?"

"Vicky, you can't be serious," McCrea said. "This is your family."

"Thank you for the reminder, Joe." How could she make them understand? Adam was the pride of her life. Her firstborn, father of her first grandchild. He meant the world to her, and McCrea was correct that he had to be returned to Ortho as soon as possible. But that didn't change the rest of the mission. That didn't change the reason why they were here in the middle of the road in the first place.

"Yes, this is my family. And the larger mission is preserving some semblance of the United States as we rebuild."

She saw the fight in McCrea's eyes, the argument that was half a centimeter from his lips, but there were no words he could say that were different than the ones he'd already articulated.

"Luke," she said, "I want you to go work with the Foster twins to transfer as much as we can out of one of the wagons. Make sure we keep the food and the water and leave enough for you guys to get back to Ortho."

"I'm not going back," Luke said. "Emma and Caleb

can take care of Adam. And you said that First Sergeant Copley was going, too. They don't need me. I'll just be in the way."

"I want you to go with your brothers," Victoria said.

She watched as Luke walked back toward his brothers and snatched his clothes from the ground. He dropped the flannel back over his head and slung his rifle. His jacket dangled from his hand.

As he passed Victoria, he said, "Not gonna happen." He kept going without pause as he headed for the wagons.

"Vicky—"

She cut him off. "We're not having this discussion again. You'll recall that my original intent was to do this on my own. I'm still willing to do that if that's what it comes to."

"Feel better?" McCrea asked with a smirk. "That's not what I was trying to tell you. Look around. You've got a crowd."

The various refugees had followed them. They numbered in the dozens now, and they were lining the other side of the road. They watched, for the most part silently.

Max Tyler stepped forward and pointed to the carnage strewn on the road ahead. "Those are the guys," he said. "I guess they're not gonna be raping anymore. Thank you."

Victoria nodded. *You're welcome* seemed somehow inappropriate.

Max pointed to the spot where they were working on Adam. "That's your boy, ain't it?"

Victoria's lip quivered. "Yes, it is. They shot him."

"I'm sorry. Can we help?"

Victoria's head felt full. She couldn't think her way through this. How could anyone possibly help? Then, "Could you please poll all of these people and find out if there's a doctor among them?"

"Happy to."

"Oh, and one other thing," Victoria said. "One of the wagons is going to take Adam back to Ortho. It's a long walk but they can lead you there. You'll be safe there. You can find shelter and food. Spread the word."

Max gave a mock salute, but he gave it with respect.

Ten minutes later, one of the Fosters had steered a mostly empty wagon up to Adam, and working as a team, Caleb, Copley, Emma and McCrea had muscled Adam into the flatbed. They had replaced the T-shirt fabric with Quick Clot—gauze that was coated with a chemical that promoted clotting of blood—and they'd wrapped a bandage around Adam's middle. They'd padded the bottom of the bed with a few blankets, and they'd wedged him in place with heavy ammo containers on either side to keep him from rolling around as they moved.

"Okay, Vicky," McCrea said. "They're all set."

Caleb and Emma planned to stay in the flatbed with Adam for the journey back. Their horses would be redistributed to other refugees for whom walking back to town would be difficult.

Victoria looked at McCrea, whose hand rested on Luke's shoulder. All the faces were grim, all knowing that Adam's chapter was closing.

She climbed into the flatbed with the others and sat next to Adam near his shoulder, her legs crossed under her. She grasped his hand, interlaced her fingers with his and stroked his knuckles. The flesh felt cold as she kissed it.

"You're a strong boy," she whispered. "No, a strong man." She pulled his hand close to her chest and rocked gently. "You have too much to live for to die today. Living is your only job now, okay? Promise me that you'll fight for that."

Adam's features remained slack. Unresponsive. He was so, so pale.

She gently placed his hand back down on the floor and bent lower to bring her mouth to his ear. In a whisper she was certain no one else could hear, she said, "I love you so much, Adam. You know that. If you lose your fight, give your dad a hug for me on the other side."

Victoria kissed her oldest boy's lips, patted his hair, then struggled to her feet. Caleb stood with her. She grasped his face with both hands and touched her forehead to his. "You be careful," she said. "And remember one thing. No matter what happens, none of this is your fault."

"I won't let him die, Mom," he said.

She folded him into her arms and lost her hand into the tangle of his hair. "I know you'll do everything you can." They hugged for a while, and then it was time. She eased Caleb away and kissed his forehead. "Try to be safe," she said.

Victoria accepted help from McCrea's hand as she climbed back down to the street. They stepped back to give room for the wagon to turn around, and she watched until it disappeared around the curve.

"Excuse me, ma'am?" It was Max. He looked solemn. "I'm sorry. No doctors among us."

She'd forgotten that she'd asked. "Okay, thank you." She looked to the gathered crowd. It seemed somehow larger than last time she'd looked. More of them were armed than before, and she realized that they'd helped themselves to the gang members' weapons. Brenda Tyler stood near the front of the crowd, a stuffed bear clutched close to her chest.

"Y'all'd be smart to keep up with the wagon," Victoria said.

"We're coming with you," Max Tyler said.

"Why on earth would you do that?" Victoria asked.

"These guys you killed here aren't all of them," Max said. "You need us."

Victoria looked to McCrea to say something, but he stood with his arms crossed. Luke's posture mirrored the major's.

"Look," Victoria said. "You've already been through hell. Take a break from it. Ortho isn't perfect, but you'll find something that feels at least a little like safety there."

"No such thing as safety anymore," said a middle-aged guy she'd not seen before. "I seen a lot of bad shit since the bombs dropped, but I ain't seen a lot of goodness outta nobody that wasn't as beat up as I am."

"You've got your brother and sister," Victoria said to Max. "If there's fighting—"

"You've got children, too, ma'am." That came from the other Tyler boy. Tommy, if she remembered correctly.

"We know what you sacrificed for us," the middle-aged guy said. "You didn't have to do none of that. You coulda turned right around, but you decided to fight." He held up an M4 rifle by its barrel shroud. "And now that I got the tools to fight with, that's what I'm gonna do, too."

Simone Tyler stepped forward. "There's no such thing as childhood no more," she said. "My kids already saw stuff—*endured* stuff—that nobody ought to see in their lifetime, and they're not yet outta their teens. We had a family meeting, and we decided that we're coming with you. If there's fighting we'll be fighting there right next to you."

"What about the little one?" Victoria asked. This whole concept felt beyond her ken. "Brenda, right? With her Buddy Bear?"

"I'm thirteen," Brenda said. "Mommy said soldiers younger than me fought in the Revolutionary War."

The middle Tyler child—Tabby, Victoria thought—said, "And that's what this is, right? A revolution?"

"Damn straight that's what this is," said Mr. Middle-Age. "The fight with the Russians or whoever the hell it were who dropped the bombs might be over, but there's still a helluva war to fight here."

"What's your name?" Victoria interrupted.

"Saslaw," he said. "Oscar Saslaw. And those punks over there"—he pointed at the looted corpses—"are the new normal unless somebody gets a hand on the wheel. That's what you're trying to do, right?"

Victoria shook her head. "Nothing that lofty, I assure you. I'm going to try to find justice for one man."

"The president of the United States," Alex Kramer said.

"That weakens the argument, not makes it stronger,"

Saslaw said with a laugh. "Though maybe I can punch the sonofabitch in the mouth if I get close enough."

"Maybe we can take turns," Alex said.

"But that's where it starts, isn't it?" Saslaw said. "Justice for everybody starts with justice for just one guy." He pointed back to the carnage on the road. "All those bodies up there is justice for God only knows how many people who've been their victims."

A lady who could have been fifty said to Victoria, "I was going to town with the wagon, but then I saw that you weren't. Your boy being so hurt, but you're staying with the fight. I heard you telling your other boy to go back, and I heard him say no. I'm sorry, I don't know their names."

"I'm Luke," the boy said. "My brothers are Caleb and Adam."

"Well, you got some spine, young Luke. You can call me Patsy."

"Restores my faith, you know?" Saslaw said. "I don't wish harm on no one, and I pray to God that your boy gets okay again, but to see people—young people in particular—willing to fight for the benefit of others, well, it makes me wonder if there's not somethin' really good on the far end of this."

"Kinda like the Noah flood," Patsy said. "Things was so bad with everybody hatin' each other, and the politicians doin' nothin' and us losing our reverence for the Lord—maybe this is the big reset."

McCrea clapped his hands, drawing everyone's attention his way. "Too much talk," he said. "If we're going to do this thing, we're going to do this thing. I want more mileage under our feet and we've got to set up some kind of camp, all before sunset." He put a hand on Luke's shoulder. "You all know Luke Emerson. Now, Kyle and Caine Foster, raise your hands."

Kyle was still sitting in the driver's seat of the remaining wagon, his brother in the seat next to him. They raised their hands.

"Okay, people, these three young men can answer any questions you may have about anything in the next few minutes. Luke, I want you to make sure that everybody knows how to use the weapons they've got in their hands. Until we all get to know each other a little better, please just do what we tell you, okay?"

Everyone nodded or made noises of consent. As Luke strode off, McCrea turned to Victoria. "Are you holding up anywhere near as well as you're projecting?"

"Of course not," she said.

CHAPTER TWELVE

*A*T 8:30 A.M. SHARP, THE GUARD NAMED JASON LED
Penn Glendale through a discreet door into the elaborate and ostentatious Crystal Ballroom. His hands were
cuffed in front, at his waist, for reasons that made no
sense to him. He was sixty-five and never much of a
runner. Where the hell was he going to go?

It was, of course, all part of the larger show.

"Don't say anything to anyone," Jason said as they
crossed the threshold.

"Where's Tay Barnes? Where's my lawyer?"

"You won't need a lawyer today. This isn't about
you."

Those words confused the president, but he didn't
ask any questions.

Barnes had prepared him for the prospect of a spectacle, but Penn had to give props to Parsons. This was
over the top. The room and its million mirrors spoke
for itself, but the Mauler had erected a three-foot dais
along the back wall, parallel to the door through which

Penn had entered. A gorgeous walnut conference table had been placed on the dais, with five chairs empty behind it. The one in the middle was high-backed while the others were low-backed, but they were all padded in leather and looked very comfortable.

Out in front of the table, still on a dais, but one level down, a stackable, padded, brass chair sat by itself. Right away, Penn put it together. That was the witness stand. Beyond that, on the carpeted ballroom floor, two tables had been arranged with chairs facing the dais. These had to be the prosecution and defense tables.

Beyond those tables—beyond the ersatz bar—dozens of desperate-looking people in various levels of tattered clothing were gathering among hundreds of padded metal chairs. None looked healthy, all looked hungry, and some looked outright sick.

"Take a look at that," Jason said quietly as he led Penn to an isolated seat away from the others. "All those people. All that misery and death. That's all on you."

Again, Penn didn't respond. In part because the kid was right. The guard's assessment wasn't exactly nuanced, but that was exactly how it would be seen by others. Instead, he asked, "Why am I not sitting at the defense table? And again, where is my lawyer?"

"This isn't your trial, Penn. This one is for Angela Fortnight."

Penn bristled at the use of his first name, but the fact that Angela Fortnight, Speaker of the House of Representatives, would be tried first startled him.

A sense of dread enveloped Penn. He thought he could see exactly how this was going to go, but he prayed that he was wrong.

As he was playing out the disaster scenario in his head, the back door to the ballroom opened with enough noise to draw people's attention. Penn figured it to be a deliberate move. Three armed men escorted Speaker Fortnight into the room, along with five other members of the House of Representatives.

"Where are the others?" Penn asked.

It was Jason's turn to ignore *him*.

Angela Fortnight looked terrified. Her shoulders sagged and she walked with a shuffle that made Penn think perhaps her legs were shackled, but they were not. She wore the same godawful uniform as he did — as they all did—but hers might not have been buttoned right. She'd aged ten years since he'd last seen her only a couple of weeks ago.

Whatever bogus charges had been levied against her—Penn presumed it to be treason, just like him—her body language told the room that she was guilty of it. If she had presumed that these proceedings would lead to her death, she looked anxious to get on with the execution.

The guards separated the Speaker to sit by herself at the defense table while the other representatives were segregated into a set of chairs near the front row of the audience.

"Ladies and gentlemen!" someone boomed from atop the dais. "Everybody stand up for the judge, Roger Parsons." The announcer—a man in his fifties who had the nose of a boxer—elongated the pronunciation of Parsons' last name to two seconds, as if, well, introducing a wrestler to a match.

As the gathering audience made their way to their feet, Penn felt Jason's hand under his right armpit as the young man tried to lift him. "That's you, Penn. Stand up."

"I don't think I will," Penn said. "How big a scene will the Mauler allow you to make?"

Jason's neck and cheeks flushed.

Parsons used stairs Penn couldn't see to climb up to the dais and he walked behind the leather chairs to the center one, which he pulled out for himself and sat. Two seconds later, two more men followed the same path and helped themselves to the chairs on either side of Parsons.

The bailiff, or crier, or whatever the hell he was, yelled, "Everybody sit down." When he was satisfied that everyone had followed his orders, the crier said, "Okay, Judge."

Parsons continued to watch the older man, clearly expecting more. The crier looked confused, and then he sort of jumped, as if physically struck with an idea. "Oh, yeah."

He pulled a piece of paper from his pants pocket and read from it in a booming voice. "This case is the people against Angela Fortnight, former Speaker of the United States House of Representatives, who has been charged with treason."

The crier looked for confirmation from Parsons, who apparently gave it because the man sat down.

Parsons then looked down to what appeared to be notes of his own. "Angela, stand up."

The speaker made a point of crossing her arms and placing them on the edge of the table. Parsons had to have seen the show of disrespect, but he chose to ignore it. "Where is your lawyer?" Parsons asked.

"I have no idea, Roger. I fired him. I figured what's

the point?" She was using her campaign voice, easily heard from all corners of the room.

"Want me to make her stand, Champ?" asked the guard closest to the Speaker.

Parsons clearly considered it, but in the end, he shook his head. "No, this is her case to screw up. Her life to lose."

Angela shot to her feet, startling her guards. "Okay, Roger, you want me to stand, I'll stand." She turned to face the gathered audience. "Do you know who we are?" she asked.

A man in an ill-fitting suit stood from the prosecutor's table. "Objection, Your Honor."

"Angela, sit down!" Parsons said.

Angela continued, as if uninterrupted. "You heard the man say it with his own mouth. I am the Speaker of the United States House of Representatives. Those other so-called defendants are likewise elected members of the House. The Senate is likewise under arrest, as is the president of the United States."

The audience erupted in spontaneous applause.

"Good!" someone yelled.

"I hope they hang the lot of you!" said someone else.

A third voice added, "Slowly!" And that drew a laugh followed by another round of applause.

"Objection!"

Someone had found a gavel somewhere, and Parsons pounded it on the table. "Order!" he yelled. "Order in this court!"

To Penn's ear, Parsons seemed to enjoy saying the words that he'd no doubt learned from television courtroom dramas.

"Hey!" Parsons boomed. "Everybody shut up! Show some goddamn respect!"

"Is this what you want for yourselves?" Angela asked the crowd. "Look at the squalor. Look at the lack of food. That man up there is the traitor." She pointed to Parsons, who was looking pretty pissed at losing the spotlight. "He's the one who committed treason. By use of deadly force, he overthrew the duly elected government of the United States. That is the very *definition* of treason."

A man in the audience stood. His skin sagged about his neck and his clothes were far too big for him. Penn figured he'd been a big man before the war. "May I say something, Your Honor?"

Parsons seemed pleased to hear the honorific directed at him. "These proceedings are already out of control," Parsons said. "So, why the hell not?"

The man sidestepped past the three people that separated him from the middle aisle and he walked with effort toward the Speaker. "Mrs. Speaker—if that's what you want to be called—all of this suffering is on you. This is your fault. And it's shared by every one of your colleagues."

"We didn't start the war, sir," Angela said.

"She should have asked him for his name," Penn mumbled.

"You shut up," Jason warned.

"The Iranians started the war," Angela continued. "And then the Russians—"

"Who cares?" the man shouted. "Who the *hell* cares who started it?"

More applause.

"We care that it started at all, and that you didn't stop it."

"You don't understand," Angela tried. "We were working on that very thing when the news of an impending—"

The man boomed, "I. Don't. Care! It doesn't matter! Look at the mess you made of the world. Are you crazy enough to think that we elected you to kill a billion people?"

"Foreign policy belongs with the president," Angela said.

Penn moaned. This was exactly the wrong time for a civics lesson.

A female voice from the crowd yelled, "Weren't you part of the same party as her?"

The man whirled on the voice. "That doesn't matter, either. Petty political games are what got us here in the first place. Maybe you liked President Blanton or maybe you didn't, but the other party didn't do shit to fix anything either. They just shouted at each other, calling each other names."

"Angela," Parsons said from his desk. "I'd like you to finish what you were about to say about working to prevent the war from happening. Start with where you were working from."

Angela took a breath to answer, then clearly saw the rhetorical snare that Parsons had set for her. She froze.

"Yeah," someone yelled. "You were here already. How did that happen?"

"Put her back in her seat," Parsons said, and both of the closest guards placed hands on her shoulders and spun her around and eased her back into her seat. She seemed to have lost all the fight she had left in her.

Parsons stood and spoke to the crowd directly. "Maybe some of you are new and don't know the whole story. Your government—the people you elected to serve you—had enough warning of the end of the world that they could get themselves to shelter, but they didn't bother to tell any of you about it. I've talked with some of the defendants, and they tell me that they didn't share the news because they didn't want to create a panic."

He leaned toward Angela. "Madam ex-Speaker, do you want to tell me that I'm wrong? Wasn't that the logic behind not warning people?"

Penn knew that the logic was more nuanced than that, but the nuances would only make things worse. The fact was that for many years, Americans had been defenseless against an organized nuclear attack. Missile flight times were eight minutes or less from submarine to target. That wasn't enough time for most families to get people to the minivan in the garage, let alone to a shelter that was unknown to them in the first place.

Angela sat tall again and said, "There is truth in what you say."

Parsons laughed. "There is truth in what I say? Is Beltway the only language you know? How about, *Mr. Parsons, what you say is the truth*?" He waved at the air, as if shooing a fly. He was done with the Speaker. He looked out into the audience. "Let me tell you people what the rest of the truth really is. Angela Fortnight and Penn Glendale and all the rest of those political maggots wanted to keep a lid on the story so that you wouldn't crowd the roads and complicate their flight to the bomb shelter that you weren't allowed to enter."

The crowd rumbled. Penn had to admit that Parsons orated well. He also cringed at the accuracy of his words. Again, the truth was nuanced, but nuanced truth was still not a lie.

"So, while we all suffered and fought and died, the people we elected to serve us and protect us lounged in comfort. Oh, I'm sure they debated and argued and stewed over what went wrong, but you know what? They slept in beds every night. They breathed filtered air. They watched on closed circuit television as we suffered and died, but did it occur to them to open their blast doors and share their food and their medical supplies? Of course not. And you know why?"

Parsons paused for effect and leaned in from the waist, drawing many in the audience to lean forward in their seats.

"They didn't share because they think they're better than you. They think that their lives are more important than yours. This whole travesty of a Government Relocation Center is a monument to their hubris. Billions may die, but God forbid that the destruction inconveniences them. They have a barber shop in that bunker! They have surgical suites! What do we have?"

Penn grew uncomfortable. The crowd was spinning out of control. The anger was as palpable as humidity on an August morning.

"This isn't new, ladies and gentlemen," Parsons continued. "Remember before the war, when cities were burning and they didn't care? When cops were being vilified and judges were being attacked and they did nothing about it because it didn't involve them? But, oh, when a protest breached the walls of the Capitol— when they felt the slightest taste of the threat that their constituents lived with every goddamn day—they threw up fences and gathered up hundreds of innocents in their giant vacuum cleaner called the Justice Department. Blood in the streets doesn't bother them, but a little broken glass and a quickened pulse was a national tragedy." A pause. Then he boomed, "These people don't care about you! These people see themselves as royalty, and they see you as subjects!"

Parsons' posture changed. He stood tall, relaxed his shoulders, put his hands in the pockets of his jeans. "Look, folks, I'm just a retired wrestler. I'm not a lawyer like all these fine men and women who are under arrest."

The crowd chuckled.

"Maybe you have to go to Ivy League schools to learn to hate your fellow Americans, but I could never afford that. I was too busy my whole life earning enough money to pay the taxes that fund the graft and greedy lifestyles of politicians. The folks here today stand charged with treason because that felt like the right charge. What else do you call it when you ignore the cries of dying constituents so that you don't have to share your gourmet food with them? I mean, maybe I'm wrong, but I feel betrayed. I feel that our elected officials betrayed their country. Aren't betrayal and treason the same things?"

A rumble of assent.

"Raise your hands if you feel betrayed."

The vast majority of hands shot up. There was enthusiasm in the shared effort.

"So, here's the dilemma we face. What do we do with people who pledged to protect us, yet deliberately harmed us instead?"

Penn had had enough. He stood. "You hold another election!" he said, as loudly as he could. "That's why we have them."

The crowd seemed confused. Some seemed to know who he was, but most did not. He took a step forward. Jason grabbed his arm to stop him, and Penn shoved him hard enough to make him backpedal and fall.

"Ladies and gentlemen, I am Pennington Glendale. I was Speaker of the House until the president and vice president were killed. Now I am the president of the United States."

"Sit down, Glendale," Parsons said. "Your trial comes on a different day."

"You said yourself, Roger, that these proceedings are already on an irregular course. Why don't you let me say my piece?"

"Because this is not your moment."

"It is *precisely* my moment because I see what you're trying to do. You want to find an excuse to hang all of us. You want your slice of revenge, and while you'll be able to revel in my death later, if I don't speak now, you're going to commit murder. I can't sit still for that."

As guards looked for direction, Penn raised his cuffed hands high over his head so that they were clearly visible.

"These hand shackles tell the whole story," he said. "Roger Parsons wants to shackle the rule of law for his own purposes. I don't pretend to know what those purposes are, but they don't have anything to do with helping your lives to get any better."

"Take him out of here," Parsons said.

"No!" a man from the audience shouted. "Let him talk."

This time the rumble through the crowd was anything but united.

"Haven't you spent enough time being told what you're supposed to think?" Penn said. "Hey, I've been a politician pretty much my whole life, and if you look at the color of my hair, you know that's a pretty long time. I remember a time when we welcomed hearing truths that differed from our preconceived notions."

Penn turned to Parsons. "I'm not going to fight your thugs, Roger. You make the call."

Parsons' face was turning crimson again. "Get him out of here."

As the guards closed in, a voice yelled, "That's not right. He should speak."

Penn wasn't going to be carried. He would leave with dignity. But as he approached the threshold, he yelled, "People were just doing their jobs, ladies and gentlemen!"

CHAPTER THIRTEEN

VICTORIA NEVER ASKED HER BOYS IF THEY WERE BOTH-
ered by the fact that she shared a tent with McCrea.
Quaint moral posturing had never made a lot of sense
to her, even before Hell Day, but since then, she had no
time at all for such things. Life had never been shorter
than it was now, and it was incumbent on everyone to
live as vividly as they could, while they could.

Glenn Emerson, the boys' father, had been one of a
kind. A devoted husband and father with a sense of
humor that never evolved past fart jokes, he was a
skilled hunter and outdoorsman. He'd loved the job
that took him to Iraq and to Heaven beyond that. If it
were possible to dim the pain of his death at the random hand of an IED, it was the fact that he'd died
doing exactly the job he loved most, in defense of the
nation that had allowed him to live the life that he'd
chosen. That they'd chosen together.

Joe McCrea could never replace Glenn in her heart,
or in the hearts of her boys, but he shared many of the

same traits as Glenn—all the ones that mattered. He was loyal, tough, honest, and, in his own way, loving. Not much of a talker, he shared very little with her about his feelings, and perhaps that was best. Who was she to say?

During quiet times like right now as she sat in a mulchy seat formed in the spot between erupting roots of a towering hardwood, it was difficult not to harbor guilt over the loss of McCrea's family on Hell Day. He had left his wife, Julia, and their kids, Tina and Toni, to fend for themselves as he followed orders to deliver Victoria to the Annex. It had to tear him apart every time he looked at Luke and Caleb, whose ages were identical to those of the daughters who no doubt had ceased to exist in the first milliseconds of the war.

Had it not been for Victoria and her family, McCrea would have been with his family.

On the other hand, had it not been for her, McCrea would be dead now. She could construct an argument in her head where he would see that as the preferred situation.

Perhaps that was why he kept his thoughts to himself. Lying was not in his nature, and he wasn't very good at shading his opinions, either. McCrea was a between-the-eyes kind of guy. Filtered thought was not his long suit.

They'd walked well into the evening without encountering any other gangs or war parties. After a couple of miles, the hills flattened out a bit and the dense woods gave way to fields. McCrea agreed that this would be the best place to set up camp. In addition to their own team from Ortho, the stragglers and refugees stopped as well. Most had no forms of shelter, perhaps because those items had been taken from them, or perhaps they had never had them.

Luke set up the tent that he would have shared with Caleb about ten yards away from the spot where McCrea and Victoria had raised theirs. The boy hadn't said much since he'd watched his brothers drive off, and Victoria didn't push him. Perhaps he was regretting his decision to stay behind. If that were the case, well, there wasn't much to do about it at this point.

As an ersatz family, they dined on venison jerky and water. It wasn't much, but satisfying meals had been hard to come by for weeks now. The jerky provided protein and enough calories to keep going, but only for a short time. Given all the additions to the caravan, Victoria thought it unwise to dig into the food stores they'd brought for the trip. There was nowhere near enough to share with the masses, and it didn't make sense to her to seed a fight over survival needs.

Instead, she assigned the Foster brothers to take the first shift guarding the wagons, with Greg and Mary Gonzales taking second shift.

When her head settled down enough for her to sleep, her plan was to take the night off and do just that. She reckoned the time to be around eight-thirty, and sleep seemed miles away for her.

She recognized the approaching footsteps as those belonging to Joe McCrea. "Do you want company or are you craving alone time?" he asked.

"That depends on whether or not you're bringing me problems to solve."

"Strictly a social call, I promise."

She patted the ground next to her tree root chair, then realized that he probably couldn't see the gesture. "Please," she said. "I'd love to have you sit with me."

As McCrea lowered himself to the ground, Victoria asked, "Do you think we made a mistake about the campfires? I worry about us being a beacon for bad guys." They'd told people that it was okay to set up fires at their campsites. The fire risk was low due to recent rains.

McCrea grunted at the effort of finding a comfortable spot for his butt. "Six of one, half dozen of the other," he said. "The light makes people feel safer, even though it might actually put them at greater risk. During the Civil War some commanders set up more campfires than they needed to give the enemy the impression that the army was bigger than it actually was."

"I don't like referring to the refugees as enemies," Victoria said.

"Everybody's an enemy until they prove themselves otherwise. I've heard you tell your boys that very thing."

Victoria wished she hadn't said that. She sounded weak and naive in a way that she was not. She found herself falling into a mindset that concerned her. It was one thing to speak in the language of preppers that it was worthwhile to have a plan to kill everyone you meet on the theory that they can pivot in an instant to pose a threat, but it was something else entirely to live that way. It was exhausting.

She said, "I worry sometimes that we trigger the fights we have. We're certainly looking for them."

McCrea didn't respond. His silence drew her head

around in the dark. They'd opted not to light a fire for their own campsite, but distant light flickered off his eyes.

"No comment?" she asked.

"There's nothing to say. You know the folly of what you just said. You know that the men and women who did what they did to these people are bad. You know that there's the binary choice of ignoring it or confronting it. Edmund Burke sponsored a lot of heroism with that quote of his."

All it takes for evil to triumph is for good men to do nothing. Victoria had thought a lot about those words in the years since Glenn was killed. Her whole purpose in running for office was to do her part to derail the evil that disguised itself as political group think.

"What's the real topic you want to talk about?" McCrea asked.

Victoria felt a surge of annoyance. McCrea was a fine man, but he had a narcissistic streak that made him think sometimes that he was a mind reader. "Sometimes a question is just a question," she said.

"There's going to be another fight tomorrow, in case that's what you were worried about," McCrea said. "There has to be. If not tomorrow, then the day after. I don't think it's possible for the remaining elements of the group we encountered today to get behind us, so that means they still lie ahead. You're not considering turning back, are you?"

That image of Adam supine in the bed of the wagon, so pale and bloody, hadn't slipped past the front of her head since she'd seen it. She saw the look of fear—horror, really—in Caleb's eyes, and could still feel Luke's wide shoulders trembling in her embrace. How could she have talked herself into believing that there was something bulletproof in the Emerson name?

"You're not answering me," McCrea said. "So, let me offer some unsolicited advice. Because you're who you are, you've decided to win the war within the war. You've decided to be that dreamer who believes that people can be driven to once again do good deeds. It's the noblest kind of warfare. You're taking on the bullies in the school yard and you're taking on poachers and rapists and murderers and God knows what else because it's the right thing to do. You're not going to profit from it, but you'll have lived up to your principles. There's nothing in any of that for you to doubt or reconsider."

Victoria wasn't in the mood for the platitude speech. "I understand all of that, Joe. I really do. And I wasn't reconsidering my commitment to this mission. Not really."

"Fine," McCrea said. "But I'm not finished yet. Your window for changing your mind closed the second you watched First Sergeant Copley drive off with your family. Do you have any idea how inspirational that was for those poor refugees? Those people who have lost everything, including their dignity and much, much worse?"

"I'm not trying to inspire people. That's the farthest thing from my mind."

"Which is exactly why it's so inspirational. Jesus, you don't even know you're doing it."

Victoria was ready for this conversation to end. It felt like a pep talk and that was not on her list of daily activities.

"I can hear you rolling your eyes," McCrea said. "And that's fine. But don't you dare discount how important it is for every person here—myself included, and certainly all of those strangers who are falling in line behind you—to be faced with a leader who's worth following. You've got skin in the game and blood in the fight, and you're still fighting."

McCrea's hand found hers in the darkness.

"There's nothing complicated about leadership," McCrea said. "It's about being honest and caring for others. It's about grunting through the pain and staying focused on the principle. Glenn died for a righteous cause."

Victoria bristled at hearing her husband evoked in this conversation.

"But he died for a cause that could never succeed because politicians didn't have the mettle to fight for the win. I caught a basketful of shrapnel in that same fight. You—we—are fighting for the real deal. We're fighting for principle. And we're giving hope to everyone who feels that they've been thrown aside to die."

"I didn't ask for that," Victoria said. "I don't even want any of that."

"Well, that's too bad, Vicky. Because it's yours. You've earned it, so you need to own it, and I know that makes you squirm inside."

Victoria didn't know what to say. The stakes were so impossibly high.

"And you know what?" McCrea pressed. "I pray that Adam comes through his injury whole and healthy, and I pray that all of us live to die at an advanced age. But if this mission costs you or me or even your boys their lives, it will have been a worthwhile trade. Living in fear and degradation isn't living at all. It's existing."

"Dying is wasteful," Victoria said. "Dying depletes warriors while it leaves holes in the hearts of the survivors. How many millions of young people have valiantly marched to their deaths over the millennia?"

Victoria knew that she was howling at the wind, that nothing would change unless someone changed it. For reasons that she would never understand, people were looking to her to be that someone.

"We should send a scouting party up ahead," she said. "Use the darkness to figure out what lies three or five miles ahead. That way we won't walk into a daytime surprise."

"I'll do it." Luke's voice, coming from the darkness, made them both jump.

"Jesus!" McCrea exclaimed.

"My Lord, Luke," Victoria said, a hand to her racing heart, "how long have you been there?"

"Long enough to hear that if we all die, it will be for a good cause."

Victoria felt McCrea pull away. "Look, about that—"

"You're right," Luke said. "You have to be right. If you're not, then I'll have been a mass murderer all these months."

Luke and his brothers were some of the best shots Victoria had ever seen. They'd taken a dozen or more lives to save the lives of—

"And don't worry, Mom, I'm just kidding about the mass murder thing. I will go ahead, though. Major McCrea is right. We need to know what's out there."

"Are you sure you're the right choice?" McCrea asked. "You've had a pretty tough day."

"Caleb's not getting any sleep tonight," Luke said. "Neither is Emma, I bet. I won't be able to, either. I can use the alone time."

"Are you sure, sweetie?" Victoria asked. She could feel the glare he shot her even though she couldn't see it. He hated it when she called him baby names. "How far ahead do you plan to search?"

"How far do you want?" Luke asked. "I'm not going to engage anyone in a fight, so I'm not going to go any farther than the location of the threat. If I find something, I'll head back and report. If it's, like, five miles out, then I'll pitch camp somewhere in between. I'll hear you coming and come out to meet you."

"Take someone with you," McCrea said.

"Who?" Luke asked. "You, First Sergeant Copley, Caleb and Adam are the only ones I'm sure know how to be quiet and observe accurately."

"What about one of the Foster boys?" Victoria asked.

"No, not one of them, either. I don't want to take the risk. I'll be okay." He paused, and Victoria knew there was more. "Or, I'll die a hero."

CHAPTER FOURTEEN

*T*HE DARKNESS INSIDE PENN'S JAIL CELL WAS ABSO-lute. Built of steel bars, the cage itself sat inside a closet of sorts with a solid steel door that his captors closed and locked at night. A big bucket with a toilet seat occupied the corner directly opposite the place where Penn laid his head to sleep. Being of a certain age, he'd learned to navigate the distance in the darkness at least once per night, sometimes more than that. Among the duties assigned to his guard, Jason, was dumping the contents of the toilet every morning. More than once, the young man had wondered aloud why the architect didn't think of running water when he designed the jail space.

Penn thought he had a good point. Perhaps it was once part of the plan, but then was cut by a bean counter.

As he lay on his back, fingers laced behind his head, he wondered whether his eyes were open or closed. In absolute darkness, it's hard to tell.

Noise at the front wall startled him. It wasn't loud—in fact, it seemed intentionally quiet to him, which made the sound somehow more ominous. Historically, his captors didn't give a shit about waking him up.

The outer steel door scraped metal-to-metal as someone pulled it open. Assuming that this was an assassination attempt ahead of his monkey trial, Penn sat up, swung his feet to the floor, and prepared to fight. He couldn't see well enough to find his shoes, and he'd laid his shirt and trousers across the foot of the bed, but there was no time.

If this turned out to be what he thought it was, he'd fight and probably die in his boxer shorts.

A vertical seam of gray bloomed in the solid black tableau before him and grew wider as the outer door opened all the way. Black stripes across the dark gray marked the location of his bars.

"Who's there?" Penn asked. He wished his tone sounded harsher, sterner than it actually did.

"Shh." A red beam pierced the blackness now. Too wide to be a laser sight —his first thought—he realized it was a filtered flashlight. "It's me. Jason. Please don't make any noise. I'm getting you out of here."

"Excuse me?"

"Shush!" the guard hissed. "Keep your voice down. Better yet, don't say anything at all."

Jason slowly and gently inserted the big key into the lock on the cell door itself. The lock turned with a clank that prompted both of them to curse.

"I'm not going anywhere without an explanation," Penn whispered.

"We thought of that," Jason said. He stepped into

the cell and handed Penn a flashlight. "Turn it on. It's got a night filter on it."

Penn fumbled with the light for a few seconds until he found the rubber button on the back that turned it on. The dim red beam somehow seemed too bright now. When he looked up from the light, he saw that Jason was holding out a folded piece of paper for him.

"It's from Taylor Barnes," the guard said.

Penn unfolded the paper, then realized he didn't have his glasses on. He'd left them on the little shelf that doubled as a desk. He put them on and read. The scrawl appeared hurried, and had the unbalanced look of something written on an uneven surface.

> *Dear Mr. President:*
>
> *You have no chance whatsoever for a fair trial. In fact, there may be no trial at all. After you left the courtroom, Speaker Fortnight and the congressmen in her company were found guilty and sentenced to death. Those six were escorted out of the hotel and hanged from the giant old oak tree in the front lawn. The rest of the House members were subsequently shot, as were the members of the Senate, without even the benefit of a show trial.*
>
> *In all likelihood, they will come at you tomorrow morning. It is of the utmost importance that you follow Jason Herringer, who will show you the way out of the bunker.*
>
> *Once outside, you will be on your own unless Jason wishes to accompany you. God bless you, sir, and God bless the United States of America.*
>
> *Yours sincerely,*
> *Taylor Barnes, Esq.*

Penn read the letter a second time, just to make sure he got the details right in his mind. "So, your last name is Herringer?"

"Ever since I was born."

"Why didn't I know that?"

"We need to get going," Jason said. "Get your clothes on."

None of this felt right. It felt like a trap. But trap or no, there was no harm in putting on his clothes. As he thrust his right leg into his trousers, he said, "I don't know whether to believe you or not."

"About my name?"

"No, about this whole offer of freedom. Why the change of heart?"

"You're talking," Jason admonished. "I asked you not to do that."

Penn pulled his pants up to his waist and fastened them. "Where are we going?"

"Out of here. After that, does it matter? Hurry up, please. I'm as dead as you'll be if we get caught."

As he shrugged into his shirt and buttoned it, Penn ran scenarios through his head. This could be a trick to "catch" him in the act of escaping and give an excuse for Parsons' people to shoot him on the spot. If that were the case, though, what difference would it make? He remembered the anger of the crowd at Angela's trial. If they shot him dead tonight, it would merely speed up the inevitable.

He sat on the bed to pull on his socks and shoes.

How could Penn even know if Taylor Barnes was who he said he was? He *seemed* like a lawyer, but so what? Anybody could do that. And he'd never seen the man's handwriting. How could Penn be sure that the letter even came from his might-not-even-be-real lawyer?

Again, a distinction without a difference. Whichever angle he considered, the only logical thing to do was to follow young Jason Herringer and hope for the best.

"All right," Penn said, "I commit myself to your hands."

Jason stepped closer, causing Penn to step back.

"You've got to trust me," Jason said. "I know you think you know where things are—"

"Actually, the opposite is true," Penn whispered. "During my weeks in here before the insurrection, I never saw the bowels of the Annex."

"Maybe that's even better. Just stay with me. If I stop, you stop. If I drop to a knee, you drop to a knee. Don't ask why. No talking. And if there's shooting, try to dissolve into the floor. Last chance for questions. Do you have any?"

"Of course I do. I've got a thousand of them. But in the interest of survival, I'll keep them to myself."

"One more thing. Keep your light off unless you need it. That's really for when you get out into the open. Try to depend on mine while we're still inside."

Jason moved cautiously, stealthily, as he led the president out of his cell and into the hallway. When the lights were on, the hallways looked like the bulkheads of a warship, with pipes and conduits stretched the entire length. In the wash of the filtered flashlight, the hall looked more menacing. The round beam gave the impression of a sewer pipe, or maybe the inside of a torpedo tube.

The shadows moved as the two men advanced down the hallway. Penn tried not to think about the vast number of dark spots that could harbor an attacker.

Jason stopped and dropped to a knee, and Penn did the same. Penn didn't see what the threat was, but he'd made a promise that he was determined to keep.

Jason shifted his light to the right and illuminated a steel door that was nestled between and among what appeared to be steam pipes.

"Hold my light," Jason whispered, handing it back without looking. "Point it at my hands."

Penn watched as the guard reached carefully into his right front pocket and retrieved a ring of what must have been ten keys.

"This'll be the tedious part," Jason whispered as he stooped to bring the keyhole to eye level.

Penn followed him down and kept the light focused on the keys as Jason picked one, seemingly at random, and inserted it into the lock in the center of the silver doorknob. It slid in easily, but it wouldn't turn.

"Like I said. Tedious."

He moved to a second key, with the same results.

As he lifted the third key, he fumbled the ring and the whole collection fell onto the tile floor. The sound of the impact registered with Penn as a tolling bell on a quiet summer night.

Jason spat out a curse. "Shit." He picked up the jumble of keys and selected a new one. "Problem now is that I don't know where I left off last time."

The key slid in as easily as the others, and the lock turned.

Penn felt a rush of elation, an urge to push through the closed door.

Jason stood to his full height and Penn mirrored him.

"That's halfway," Jason whispered. "One of two."

Penn saw the keyhole to a deadbolt at shoulder height.

Jason selected a key. It slipped in, didn't turn.

"Maybe you should drop the key ring again," Penn quipped.

"You're talking."

This time, the fourth key did the trick. The deadbolt turned, but apparently with some effort. Jason used both hands to make the key turn all the way.

"Why can't it ever be easy?" the guard muttered.

Nearby, a different steel door opened and closed.

Penn and Jason dropped to a knee in unison. Jason had to sweep the muzzle of his carbine to the side to keep it from hitting the floor. He killed the flashlight, and absolute darkness returned.

"Shhh . . ." Jason's hiss was barely audible.

The hallway exploded in light. "I wish they wouldn't turn these things off at night," a voice said.

Another voice said, "When the fuel for those generators is gone, this place will be dark forever."

The footsteps and voices were coming their way.

"I don't like all this killing," the first voice said. "It doesn't feel right."

"It'll be over soon. One more day. Once all the old school is dead, we can move ahead with other stuff."

Hearing talk of his impending execution didn't bother Penn a bit. But the fact of being shot in the bowels of a facility like this terrified him.

Jason made eye contact with Penn and placed a forefinger on his own lips. *Keep quiet.*

Then, keeping his back straight and pressed against the door, he rose to his feet and carefully slid his rifle out of the way. He unclipped a folding knife from the edge of his pants pocket, opened it, and then slid his hand and knife back into the pocket.

Jason reached past Penn and put his left hand on the doorknob. Steadying himself with a big breath, he opened the door, then closed it with a slam before stepping out into the hallway.

"Stop!" one of the others yelled. "What the hell!"

"Easy, gents," Jason said.

"What are you doing down here?" one of the new arrivals asked.

"That's my question for you," Jason said. "As long as Glendale is down here, this hallway is supposed to be empty."

Jason hadn't moved, but the others' voices continued to crescendo. They were very close.

"There is too much weird shit going on with this Parsons guy," the other talker said. "I mean, I guess he's in charge, but all this sneaking around and shit is creeping me—"

Penn saw the speaker at the same instant the speaker saw him.

"Holy shit!" The guy raised his rifle.

Jason moved with blistering speed. His knife hand snatched out of his pocket and moved in a wide arc. Penn couldn't see what he did, exactly, but the other man dropped straight down as blood spray-painted the walls and ceiling.

The second guy was still standing there, his jaw

slackened as Jason slashed him across his face, and then pounded the blade five times into his gut. Penn sensed that the guy was already dead before the last couple of thrusts.

After the second guy hit the floor, Jason turned back to Penn. His hands were soaked with the dead men's blood, and his face was spattered with it.

"I guess that means I'm coming with you," Jason said. "Help yourself to a rifle."

Penn found himself gaping at Jason, his jaw slack. He'd never seen anything like that. The speed of the attack, the violence of it, was terrifying.

Jason reached out and grabbed Penn under his arm. "Come on, we're not out of here yet."

"What did you just do?"

"I just saved our lives. And, if I'm to believe everything your lawyer says, I'm somehow saving the American dream. On your feet. We really need to get going."

After Penn was on his feet, Jason bent down to one of the bodies on the floor and unstrung the black rifle from around the corpse's head and shoulders.

"This is an AR-fifteen," Jason said. "Ever shot one?"

"Yes, I have."

Jason handed it over. "It's the same weapon that you and your asshat politician friends liked to call an assault rifle, which it is not but I wish it was." He patted down both bodies and was able to produce three extra magazines filled with ammunition. He kept those for himself.

"Point to the charging handle," Jason said.

Penn pointed to the T-shaped handle at the rear of the receiver.

"Is the safety on or off?"

Penn looked, verified that the safety near his thumb was parallel to the barrel. "It's on. I really have used these before."

"Yeah, well, forgive me if I get nervous being with a guy who's never had a real job and is carrying a gun he doesn't want other people to have."

"Really?" Penn said. "This is the time for political talking points?"

"No, sir, that time passed when you killed a few billion people." He pointed at Penn's weapon. "You keep the safety on until you're ready to shoot someone. And I swear to everything holy that if you point that thing at me one single time, I will drop you on the spot. We good?"

Jason didn't wait for Penn's answer. He turned back toward the unlocked door, opened it, and stepped through. Penn followed, feeling clumsy as he fumbled with the rifle's sling. "Jason!" he whispered.

The guard turned, saw the nature of the president's problem, and smiled. "Stop," he commanded. "Raise your right arm and hold still."

Penn did exactly that as the guard draped the rifle so it dangled right to left, with the muzzle pointing down. "Ask me again why I'm a little nervous. Keep your flashlight close, we're going dark again when I close the door behind us."

Penn was ready with his filtered flashlight when darkness returned.

Within a few steps, Penn realized that he was once

again in familiar territory, surrounded by potable and nonpotable water tanks and massive fuel tanks. This was the guts of the Annex—the utility complex that Solara used to oversee. In the far wall, a circular blast door hung wide open. Beyond it lay a tunnel that would lead to an exterior door.

"This was the door that Parsons used to invade the place," Penn said.

"I remember," Jason said. "I wasn't on the first wave, but I was here."

"My chief of staff was killed that night."

"My whole family was incinerated under a fireball a few weeks before that," Jason said. "But I'm sorry for your loss."

The dismissiveness of the tone pissed Penn off more than anything else. Yes, the politicians put the world in a place where no one wanted to be, but he was president of the United States, for God's sake. That qualified him for some modicum of respect, didn't it?

Jason kept going, leading the way through the hatch and into the space beyond.

Arlen Strasky, Penn's longtime chief of staff, had volunteered to travel outside the sterile bunker to get a feel for what the conditions were for people who were stuck outside. He was to have been gone an hour and then return. Penn had no way of knowing what had transpired that afternoon, but when the hour expired, Parsons led his assault on the Annex, and here they were.

"What's on the other side out there?" Penn whispered.

"Unfiltered air and angry people," Jason said. This area between the hatch and the exit door looked like it might have been used for storage at some point. Now, it was largely empty.

As they came to within a few feet of the door that would dump them outside, Jason stopped short and turned to address the president. He lit his own face, as if on Halloween, the red light creating shadows where his eye sockets lay.

"Mr. Glendale, you need to listen closely to me, okay?" His voice was barely audible. "I don't like you, but I don't have anything against you, either. I accept that you were trying to do your job, but as far as I'm concerned, you were really shitty at it."

"Now, wait—"

"I don't care about any of that shit. What happened, happened. Up until a few minutes ago, when I killed those guys, my future was pretty damn safe. Well, as safe as it can be when the air is radioactive."

Penn didn't bother to tell him that the atmosphere was fine by now.

"Now, I'm on the run just like you. When these doors open, my responsibility to you ends. Are we clear on that?"

Penn said nothing, choosing instead to wait for the rest.

"If you want to come with me, that's fine," Jason continued. "But understand that that's on you. I don't owe you a thing, and you don't owe me a thing, either."

"Where are you going to go?"

"Someplace other than here. I promised your attorney friend that I would get you this far. I thought I was going to open the door, release you and then close it again after you were gone. Now I can't do that."

"Can I ask a question now?" Penn said.

"Go ahead."

"Why are you doing this?"

"Ask a different question," Jason said. "I have reasons. That's all you need to know about that."

What an odd young man, Penn thought. Clearly a trained killer, he also had a heart. But he wanted to pretend otherwise. There was a story there that Penn wanted to hear, but now was not the time.

"I'm ready when you are," Penn said.

Jason handed his light to Penn and turned to the door to address the steel crosspiece that rested in brackets that had been set in the concrete to brace the interior. From the effort, it appeared to be damned heavy. He set it to the side.

"This is where it gets exciting," Jason said. He opened the door a crack and cast his light out the opening.

"What are you looking for?" Penn whispered.

"Anything that looks like a threat. As you know, this is the weak spot into the bunker. Sometimes, Parsons posts a guard out here. I think it's just to give someone something to do. There's no way to open the door from the other side."

After scanning the night for a few seconds, Jason announced, "We're clear."

As the door opened, the metal-on-concrete screech sounded to Penn like a woman's scream. He cringed. "Good God."

"Yeah. Stealthy we ain't," Jason whispered. As he led the way out, he stopped. "Hold the door."

Penn used his foot to keep the heavy panel from closing while Jason bent at the waist and picked something up off the ground. When he stood again to his full height, Penn could see the grin even through the dark. Something heavy dangled from a two-handed grip at the level of the guard's crotch.

"Is that a rock?" Penn asked.

"Yep. Want to really piss Roger Parsons off? We're going to leave his security door open." He placed the rock on the ground next to the door, where its weight would keep the panel from swinging shut.

"What will happen to the people who enter unannounced?"

"Hard to say. Depends on Roger's mood. Somewhere between a beating and a bullet through the brain. I've seen it go both ways. But that's okay, the people know the stakes."

"Suppose they don't and they get seriously punished?"

"Then they'll learn. This is how the bad guys win, you know. They make people afraid to try to do what they know is right." As Jason rose to his full height, he squared off to Penn, face to face. "Of course, you're a twenty-first century politician. You know all about making people afraid to do the right thing."

With that, Jason stepped out into the night.

Penn followed.

CHAPTER FIFTEEN

*L*UKE ENJOYED NIGHTTIME. HE LIKED THE QUIET OF IT, the darkness. In the weeks since Hell Day, he swore that his eyes had adjusted to the darkness of the night unmarred by electric lights. The stars were brighter, as was the moon. Once he oriented himself to the roadway, he took note of the black ribbon that was the paved surface. He carried a flashlight in his pocket, but he intended not to use it unless there was no alternative. Not only did the beam destroy night vision, it also told potential bad guys that you were approaching. Plus, batteries were a finite commodity these days.

He carried his M4 slung across his chest and a Glock 42 pistol on his right hip. He'd lifted the Glock from one of the bodies at the roadblock where Adam had been wounded. The .380 caliber round was generally disrespected by the pistol snobs before Hell Day, but Luke liked the small size and light weight. Plus, the dead guy he took it from had a holster for it and two extra mags, both loaded. That would give him nineteen rounds to throw downrange before the empty pistol became a paperweight. Or maybe a hammer. To his knowledge, no one else in their caravan was carrying .380.

Luke's plan was to keep his horse, Rover, in the center of the road and to walk slowly. His backpack carried only water and jerky, plus two extra thirty-round mags for his M4. With the one in the mag well and the quick-access spare in his back pocket, that gave him 120 rounds of 5.56 millimeter if things went to shit.

And why wouldn't things go to shit? It had been that kind of day.

He'd been at it for over two hours now, and he'd seen nothing. Literally, nothing. No people, no animals. He'd heard a few screeches from owls, but overall, the quiet was spooky. It made Rover's own footfalls sound louder than they should. Trees lined both sides of the road, but the heavy forest had given way to what appeared to be broad fields. Somewhere in the darkness, he imagined that there were houses and cars and boats and RVs, all but the houses useless to their owners. There were probably bodies out there, too, though his nose didn't detect any traces of them.

His mission was simple enough. He'd walk through the night until he found people. Then, when he found them, he would watch them for a while. Were they a threat, or were they just more refugees? If they seemed safe, he would approach and see what he saw. If a threat never materialized, he would move on.

Luke needed to find the rest of the crowd that was responsible for killing Adam. He knew it was wrong to think that way—that there was always hope, and that until he knew that the news was bad, he needed to assume that the news was good. That had been driven into his psyche with a sledgehammer by both his mother and his father. But he had also seen the bullet wound, and he'd studied enough anatomy and physiology to know what organ systems lay in the gut. That was stuff you had to know if you were going to be a good combat shooter. Hell, it's good to know even if you're going to be a hunter.

Most hunters aim for the spot behind a deer's right shoulder in hopes of hitting the heart, his father used to tell him. *Good hunters know where the heart is and know how to hit it. Great hunters aim for the left ventricle of the heart and nail it.*

Luke actually preferred going for the head shot with deer. He was a meat eater, not a trophy taker. Put a .308 round just forward of Bambi's ear and the critter will drop straight down, dead before its knees buckled. And you won't have to deal with the trench of shredded meat through the beast's chest.

Instant death was the dream. No suffering, no pain. Just there, and then not-there.

Luke also saw the look in Caleb's eyes. His words said that he'd keep Adam alive, but words never kept anyone alive.

Now, Luke was going to bring justice to the assholes who hurt his family.

When all of this was over—whatever that meant— he was going to write about it. He was going to let the world know how they'd fought and how they'd survived. He'd show them how random life and death was.

Back when his mom was in the House of Representatives, he thought it was cool to be so close to the seat of power. That's what she called it, the seat of power. She believed in democracy, and she believed that people were good. Luke wondered how she could continue to believe it still.

He hoped he'd have the talent to show people that when the world collapsed, all that mattered was survival skills. It blew his mind that so many of the new arrivals in Ortho were clueless when it came to doing anything with their hands. Because they were in West Virginia, he supposed, most people at least knew which end of the gun a bullet came out of, but even for many of the locals, that's where the knowledge ended.

He couldn't imagine what it must be like in cities, where nobody did anything useful. Stock brokering and money handling didn't mean anything in the end.

From what Luke saw in Ortho, though, people could learn when they wanted to. Or, maybe when they had to. It was hard to tell the difference anymore.

Over the course of maybe ten minutes of walking, he became gradually aware of a lightening of the darkness. At first, he thought it was a trick played by the moon and the stars, but the glow was too pronounced for that.

As he walked along a curve in the road, the aura of light disappeared behind the wall of trees, but when the curve turned back to the right, the aura returned, brighter than it was the last time.

That made it man-made.

The alternative, he supposed would have been a forest fire, but the glow seemed wrong for that. He remembered the anger of the reds and oranges on the horizon on Hell Day, and this was not that.

It was time to be hyper alert.

If this was another roadblock, or maybe a pop-up community, and if it were run by the likes of his mom and Major McCrea, there'd be watchers deployed on the outskirts of the place, especially at night, when every danger was the greatest.

Luke moved to the right-hand edge of the roadway and slowed his approach even more. If this was a group of people, they would either be looking for new victims to terrorize, or they would be people fearful of being victimized. One way or the other, they would not be pleased to see an armed stranger approaching out of the darkness.

That's why he moved to the side, where the shadows were darker. That's also why he moved more slowly. He knew from his childhood of training that humans were cursed with terrible night vision, certainly relative to other mammals. Over the centuries, though, we'd learned to adapt by having the other senses take up the slack. Our hearing got sharper, and our noses became more discerning. But even with decreased sight, we became more adept at sensing motion.

Luke swore it was a supernatural thing. He sensed people. He knew when he was being approached, even when he couldn't see a thing. He wouldn't know who it was, or even what it was, but he'd know that something was there. He'd always assumed that other people were the same way.

He decided it was time to dismount. After lifting himself out of the saddle and down to the ground, he let Rover's rein dangle. She wasn't a wanderer. Five minutes later, deep in the shadows now, he squinted into the night, trying to tune his ears to the sounds around him as he strove to remain invisible.

As he lifted his foot to take a step, he froze, then gently laid his boot back on the ground. The hairs on his neck went to full alert as *that feeling* overpowered him. He felt eyes on him.

Was he being watched, or was he being targeted?

Slowly—oh, so slowly—he let his knees fold and he lowered his body to the ground, till his butt was resting on his heels. God had a cruel sense of humor when he wired the heart directly to the ear drums. As his chest pounded, the rush of each pulse left him feeling deaf.

He took a deep breath and held it, trying to tame his racing heart.

A flashlight jumped to life off to his right. He went flat on his stomach, trying to dissolve into the gravel shoulder.

The beam was close, but they hadn't nailed him exactly, falling too far to the right, about ten feet forward of the top of Luke's head.

"Who's there?" a female voice said.

"Show yourself or we'll shoot," a male voice added.

Three seconds later, a single gunshot ripped the night. It was a rifle for sure, and Luke thought it was a big one, a hunting rifle perhaps. The bullet didn't come anywhere near him, and the fact that it was a single shot made Luke believe it was a bolt-action weapon.

"I missed on purpose," the man said. "Next time, I won't."

"We don't want to hurt you," the lady said. "We just don't want to be snuck up on."

This sucked. Of the many drills and speeches his parents had pounded him with over the years, the one that registered most loudly now was the one about never surrendering.

The best fight is the one you never engage in, he remembered his mom telling him not too long ago for the bazillionth time. *If walking away is an option, that's always the best choice. But if you have to fight, you fight to win. Surrender is never an option.*

Once you put yourself into the hands of an enemy, you've surrendered your free will. War crimes and tortures have always been preceded by surrender.

But he'd screwed himself by dropping to his belly. He couldn't see his surroundings, and he couldn't get up and run without rising first, and that would give the shooter an extra second or two to take him out.

"We just want to see who you are," the lady said. "We want to talk to you. You know how unsettling it is out here at night."

"I'm going to count to three," the man said. "If you're not up by three, I'm going to kill you."

The flashlight remained fixed on the wrong spot.

That was Luke's only advantage here.

"One . . ."

The woman whispered something.

"He's the one making the choice," the man replied, not in a whisper. "Two . . ."

Luke's mind raced. Something had to change here. Shooting at the wrong spot would keep him alive one shot at a time, but that wasn't sustainable. If he could use the two seconds it would take for the shooter to work the bolt—

"Three!"

Two seconds passed, and then the rifle boomed again.

This was it. Luke jumped up to a squat, pivoted on his right foot and dashed into the woods on the same side as the shooters, but in a different direction.

"Hey!" the lady yelled. "There! He's running."

Luke kept his head low and squeezed his rifle to his chest as he charged through the branches and ferns and ground cover. He held his left forearm in front of his face, cocked vertically at the elbow to protect his eyes from unseen branches and vines.

The rifle fired again, and this time, Luke heard the bullet hiss past his head, drilling through the autumn leaves.

That was too close. He made a hard turn to his left and plunged twenty yards deeper into the foliage before his right shoulder collided with a tree and spun him around. He landed on his back, where a protruding rock found his short ribs on the right side.

Another shot, but it was nowhere near him. It was time to settle in and become invisible.

"What the hell are you shooting at?" a third voice yelled.

"There's someone out there," the lady said. "He wouldn't show himself, so we shot him. He was coming up the road."

The new voice clearly belonged to someone in charge. "Did you hit him?"

"I don't think so," the male said.

"Then you didn't shoot him, did you? You only shot *at* him."

"Yes, sir. I suppose so."

"I knew it was a mistake to put you out here. Where is he now?"

"Out there somewhere."

"Well, no shit. Point to where."

A pause, during which Luke could imagine the shooter pointing into the woods.

"Was he armed?"

"I don't know."

"Did he shoot back?"

"No, sir."

"Well, that's a hint, don't you think?"

"I think he was young," the lady said. "He moved very fast."

"What does *young* mean?"

"Teenager, I think," the lady said.

The boss's voice boomed, "Hey! Kid! If you're alive, I know you can hear me. And I swear to God you don't want me to come out there and find you. I swear I'll strip the flesh from your bones with a dull knife. Now, show yourself and stop this nonsense."

Luke willed himself not to breathe as his mind raced through his options. He needed to get out of here, but he also needed not to move.

"I'm going to send a bunch of people out there to find you, kid. You are a kid, right? I am not a man to mess around with. So, let's just make this easy, okay?"

Maybe he should roll the dice and give up. Who knows? Maybe they're just a bunch of scared refugees who were trying to protect themselves. Wasn't this exactly what he would do if he were standing sentry outside Ortho, as he'd done God only knew how many times?

No, it wasn't. The Ortho militia had rules of engagement. You never fired on anyone who didn't pose a threat.

But you also returned fire on those who did.

He didn't see an upside in returning fire right now.

But he also didn't see an upside to handing himself over to a bunch of angry strangers.

"Well, shit," Leader Man said. "Okay, what's your name again?"

"Melissa."

"Right. Melissa, go back and bring back five of the most pissed off people you can find and we'll root this sumbitch out and crucify him."

Luke felt a chill. Could this guy be serious?

"You're not serious," Melissa said.

"Goddamn right I'm serious. We'll hang him from a limb down the road as a warning to others."

Shit, shit, shit.

Maybe the guy was only bluffing, but it was the kind of bluff Luke wasn't going to call. He needed to get the hell out of here, and he'd better do it before the woods were full of people with flashlights and guns and attitude.

Two flashlights came to life this time, and they were sweeping a section of woods where Luke had been before he jinked to the left. The beams were off by yards this time, not merely by feet.

This was his chance. He didn't have time to get away, but maybe he had time to find a place to hunker down and hide out of sight. That was easier to do at night than it would be after the sun came up, but now he was all about buying time. If they organized a good search, they would sweep an area and then move on when they didn't find anything. All Luke needed to do was make himself invisible for the time it took to sweep this one spot in the woods. Then, once they passed him, he would move into one of the areas they'd already searched. That would buy him still more time.

Within the next few hours, the sun would come up, and by that time, if everything went well, he hoped he'd be able to relocate enough times to be completely free of the area. He wouldn't have much to report back to the major and his mom, but at least he'd be able to say where the bad guys were and be alive to do it.

What if they had dogs?

The thought chilled his blood. He'd seen hunting dogs tear into prey. He wanted none of that.

Screw it. Nobody has dogs anymore. They'd all been eaten, he presumed. He hadn't seen any pets around anywhere for weeks.

This had to happen now, while the lights were confused and the woods were still relatively empty.

Crawling would take too much time and make too much noise, so he rose again to his feet and bent low at the waist to head deeper into the woods, away from the road. The Leader Man and the guy who'd shot at him were talking and making threatening noises, which gave him some forgiveness on moving stealthily. That meant he could move with some speed, but he couldn't be careless. One loud noise would ruin everything.

As he scooted through the underbrush, he tried to make out places where he could lay low. Through the shadows, he could see an outcropping of rocks, jagged things that had erupted out of the earth God knew how many millions of years ago. In the non-light of the nighttime, they looked like dragon teeth, pointy and arranged at odd angles. The shadows between the teeth suggested the presence of caves that could provide him all the shelter he'd need.

They'd also be seen by the search party as the most logical place for him to seek shelter. Even if they didn't want to go and explore the caves—or the crags or whatever the hell they were called—they only had to fire shots down into them. Between bullets and rock fragments, having no place to go seemed like a bad idea.

Okay, every logical hiding place would be a bad idea, wouldn't it? They'd assume that he was scared shitless, which he was, but they'd also assume that he would panic and hide someplace obvious. That meant he needed to go to ground someplace that was not obvious. But to buy a few minutes, he needed to convince the coming search parties that he was someplace he wasn't.

In theory, while they were diverted, he could make a break and escape.

To divert them, though, he needed a diversion. A hand grenade would come in really handy right now. So would a bunch of people who were on his side.

The caves.

He couldn't hide in the spaces between and among the jutting rocks because it would be too obvious, so why not sell that as the place he needed to be?

Noises crescendoed back toward the road as the searchers gathered. Luke picked up his pace. He button-hooked to his left and returned to the jagged rocks. He shrugged out of his backpack and laid it off to the side of one of the narrow gaps in the rocks. He removed his flashlight from its pocket in the side of the pack. Covering the lens with his palm to deaden the beam, he thumbed the light to life.

Keeping the lens covered, he laid his belly across the top of one of the rocks and leaned way over into the maw of the opening. Then, he let go of the light and watched as it rolled down the side of the rock and into the mouth of the cave at the bottom. When it came to rest, the beam pointed perfectly into the cavern.

Luke talked himself into believing that it looked like the light was of a scared kid trying to stay out of sight.

The sounds were getting louder. He could hear words now. Something about not hurting him until they had a chance to talk to him.

Luke pushed away from the rocks and headed deeper into the woods. He left his backpack where it was, in hopes of alerting the searchers to his fake hidey-hole. Keeping low at the waist, he scooted twenty or thirty yards and stopped at a deadfall, a thick hardwood that had rotted out at the bottom and gave him pretty decent cover. It wouldn't hold up to a daylight search, but he had no intention of still being here when the sun rose in the morning.

The hardwood had toppled against an upright tree, presenting a pretty good spot where he could nestle in, stay out of sight, yet still be able to see what was happening.

"All right," someone yelled. "Let's find this kid, take care of him and get back to camp."

Luke hadn't seen that many flashlights in one place in a long time.

As the search party approached from the road, Luke

saw them only as dancing light beams, each one casting bizarre, mottled shadows that swirled like phantom bats through the foliage.

"Honest to God, wherever you are, it's so much easier for you to come forward than it will be to wait for us to find you!" Luke thought the voice belonged to Leader Man, but he wasn't sure. Everybody sounds kind of the same when they shout.

"We don't like sneaky strangers," another voice shouted.

"Except for breakfast," another one said. "Fry 'em up with a little bacon, and that's a morning taste treat." That one brought laughter from the others.

"And young flesh is the best there is!"

Luke knew they were trying to freak him out and flush him out, but that wasn't going to work. Not yet anyway.

They were coming straight at him now, but across a wide arc. If his ruse didn't work, at least one of those flashlights was likely to come right at him. If that happened, there'd be some decision making to do.

In his haste to move away from the cave, Luke had lost track of where the rock outcropping was. He knew it was in front of him somewhere, and he thought it was right of center, but he couldn't be sure. Not that it mattered. This thing would work or it wouldn't. He'd know for sure in just a minute or two.

"Oscar!" someone called. It wasn't a shout, exactly, but not a whisper, either. It sounded conspiratorial. Then a flashlight made a circular motion in the air. "I found something!"

The light was ahead and to the right. Had they fallen for it?

Other lights turned in that direction. They started converging.

"What is it?"

"A backpack."

Yes!

Most of the lights hurried that way.

After ten or fifteen seconds: "Hey! You down there! I see your light! Come on out or we'll open fire."

This was Luke's cue. This was his chance.

Again staying low, he rose from his cover and darted away from the commotion. If his sense of direction was calibrated right, he was heading parallel to the road where he was first shot at. Straight ahead, sooner than later, he'd come to the dogleg of the switchback, and then he could return to the solid surface and run for real.

Now it was all about time and distance.

He hadn't done anything to truly offend anyone, so maybe they wouldn't pursue him. He hoped they'd just get bored with the search, and when that happened—

A bright white light nailed him in the face, causing him to skid to a stop.

"If your hands go anywhere near a weapon, I'll kill you right here."

CHAPTER SIXTEEN

*T*HE NIGHT WASN'T AS DARK AS PENN HAD THOUGHT IT would be. It was clear and chilly and the moon hung high, casting blue light and dark shadows. Small fires burned everywhere, marking the locations of individual campsites, he imagined. The smoke from the fires stung his eyes a little, and the smell irritated his sinuses.

But it wasn't just the smoke that polluted the air. There was something . . . rotten.

"The cremation pits are up there to the right and around the corner," Jason explained before Penn could ask the question. "The people here live like pigs. I don't get it. I understand that these are tough times, but there's never an excuse to surrender your humanity."

Penn followed as Jason turned left out of the steel door and started down a narrow roadway. In the dim light, the black strip against the charcoal gray tree lines could have just as easily been a stream.

"What's it like inside the hotel itself?" Penn asked.

"A little better. But you have to be a friend of Roger's to be allowed in there. As you might guess, that's a pretty small list."

"Why do the people stay here?"

"Where else are they going to go? Most of these folks traveled for days or weeks to get here. I guess they feel safer surrounded by other people."

"You sound like you disagree."

"Damn straight I disagree. You can smell the shit in the air. This place is a disease factory. Some of the toilets inside the hotel still flush, but you have to prime the tanks with water first. There aren't enough toilets for all the people on the grounds, and even if there were, I don't think a lot of them would bother to use them anyway. They just drop trau, squat and let it rip. It's disgusting."

"How many people are here?"

"Oh, hell, I don't know. Hundreds, but I don't think a thousand. It's a pretty big bit of property."

"How do they feed themselves?"

"I don't think I want to know. Remember, I was an FOR—friend-of-Roger. I didn't have to deal with the shit that these poor folks do. Given the awfulness of the times, I had it pretty comfortable."

Penn found it difficult to comprehend that he'd had no idea of the scale of the desperation that teemed just outside the Annex. Scott Johnson, and the others in Solara who ran the operation of the physical plant, had made reference to hearing and seeing signs that people were moving around the grounds of the resort, but there'd been no indication of hundreds.

Or maybe Johnson had known exactly how desperate the situation was, and he'd chosen not to share it with the residents of the Annex. What good would the knowledge have done when there was no option to open the doors before a minimum of sixty days had passed?

Jason walked quickly, fast enough that it was hard for Penn to keep up. He blamed his stiffness on the weeks of inactivity while wasting away in the jail cell. "Can you shorten your strides a little?" he asked.

"Are you sure you want to? If you get seen out here, you'll get dead real quick."

"I'm not suggesting we stroll," Penn argued. "Just take a little of the edge off."

Jason slowed his pace. "Just so you know, our guns are going to mark us both in people's minds as Parsons' guys."

"Is that good or bad?"

"It's real bad if the person we see is *really* one of Parsons' guys. For everybody else, it shouldn't matter much. Like I said before, they're scared of being anything other than scared."

As they moved past the trees on both sides of the narrow roadway, Penn swore that he could feel people watching them. Shadows moved, snippets of discussions disturbed the silence.

Jason said, "I'm told the roads on the campus here are dangerous this time of night. This is where the thieves and the muggers hang out. Rapes and other assaults are through the roof. I suppose that's why we haven't seen anyone else walking on the road."

"Who's doing all the raping and pillaging?"

"Nobody knows. Not sure anybody cares. Not officially, anyway. Murders happen every night. Who's to say if the dead guys were attacking people or defending themselves?"

"What does Parsons say?"

"Nothing, I don't imagine." Jason's tone showed indignance. "Why would he? It's not his problem."

"But he runs the place, right?"

Jason chuckled. "You really don't get it, do you? Parsons doesn't give a shit about anybody but Parsons. If you ask me, that's the healthiest attitude to have. My problems are mine and yours are yours. Roger has declared the hotel to be his little kingdom. He owns the palace, and he's surrounded himself with a bunch of thugs to defend him. If you're not a spoke in that wheel, you're screwed."

"So, of the rapists and pillagers, what percentage do you guess are Parsons' acolytes?"

"I don't know. Some, I'm sure. I mean, a man's got needs, right?"

Penn's stomach tightened at the violence of Jason's words. That such things happened was not a surprise in the aftermath of a war and the deprivations that followed, but to hear it taken so lightly angered him. But he kept those thoughts to himself. Like it or not, he needed Jason on his side.

"That explains the lack of talking, too, I guess," Penn observed. "I've noticed that conversations stop as we pass. They must be wondering if we're coming to hurt them."

"I imagine they are."

Ahead and to the right, along the tree line, a match flared as someone lit a cigarette.

"Take the safety off your rifle and get ready to shoot," Jason said as he brought his rifle to low ready, the butt plate nestled in his shoulder. "Only Parsons' guys have cigarettes. Every other smoker burned through theirs weeks ago."

Penn's thumb found the selector switch and moved it from its horizontal position to a vertical one.

"Don't address the guy, don't say anything," Jason instructed at a barely audible whisper.

"Strolling awfully late, aren't you?" said the man in the dark.

The world turned bright white as a flashlight beam nailed them straight in the eyes.

Penn reflexively turned away from the light.

"Get that goddamn thing out of my eyes!" Jason barked.

"Herringer?" Shadow Man said. "The hell are you doing all the way out here? I thought you were guarding Numb Nuts."

Penn sensed that this was going to go bad, and fast. Keeping his back to the light as best he could, he rotated his body and ducked out of the beam, circling around to flank Shadow Man, but the beam followed *him*.

"Hey, you're him!" Shadow Man yelled. "You're Glendale!"

Blinded by the light, Penn couldn't take a shot without risking a hit on Jason. Instead, he dropped to his stomach on the street to make as small a target as possible.

He'd just hit the ground when a rifle boomed. In the silence, the report was the loudest thing Penn had ever heard.

Penn felt no pain, so he expected another shot. But it never came.

"Bad guy down," Jason said. "You okay?" He made no effort to help Penn rise back to his feet.

"I'm good," Penn said.

"Okay, they heard the gunshot in Florida," Jason said. "I think it's about to get uncomfortable around here. We need to quicken that pace again."

"You!" someone yelled from the darkness.

Penn whirled on the sound.

"Don't shoot! I got no gun. Assholes took it from me."

From Penn's left, Jason aimed the white beam of his Mag Light at the approaching man. A woman walked by the man's side. They both winced at the blast of light and shielded their eyes.

"For Christ's sake!" the man said.

Jason lowered the beam, so the hot part of the circle was at the man's chin.

"State your business," Jason said.

"Are you Pennington Glendale?" the man said. "Ex-president?"

"Who are you?" Jason asked.

"You first," the man said.

"I'm the man with the gun," Jason said, "and I'm kind of in the groove for killing. You'd do well to take a step back."

The man seemed unafraid of getting shot. He kept his eyes on Penn as he said, "I'm Bruce Cauthen. Was visiting this place from Harper's Ferry when you ordered the world to be killed."

In the wash of Jason's light, Penn read seething anger in Cauthen's eyes. "Sorry, Mr. Cauthen. You've got the wrong guy."

"I was at the congressbitch's trial today," Jason said. "You were there."

"You're the third person tonight to confuse me with the president," Penn said. "I guess I just have that kind of face."

"You shithead," Cauthen said. "You're such a coward, you can't even admit to who you are. It's not like I can hurt you. You've got the guns."

Penn had dedicated his adult life to reading when it was time to speak and when it was time to stay silent. This moment had silence written all over it.

"I think we should be moving along now, Mike," Jason said to Penn. "When we find a plastic surgeon, we'll have to get you a facelift."

"You don't even have the stones to stand trial. You've got to run away like the little bitch that you are. That's the thing about politicians, isn't it? None of them have the courage to be held accountable for all the terrible shit that they do."

"It's not all terrible shit," Penn said. The sound of his own words nearly startled him. "There would be no infrastructure but for politicians. No justice, no laws."

Jason stepped closer, put a hand on Penn's arm. "Um, Mike? I don't think that Mr. Cauthen is in the mood for a discussion of civics. We really need to be moving along."

"You mean we'd have none of the stuff that we used to have but don't have no more," Cauthen's female associate said.

"Hey, everybody!" Cauthen yelled. "I got the president of the United States over here. He's making a run for it. What should we do?"

As the shadows closed in around them, Penn realized that he'd waited too long. He stopped resisting Jason and started pressing his way through the crowd.

"I think we should take him back to stand trial," Cauthen said.

Penn hovered his finger over the trigger.

"Don't be crazy," Jason said. "Don't die over a lost cause."

"Why are you helping him escape?" Cauthen asked. "You killed your own friend to help him."

"That man was about to kill us," Penn said, and again, he regretted his words. They sounded weak. He didn't owe anyone an explanation.

"Missing your Secret Service detail?" someone said from the crowd.

"Keep moving," Jason said. "Don't slow, don't engage. If someone puts hands on you, or if you see a weapon, shoot. Otherwise, let's walk our way out of this."

Jason took an aggressive stance with his rifle. He held it up to his shoulder, the muzzle sweeping the crowd at chest level. Penn kept his muzzle low and scanned the crowd.

"Anybody got a rope?" someone else called. "We can take care of things now and skip the formalities."

"If anybody touches either one of us, I will shoot everybody in this crowd," Jason said.

"What do you say, *Mr. President*? Do you agree with him? You willing to kill people directly, or do you only do that by remote control?"

Penn picked up his pace. This crowd was hot and about to boil over. Did he have the commitment and courage to follow through with Jason's threat?

Yes, he did, he decided. But courage had nothing to do with any of it.

"Do you really think you can survive this?" Cauthen asked. "You've seen the pictures of what the crowd did to Mussolini when they got their hands on him, right? And Gaddafy? Why don't you do yourself a favor and kill yourself so you don't have to suffer that humiliation."

Penn had never been this terrified. The hatred seemed to have physical weight, physical force. These people didn't understand the reality of what had happened, but they also didn't want to. They had lost so much, and in their minds it was all his fault.

"Don't shoot unless I do," Jason said.

Penn understood the context. The threat of violence was a far better deterrent than violence itself. Once the killing line was crossed, the crowd no longer had anything to lose. The bitter truth was that if they fired every bullet they had, the crowd would ultimately have the upper hand when the ammo was gone.

"You know," Cauthen said loudly for the crowd, "Roger Parsons would probably let us into the hotel if we brought him this guy's body."

"We're not bringin' nobody no body," said a man from the shadows. An enormous shadow stepped forward but kept his distance from the rifles. He stood six-five, and still carried a good bit of girth. To Penn, he said, "You two better get git while you can." Then he addressed the crowd. "Ain't none o' you is gonna lay a hand on them because you don't want to die tonight, and because when we all lay our heads down tonight, we want to be able to tell ourselves that we're better than the people who put us here."

"No," Cauthen said, "I think I'd sleep just fine knowing that the new Bin Laden is dead."

"Stop listening to the debate," Jason whispered to Penn. "A closed window just opened up again for us. We need to climb through it."

Roger Parsons made a point of being showered, shaved and dressed in freshly laundered clothes when Mason Goode escorted Taylor Barnes into his suite of rooms. Parsons sat at the head of the dining room table, his feet propped on the adjacent chair, pretending to read a book on the history of the Hilltop Manor Resort, and did not look up as he commanded Barnes to sit in the seat at the far end.

"He was already up and wandering around," Goode said. "Took a little while to find him."

Parsons still avoided eye contact. "Where was he?"

"Out on the front lawn. I saw him coming up the hill past the cremation pits."

"What do you have to say for yourself, Taylor?" Parsons asked as he turned a page.

Barnes remained silent, drawing Parsons' gaze. "Rudeness is never appropriate," Barnes said. "If you want to talk to me, talk to me. I'm not going to perform for you."

Parsons made a show of closing the book and laying it on the table. "Very well. Why did you do it?"

Barnes gave a smug smile. "I might not be the best lawyer in the world, Roger, but I know better than to answer a question like that. Could you try being more specific?"

"Two of my people are dead down in the catacombs, and your primary client is missing, along with the man assigned to guard him."

Barnes replied with a deep scowl. "That's terrible. What happened to them?"

Parsons was ready for the attitude. He nodded to Goode, who moved with startling speed to pull Barnes's left ear out straight and swipe down on it with a razor-sharp knife blade. As Barnes howled in pain, Goode tossed the hunk of severed cartilage onto the table in front of the lawyer. Blood poured down the side of Barnes's face and through the fingers he'd pressed against the wound to stanch the flow.

"Mason, if you don't mind, do me a favor and get Mr. Barnes a towel from my bathroom. He's making quite the mess of my carpet."

"Are you out of your mind?" Barnes yelled. "He cut my ear off!"

"Not all of it," Parsons corrected. "Just the top half. Sounds like a detail you should keep in mind. You've got many parts and pieces of parts that Mr. Goode can cut away from you." He leaned closer and grinned. "No skin off my nose, as they say."

Reflexively, Barnes's hand shot to his face.

Parsons tossed his head back and laughed to the ceiling. "Now you're getting it," he said.

When Goode came back with a white hand towel, he tossed it to Barnes, who shoved the cloth against his ruined ear.

"Are you tired of the games yet?" Parsons asked. "I'm good with carving on you for hours because I know that sooner or later you're going to answer my questions. The challenge for you is to decide how much tissue you want to still be hanging off your bones before you get to it."

The glibness was all gone from Barnes's face, replaced by fear.

"Let me give you a head start on not bleeding out," Parsons said. "I imagine that as a point of honor, you'd be inclined to lie in an effort to cover your tracks. Don't bother." Parsons held up a piece of paper he was confident the lawyer would recognize. "When you're going to betray my trust in you and trigger the events that would inevitably result in people being killed, you really shouldn't leave a signed note."

Barnes looked horrified.

"Yeah, we found this next to one of the dead men. Lost in a struggle, perhaps. That's what I imagine happened."

"Are you going to kill me?"

"I'm angry enough to do that, yes. But to be honest, it wouldn't make a lot of sense, and it really wouldn't solve my problem. So, where did you tell Glendale |to go?"

Barnes pulled the soaked towel away from his head and looked at it. "I'm going to need another one of these."

"Not if you don't start talking to me in a serious way," Parsons countered. "In about thirty seconds, all you'll need is a bucket to carry your brains in."

"I didn't tell him anything that you don't see on the note," Barnes said. He accepted the replacement towel from Goode.

"The question on the floor is why, Counselor."

"Because he's my client. I'm not going to let you railroad him and make a show of killing him. What you're doing is wrong, Roger."

Parsons took a breath to argue, but Barnes cut him

off before he could get a word out. "You're going to say you're bringing justice, but even you know that's bullshit. You're throwing a temper tantrum and giving a lot of desperate people a bloodshed show."

"I didn't see people turning away when we hung those congressmen and women," Goode said. "All I heard was cheering. Did you see them whacking that Fortnight chick with sticks like a piñata while she was dangling from that oak limb?"

"Isn't giving people what they want the very essence of justice?" Parsons asked.

Barnes started to say something but chose not to.

"How did you talk my man into going along with it? Jason Herringer. He was loyal till you got to him."

"Where is Jason now?" Barnes asked.

"You tell me. And thanks for confirming my suspicions. It only made sense, him being the only person to get physically close to Glendale. Well, him and you. How did you flip him?"

"It wasn't hard, really," Barnes said. "Not everybody who cheers is cheering because they want to. They cheer because they think they're supposed to. They see a lot of angry people and they don't want the fight, so they cheer."

"Jason Herringer is no coward," Parsons said. "Apparently, he's a traitor and a liar and a murderer, but he's no coward."

"What you call cowardice is what I call strategy. It's like those times a few years ago when we called riots peaceful protests and peaceful protests were labeled as riots? Everybody knew it was a big lie, but they perpetuated the lie because that's what their friends were doing, and nobody wanted to lose their friends. Take that same kink in human nature and insert it into the misery people endure every day out there, and you've got a recipe for getting people drawn and quartered if they don't cheer."

"You just told me why *you* betrayed me. You didn't say why Herringer did it."

Barnes's expression said that Parsons wasn't very bright. "You really don't get it, do you? Okay, then, here's the bottom-line truth to it. Jason obeyed your orders to the letter, but you got a different result than you wanted, and he never shared it with you. When I told him to leave the president and me alone to discuss his case, he stayed close, but out of sight. He heard the president's side, and I guess he had a conscience."

Parsons considered what he was hearing and cursed himself for repeating a past mistake. This was the same thing that Jerry Cameron had done when he ran off to deliver that damn letter to the bitch down in Ortho. It made sense, he supposed, now that he thought about it. Politicians get elected by being persuasive. It had been a mistake to assign the same people as guards day after day.

"Where do you reckon he's headed to?" Parsons asked. "And don't let loyalty get in the way of your survival instinct."

"I honestly have no idea, Roger. I didn't want to have an idea. I just wanted him to have a chance to get away. Everything after that is on him. It's the least I could do. It's also the most I could do."

"I think he's headed down to his friend in Ortho," Parsons said. "Where else would he go?"

"I thought she was headed this way," Goode said.

"Maybe," Parsons said. "I wouldn't if I were her. It'd be too dangerous a trip, and why would she walk away from *Eden*?" He rolled his eyes as he said the word.

"So, are we going to chase him down?" Goode asked.

That was a tough question. A tough decision. Parsons had a good gig going here. Was it worth walking away, even for a day, if it risked losing control? Somebody needed to have a hand on the tiller, right? Someone needed to keep order.

"I'll keep things running here," Stony said. "You have no choice but to go after Glendale. If you let someone that high profile escape, everybody will see it as a failure. It'll be seen as weakness, and the way you built this up as a big show for everybody, there'll be a lot of disappointment. This could be your big leadership moment. I mean, think about it. You'll have beaten the most powerful person in the Free World."

Parsons suppressed a smile. The concept of a Free World—any world, really, in the sense that the world used to exist— seemed quaint and naive. But Stony had a point. Whatever power Parsons held over the people there at the Hilltop Manor was as fragile as their impressions of his infallibility.

"How about I stay behind, and you and Goode take a recovery party out to get him?"

Stony crossed his arms, gave a disapproving look. "Do you want to be the guy who brings him in, or do you want to be the guy who told other people to bring him in? People are gonna be watching, and they're gonna talk."

Parsons wandered back to the window. He placed

his hands on the sides of the frame and did standing pushups as he thought this through. Perceptions were important, but so were survival skills. What Stony was suggesting—what Parsons more and more understood to be his only option—was essentially to form a small army and hunt down the president of the United States. Parsons had heard the stories of what lay out there, of the danger. That wasn't something he was anxious to wade into.

"The longer you wait, the harder it's going to be to catch up to him," Stony said.

Parsons turned back to face his old friend. "How many people do you think I need to take?"

Stony looked at the ceiling as he silently ran calculations through his head. "Last count, I think we had forty-five men in the Hilltop Security Force." That was the lofty name that Parsons gave to the people who proved their loyalty to him, and whom he allowed in turn to carry rifles and sleep in the relative comfort of the hotel. "You can spare twelve to fifteen of those for a day or two."

"Jesus," Barnes scoffed. Parsons had nearly forgotten that he was in the room. "It takes fifteen people to murder one old man?"

Something in the man's tone burned through Parsons' gut. The smug smarminess in his words. The foolishness of the timing. Parsons pulled the cheap knock-off 1911 .45 from its holster on his hip, thumbed off the safety and leveled the muzzle at Barnes's forehead. Goode jumped to the side to get out of the bullet's pathway.

Barnes didn't move. He stared down the void of the barrel and gave a little shrug. "Go ahead," he said.

"You're going to do it to me anyway eventually, so why not get it over with?" He took the towel away from his ear, which had mostly stopped bleeding. He folded the cloth carefully, placed it on the table and then folded his hands on top of it.

"Any time," Barnes said.

Parsons willed his finger to press the trigger, but it didn't seem to want to work. Finally, he made a show of re-engaging the safety and stuffing the pistol back into its holster.

"I don't need the mess on the carpet. Goode, take this piece of shit outside and cap him."

"Hear that, guys?" Barnes said. "Remember that stuff about perceptions of grit and leadership? Roger Parsons is fine having you do the dirty work— "

Parsons drew the pistol again. "Shut up, Counselor."

"—but apparently he doesn't have the stones to do it himself."

Parsons felt the heat of the others staring at him, watching what he would do. Watching what he wouldn't do.

Barnes kept going. "Maybe the best advantage you can give to Penn Glendale is to have Roger lead the posse to bring him back. What do you say, Roger? Do you think something might go wrong that will cause you to turn back and return empty-handed?"

"I swear to God that I will shoot you," Parsons said. He felt his pistol hand tremble. He hoped the others couldn't see it.

"I'm *asking* you to shoot me! What more do you want me to do? I'm not going to shoot myself. This is as close to suicide as I get."

Goode said, "Roger, put your gun away. I'll take this sonofabitch outside and shut him up."

"Yeah, Roger," Barnes mocked. "Put your gun away and let—"

The pistol bucked in Parsons' hand. The room pulsed with the boom of the gunshot and filled with the smoky stench of gunpowder.

Barnes jumped in his seat. He reflexively brought his hands to his ears and his face showed pure amazement. How was that possible?

"Holy shit," Barnes said with a laugh. "Did you miss?"

Holy shit, did I miss? Was that even possible at this range?

Then he saw the hole in the wall behind the lawyer's head.

To his right, Parsons saw Goode leveling his own pistol at the side of the lawyer's head.

"No!" Parsons yelled. "Absolutely not."

Barnes's demeanor had changed. He showed fear now. Maybe a taste of survival was all that was needed to derail a commitment to die.

Parsons leaned in close, even as Barnes was leaning back far enough to bring the chair's front legs off the floor.

This time, when Parsons pulled the trigger, he got a mouthful of Barnes's blood.

CHAPTER SEVENTEEN

*A*ND THIS WAS WHY YOU NEVER SURRENDERED. LUKE sat on an eighteen-inch hearth in front of a blazing wood stove in the living room of a squatty one-story house that was no doubt older than his grandparents. The acoustic-tiled ceiling hung low and displayed a sepia-toned map of water stains. Nine people crammed the room—at least three too many for the size of the place—driving the heat and humidity to tropical levels.

They'd tied his hands with the paracord they'd stolen from his own backpack—the ultimate irony and humiliation. A staple of every survival kit, paracord was the nylon rope that attached a deployed parachute to the paratrooper. Made of nylon and about a quarter inch in diameter, the stuff had all kinds of uses. At least they'd bound his hands in front and not behind his back. Utilizing a trick he'd learned ages ago during the stranger-danger lessons of his childhood, he'd kept his wrists sightly arched as his captors wrapped them, such that now that they were done and he relaxed, he had some slack in the rope. It wasn't enough to be obvious—certainly not in the dim light of the paraffin lanterns—but it kept circulation flowing and maybe left him with an opportunity to break out if the chance ever came.

The man who'd captured him was called Smitty. He'd relieved Luke of all his weapons, including both his knives, and walked him back through a serious encampment to this little house at the end of a long driveway—every bit of one hundred yards. This wasn't a pop-up camp. This one was intended to be here for a while.

The guy in charge of things called himself Primo. Luke didn't know if that was a real name, or a claimed one, but it didn't matter. This was the guy that Luke had previously thought of as Leader Man. The others seemed to be afraid of the guy.

While being walked to the house, it was hard to get an exact count of the number of people in the yard, but Luke estimated that the encampment housed upwards of twenty, twenty-five people, maybe a little more. They were not shy about using lanterns and campfires for illumination, either. Tents and improvised lean-tos provided shelter, but from the stench, he guessed that they hadn't figured out what to do with human waste.

Primo took a seat on a stout coffee table that rested between the hearth and a facing sofa that sagged under the weight of three occupants. Primo wore a 1911 model .45 pistol on his right hip, and he had Luke's rifle and pistol in his hands. In the deflected, dancing light of the lamps, Primo had a gaunt, skeletal look about him. The yellow cast of the light made him look ill.

Luke looked around to see who was listening, who was threatening him. A few of the living room's occupants clearly were eavesdropping, others appeared to be intentionally looking away. Most, though, appeared to be sleeping where they sat on the floor, propped up against the plaster walls.

"So," Primo said. "What's your deal, kid?"

Never answer a question when you don't know exactly what it means. He waited for the man to rephrase it.

"Don't play games with me. Let's start with the simple stuff. What's your name?"

"Luke."

"Luke what?"

"Wayne." Batman and Bruce Wayne were the first names that jumped into his head.

"Luke, then. What are you doing sneaking around at this time of night? Don't you know the roads are dangerous?" His smirk spoke more clearly than his words.

"It's hard to think of anything that's not dangerous these days," Luke replied. "I saw the light on the horizon and I thought I should approach cautiously."

"Why did you try to run away?"

"Because your friends threatened to kill me. Then, you threatened to skin me alive. What would you do?"

Luke knew that the next few minutes, hours and maybe days would depend on his ability to think fast on his feet. He had to find that line that kids everywhere were forced to deal with: He didn't want to cower and show fear, but he also didn't want to be the cocky jerk who pissed off the adults because they thought they deserved more respect. It was a line that Caleb crossed all the time, and Luke had seen him get his ass kicked for it.

"Where are you coming from?" Primo asked.

"Who are y'all?" Luke asked.

"I'm asking the questions," Primo said. "Where are you coming from?"

"Down the mountain. I've been wandering, just like everybody else. Do you have any food to share?" Luke thought that last part helped sell his lie.

"Nobody's got food to share," Primo said. He hefted Luke's M4 and turned it over in his hands. "This is a nice rifle. Where did you get it?"

"I had it before the war started."

"So, you live nearby?"

Oh, shit. The first crack appeared in his story, and it was a big one. Why was he wandering at all if he lived nearby, and why would he have had the guns on him if he'd been away from home when the bombs dropped?

"Fifty, sixty miles, I guess." Lying was not one of his strong suits. His mom always knew when he was doing it. She said the word *liar* appeared on his forehead when he tried.

"Why are you out on the street, then?"

"Because of the gangs. They burned down our house. Killed my parents." It had happened enough to others that he figured why not to his, as well?

Primo showed Luke the backpack he'd dropped near the caves. "Lots of ammo, too. You want me to believe that you've been wandering around for all these weeks, minding your own business, with this kind of weaponry?"

"It's only been a couple of weeks," Luke said, and instantly wished he had not. The more layers you pile on a lie, the harder it is to keep track of it. "And it's not like I'm the only one. Everybody's got guns."

"How come nobody's taken them from you?"

Luke smelled danger. Primo was trying to get him to confess to killing people. He stared back without saying anything.

"I bet people tried, didn't they?" Primo asked. "I bet it didn't go so well for them. I bet you killed people who tried to take your stuff. That's what happened, isn't it?"

Luke tried a noncommittal shrug, but he didn't think he pulled it off. Primo saw something in his face. Across the room, a girl a little older than him seemed to be following an escort as she entered the room and took a seat on the floor next to the sofa.

"A gun like this would've sold for a thousand dollars back before the war," Primo said. "You want me to believe that you owned a thousand-dollar rifle?"

Luke cleared his throat. He couldn't just sit silently. "I don't know what to say. You're going to believe what you want to believe. But yes, I owned that before the war."

"What do your parents do for a living?"

"I told you they were killed."

"By the gangs."

Luke looked down, tried to look sad.

"Tell me about that," Primo said. "About the night your parents were killed. What was your address?"

Luke tried to sound natural as he rattled off the house and street number from the house they lived in before his mom got elected to Congress and they had to shift over to rentals.

Primo recoiled from the words. "That's got to be three hundred miles from here."

Luke shrugged.

"Show me the soles of your shoes," Primo said.

Luke lifted his foot. *This is weird.*

Primo's eyes showed nothing. "So, why here?"

"Excuse me?"

"This is a big state," Primo said. "Hell, it's a big country. How did you end up right here on my doorstep?"

"Smitty brought me here."

"Be careful, Luke," Primo menaced. "Being a smart-ass is not a smart play."

"I didn't plan to come here. I've just been wandering. Trying to survive."

"All by yourself?"

"Not always. Sometimes I'd hook up with another group of people, but mostly I'd be by myself."

Primo spread his arms out to his sides to form a kind of tripod where he sat on the table and leaned back. "Smitty tells me you were coming up the mountain, up Mountain Road, is that right?"

"Yes." Even though the question seemed innocuous, it felt bad to tell the truth, like he was sharing information that should have been kept secret.

"Did you come through a town called Ortho? Some people call it Eden?"

"You kind of have to," Luke said. "Yeah, I was there."

"Tell me about it."

"There's not much to tell. It's a nice enough town, I guess. Lots more people than I've seen in other places since Hell Day."

Primo cocked his head and might have smirked. "Are you lying to me, Luke Wayne?"

"No, sir." Luke thought the *sir* to be a good idea. Certainly, it was never a *bad* idea to suck up a little.

"You're a plucky young man, aren't you?"

Luke wasn't sure what *plucky* meant, but it didn't sound like a bad thing. "I'm a survivor," he said.

"And a fighter, too?"

"I suppose I can be."

Something changed in Primo's eyes. He laid Luke's M4 on the floor next to the coffee table and changed his focus to the Glock that Smitty had taken from Luke's holster. Primo dropped the magazine from the grip and cycled the action to eject the cartridge from the breech. He caught it in the air as it twirled out of the ejection port. Then he held the round in his fingers and examined it as if it were a gem in a jewelry store.

"What kind of ammo is this?" Primo asked.

Luke honestly had no idea. He'd never looked at the magazine after he lifted the pistol from the body of its previous owner. "I don't know."

"It's got a strange-looking bullet, don't you think?"

Luke felt himself getting ensnared in a verbal trap. He said nothing.

"You loaded the magazine, didn't you?" Primo pressed. "You'd know what the bullet looks like."

"It looks like a . . . *bullet*."

Primo handed him the round. Luke took it with his bound hands.

From the dimensions, Luke recognized it right away as a .380 caliber cartridge, but on closer examination, he saw that the bullet face itself was strange. Rather than coming to a conical point like most bullets, the point on this one looked like a plus sign.

"That's a Black Hills HoneyBadger Plus-P," Primo said. "I've read about them, but I've never seen one before. Expensive round. If that gun is yours, that means that you loaded the magazine. And since you loaded the mag, I figure you had to know what your ammunition looks like. Does that make sense to you?"

Luke shifted his butt on the hearth. He didn't know exactly where this was going, but it didn't feel like it would end in a good place.

"How about you tell me where you got this pistol?"

There was no reason for Luke to do that.

"Let me tell you my theory," Primo said. "You go ahead and stop me if you want to call bullshit, okay? A week, maybe two weeks ago, a good friend of mine— his name's Buster—took a Glock forty-two just like this one from a guy who didn't want to share and ended up getting beaten to death. Stupid reason to die, don't you think?"

This guy was crazy. Luke could see it in his eyes. They opened wider when he talked about beating the guy to death.

"In fact, it was the old guy who owned this very farmhouse. The body isn't far from here, still rotting away if you want to take a look." He leaned in closer. "Or if you want to join him."

"No, sir," Luke said. "I wouldn't like that."

"No, I wouldn't think you would. But there's even more coincidence here. On that Glock forty-two that my friend had, guess what kind of ammo he found in the magazine."

Luke said nothing. As his heart pounded and tears pressed behind his eyes, he couldn't think of a way out of this.

"I want you to guess," Primo said. "Seriously, just take a guess."

"The same as that." Luke heard the shakiness in his voice.

Primo slapped Luke's leg and the boy jumped. "Exactly! I mean, what are the chances? You and my friend Buster carrying the same pistol with the same ammunition. It's mind blowing." To emphasize his words, Primo pantomimed an exploding head with his fingers.

Clearly, Primo had connected the dots, but what should Luke do? Should he fess up in the hope that if he shared some details these people would show him some mercy? Or should he double down on the lies?

Primo wasn't done. "You know, since the war wiped everything away, the world has gotten really quiet, have you noticed that? Here's what I'm wondering now. A few hours ago, the wind brought the sounds of a gun battle from the direction you were coming from when you tried to sneak into our camp. My friend Buster happened to be on a foraging trip at about that time, and I'm thinking maybe you and him crossed paths. If that's what happened, and you're carrying his pistol, I figure that means you killed him. Is that what happened, Luke?"

Luke gaped. He wondered if he was going to throw up.

"You can tell me," Primo said. "It's what I assume, anyway, so it really doesn't matter one way or the other."

Luke inhaled to speak, but Primo cut him off.

"Oh, and before you choose your next words, I noticed something you said a few minutes ago. You referred to the war as Hell Day. Did you hear yourself say that?"

"Not really, but so what?"

"I've only heard it referred to that way by a couple of people, and those people had one thing in common: They came up from Ortho. And word has it that those Ortho people are real bad-asses. I've heard stories of wholesale executions. That mean anything to you, Luke?"

Luke felt his jaw locking as anger brewed in his gut.

"Say what's on your mind, kid," Primo baited. "No, wait. Not yet. I'm enjoying this too much." He turned to his left and motioned for the newcomer to the room—the young girl—to stand up and sit next to him on the table. "Allison, honey, would you come over here, please?"

The girl looked at the floor briefly as she rose to her feet. Her eyes stayed down as she walked with hesitant steps over to the spot on the table where Primo was patting. Up close, in the lamplight, she looked older than she'd seemed before. Maybe early twenties.

"Allison, do me a favor and take a good look at Luke."

She raised her eyes, but it was more of a quick glance than a good look. She was vaguely familiar to Luke, but in that way that everyone looks vaguely familiar when you think about it hard enough.

"Do you recognize him?"

Allison nodded. "That's Luke Emerson."

Luke felt a shiver.

"And why should that name sound familiar to me?" Primo asked.

"Because his mother is Victoria Emerson, the leader of Eden." Allison refused to make eye contact with

Luke. Could she be ashamed that she was ratting him out?

Primo patted the young lady's thigh. "Thank you, Allison. Go back to my room and wait for me. I won't be too long."

As Allison left the room, she shot a last quick look toward Luke before the man who'd escorted her into the room fell in behind her and followed her out.

"So, Luke Emerson," Primo said. "Are you going to continue with the lying games, or are we going to speak like men?"

Luke's mind was spinning too fast to produce words. He'd been made, caught in lies, and now he'd pay whatever price would be exacted.

"Let's start with the pistol," Primo said. "You took this from Buster, didn't you?"

"I don't know his name."

"But you took it from a dead guy."

"Yes."

"A guy you killed."

Luke had seen countless cop shows in the before times when this was the point where people asked to speak to their lawyers and the questioning got shut down.

Screw it. "I have nothing to be ashamed of," Luke said. "Your friend shot my brother. Probably killed him. He would have killed me if I hadn't shot him."

"Why were you engaging him? How did the shoot-out start?"

"It wasn't just one guy. It wasn't just your friend. There were a bunch of them."

"I know who they were," Primo said. "I sent them

down there. They report to me. Their job is to provide supplies to me so that I can send them back up to my boss."

These words surprised Luke. Primo didn't seem like a guy who would have a boss or even tolerate the thought of being bossed.

Primo wouldn't be distracted from his questioning. "Buster didn't come and find you," he said. "He wouldn't do that. It wasn't his style, and he was too lazy. So, my question to you is why did you confront him? Why did you leave the safety of Eden and travel the miles it took to get where my people were?"

Luke's brain struggled to find the handle that would allow him to answer that question.

"Buster's a hothead," Primo said. "He's a little bit out there on the batshit crazy spectrum, but he's not a cold-blooded killer. He has to be provoked before he goes postal. What did your brother do to him?"

"Nothing. I think he probably startled them. But they were planning to engage us before that."

"*Engage* you? Who talks like that?" Primo forced a derisive chuckle.

Luke decided to go for broke. "Your friends are rapists and murderers."

The words amused Primo, triggering a blast of what sounded like genuine laughter. "Oh, for God's sakes, Luke, we're all murderers, aren't we? I mean, you're a murderer, too, right? Isn't that where all this fine weaponry came from? You lifted it off the carcasses of people who didn't need it anymore? And the reason they didn't need it was because you made them dead? Am I right, or am I right?"

Of course he was right, but there were differences.

"If I have to kill, I do it in self-defense," Luke said. "You people do it to take other people's stuff. And to hurt them."

Primo crossed his arms and sat taller. Straighter. He looked satisfied, as if he'd just solved a problem. "I get it now," he said. "You and your brother are social justice warriors, aren't you? You were going to teach my friend Buster a lesson for doing bad things to good people? Is that what was happening?"

Luke stared.

"So, you and your brother were going to talk sense into Buster's head and get him to be a better man? Maybe you were going to bring Jesus into his heart? Just talk, right? No violence. Once Buster saw the evil of his ways, you figured he'd throw up his hands, apologize and be reformed?"

Primo laughed again, and then he turned very serious. "But you know what I think? I think you had no intention of talking. I think you planned all along to take your *revenge* by ambushing him and shooting him down like a dog. Not bringing justice. Meting revenge. I'm close, aren't I?"

No, he wasn't close. He was making Adam and him sound like the same kind of murderers that this Buster guy was, but that wasn't true. They didn't go to that roadblock to kill, they went to stop them from hurting other people. But Primo wasn't going to be interested in any of that.

"I see it in your face, Luke. I see that I'm laying everything out there just as it happened. You can go ahead and admit it."

"You abuse kids," Luke said. "You rape boys and girls."

He never saw the slap coming. It was a roundhouse, open-handed stunner that landed just in front of his left ear and spun him off the hearth and into the dusty wood floor. A few seconds later he felt a trickle of blood tracking over his lips and down his chin.

"Don't press your luck, young man," Primo said. His tone remained calm, his demeanor businesslike. "Get up and sit back on the hearth."

Luke rolled to his stomach and found his feet. As he moved to stand, he raised his hand to wipe his nose.

"No, don't touch the blood," Primo commanded. "Let it drip. It'll be a good reminder for you to watch your mouth."

Luke used his bound hands to steady himself as he turned and sat back down on the brick. He turned and snorted, spat a wad of bloody snot into the firebox.

"Do yourself a favor and be careful of your attitude," Primo said. "I know you're scared and trying to put a tough face on a bad situation, but there are limits on what I'll tolerate." He leaned in until he was inches from Luke's face. "You okay? I didn't hurt you too bad, did I?"

"I'm fine."

"What happened to the others who were with Buster?"

Luke looked down.

"Ah," Primo said. "All of them?"

Luke nodded. What was the point in trying to hide the facts now?

Primo wasn't buying. "You want me to believe that you and your brother, working alone, killed all of my people?"

"They'd've killed us both."

"Yeah, well, that happens when you go out looking for a gunfight. Sometimes, you find what you're looking for." Primo rubbed the sides of his head, just above his ears, then rested his forearms on his knees. "So, here's the big one, Luke. Why are you here? You bring bloody justice to Buster and his crew. Your brother gets shot, maybe killed. What could possibly make it feel like a good idea to come farther? Why didn't you stop with the win and go on back to Ortho-Eden? Why were you really sneaking around here?"

All the lies fell apart in Luke's head.

"You're on a scouting mission, aren't you? Want me to tell you who you're scouting for?"

Luke offered what he hoped came off as a noncommittal shrug.

"A very good resource told me that the vaunted Victoria Emerson— your very own mother—is on her way to my boss's camp up at the Hilltop Manor Resort, and that she knows we're in the way between where she is and where she wants to be. How's that?"

Jesus, it was spot-on. "Who told you that?" Luke asked. He tried to make the question sound indignant, but he knew that he'd flubbed it.

"The source doesn't really matter. How big a group is she with?"

Luke couldn't decide quickly enough whether he should lie and say that the caravan numbered in the hundreds, or that Primo didn't know what he was talking about—that no one was coming.

"Is it your mommy's mission to just talk with us the way that you just talked with Buster?"

Luke remained silent. Primo obviously had the entire plan figured out. There was going to be shooting tomorrow. All that mattered was the magnitude of the engagement.

Since Primo knew the fact of the mission, he had to likewise know the reason why. What might he do?

"You know, Luke, you put me in an odd position. You bring aggression to my home, but I like you. You seem like a nice kid who's scared shitless, which is entirely appropriate. Would you like me to tell you what my plans are when your mother arrives with whatever army she's coming with?"

Luke said yes because it felt like the only correct answer.

"I'm going to say *Happy trails, Mrs. Emerson. Travel safely.*"

Not what Luke was expecting. "Bullshit."

"It doesn't have to be, but she has quite the reputation for violence. I've heard rumors of mass executions. What can you tell me about those?"

Luke decided to embrace this one. "People from another town were spun up by an Army guy to attack Ortho. They set fires, killed a bunch of people. We fought back and at the end, there was a trial for the survivors from the other side."

"And they were found guilty, I presume?"

"Yes."

"Of what?"

"Murder. So, they were executed."

Primo raised his chin and looked at Luke as if through reading glasses on his nose. "Were you the executioner?"

"No." Major McCrea and First Sergeant Copley took care of the executions, but this guy didn't need to know that.

Primo shook his head slowly and scowled. "All of this killing, and you think that my friends and I are murderers."

"Murder and justice are different things," Luke said.

"I think that depends on which spot on the guillotine you're assigned to," Primo said. "Let me have your shirt."

The request startled Luke. It was such a non-sequitur. "What?"

"Your shirt. Take it off."

"Why?"

"I want to start a negotiation with your dear mother, and I think I can influence her with the fact that we're holding her baby boy captive."

Luke sat there, considering. The words all made sense by themselves, but the context confused him.

"Look, kid," Primo said. "You can take it off the easy way, or I can take it off the hard way with an ax to your arms. What's your preference?"

Luke held up his bound wrists. "You'll need to untie me."

Primo reached under his shirt and withdrew a nine-inch Bowie with an edge that gleamed in the lamp-light. "Hold 'em out and stay real still."

Suddenly, this seemed like a bad idea. Luke held his arms straight out from his shoulders and he spread his palms as wide as they would go, exposing the gap between his wrists.

Primo laughed. "Look what you did. You kept your wrists spread when they tied them. That's good thinking. I might recruit you for our side."

His words sounded light, but his eyes remained intense as he slipped the blade between Luke's wrists. The paracord fell away with zero effort.

"You never want to work with a dull knife," Primo said. "Now, the shirt."

Luke shrugged out of his coat and then set about unbuttoning his flannel shirt.

"Whose blood are you splashed with?" Primo asked. "Is that my friend's or your brother's?"

"Probably my brother's." Luke's voice cracked as he said the words, and that pissed him off. "And his name is Adam."

Having donated his T-shirt to tamponade Adam's wound, handing over the shirt left him bare chested and cold. He moved quickly to put the jacket back on before Primo demanded that, too. "Now what?"

"Now, we wait and see how much your mommy loves you." He looked at one of the tougher-looking dudes in the living room and beckoned him forward with two fingers. "Hey, you."

The man stood. Maybe twenty years old, he had a menacing look about his eyes that put Luke on edge.

"You've got a stupid name if I remember right," Primo said.

"Spanky. Spanky Harrison."

"Good Lord Almighty," Primo said with a laugh. "When the world ends, that's an opportunity to change the stupid shit you've been burdened with your whole life." He waved away the stupidity, as if waving off a fly. "Take Mr. Luke Emerson here down to the cellar."

Primo stood and slid a key off the fireplace mantel. He handed it to Spanky. "This is for the lock on the door." He pointed to what looked to be a Ruger 10/22 propped against the wall. "Take that with you. If the little shit gives you any trouble, shoot him in the balls."

If those words had been intended to be intimidating, it worked. Luke felt a fluttering in his gut. He was just standing when he heard commotion outside the front door, which continued while he was being escorted out the back, through the kitchen.

Someone he couldn't see yelled, "Primo! You're not going to believe this!"

CHAPTER EIGHTEEN

*V*ICTORIA'S CARAVAN SET UP CAMP IN A SPRAWLING field that no doubt had once housed cattle and perhaps grew crops. The tiny farmhouse at the end of the driveway had burned some time ago, and there was no evidence of other inhabitants. Those who had tents or other forms of shelter deployed them as they wished, while others slept in the grass.

Victoria lay on her back with her sleeping bag pulled to her chin, staring into the darkness. What the hell was she doing? And why the hell was she doing it? Why was she driven to live as if every fight were hers when in fact virtually none of them were?

"You're not sleeping," McCrea whispered from the slice of darkness to her right.

"I'm thinking of the boys. Wondering just how bad a mom I am." She said that last part with a smile, but the words carried a lot of truth.

McCrea issued a large sigh. "I think the metrics of

parenthood have changed. Childhood isn't a thing any-more. There's only survival." He pulled his hand out of his sleeping bag and patted the outside of hers. "For what it's worth, I think you're doing a great job. Not that there's much to do anymore."

Victoria uncovered her arm and found McCrea's hand. She squeezed it.

"You did all the heavy work before Hell Day," he continued. "You and Glenn raised them to be strong, independent fighters."

"All the things that were considered toxic and harm-ful before reality happened," Victoria said. "It's hard to be apart from them all."

"I know all about that," he said. "I think of Julia and the kids every day. I know they're gone, and I believe that Heaven is real. I'm confident that they're there, but I don't know what to do with the doubt."

Victoria said, "I wonder sometimes if it wouldn't have been simpler to stay in DC and get incinerated."

"Don't say that. You don't mean that."

"Yeah, I think I do. It's not that I want to die or be dead. I just think it would be a lot easier not to have to relearn how to live every day."

It was exhausting—mentally and physically—to be ever aware that safety no longer existed in the way it used to. Not only was every new personal interaction a potential confrontation, but every bruise or nick of the skin was potential cellulitis or sepsis. With the practice of medicine now knocked back to the nineteenth cen-tury, there was no way to stop disease. Water had to be boiled. And to be perfectly honest, she was tired of never being comfortable.

"It's no wonder that our grandparents were often grumpy," she said with a chuckle. "Life without conveniences is hard."

"I'm beginning to think that maybe life is supposed to be hard," McCrea said. "The world got fat, self-reverential and lazy. We stopped listening and we let meanness go unchecked. And here we are. Maybe billions of people are dead, but the survivors all need each other again."

"So, this was all for the best, right?" she teased.

"Who knows? Mysterious ways and all that."

Victoria rolled to her side to look at the man who remained invisible in the darkness. "That's pretty thought-y stuff for an old Army mule."

"I try," he said. "I have to find some good in all of this awfulness. The reset on everyone's lives has to be for a positive reason, or else there's nothing left but sadness."

"I should have sent someone with Luke."

"He's a pretty stealthy kid," McCrea said. "Two people make more noise than one. That was the call."

"I advise you not to call him a kid to his face," Victoria said. Caleb and Luke had both advanced to manhood overnight. Like flipping a switch. Was this the way of things back in colonial times? she wondered. When there was work to be done, and someone was strong enough to do it, their fragile psyches could not have been a driving concern.

"I told you, you should be proud of your parenting."

She knew that McCrea was right, and in fact she *was* proud. But this breed of pride brought fear that edged toward terror. She sent her boys into harm's way because they were clearly the best choice to do the things they were sent to do. Now, she was facing the reality that had been so easy to push away—that harm's way brought harm.

"Everybody will end up where they're supposed to be," McCrea said. As always, he had an incredible way of reading her thoughts. "That's part of my new world view. I don't know if God wanted this war to happen as part of a modern-day Noah-like reset, but I do think that He's opened His gates for a tough night at the check-in counter."

"Are you telling me that Adam getting shot was ordained?" Victoria had never heard this level of philosophical discourse from McCrea. On the other hand, they'd never been this alone together before.

"I think *ordained* is a loaded word. What I'm saying is that it's the thing that had to happen. It's part of a plan that we can't understand. I don't think we're *supposed* to understand it."

Victoria saw that McCrea was rationalizing. She herself had never been particularly religious, though she checked the box as Christian. She wasn't comfortable with God being the vengeful sonofabitch that He was in his Old Testament persona, and it angered her that any father—divine or otherwise—would plot a career path for His Son that would include unspeakable torture.

If Adam conquered his wounds—*when* he conquered his wounds (positive energy was important)—any limp or complications would have nothing to do with a holy plot for the greater good. It would have everything to do with his metabolism and his strength. If he didn't conquer them—which he *would* if only because Victoria didn't know if she could cope with the alternative—his death wouldn't be symbolic of anything. No deaths were symbolic of anything. They were mere facts that left families and survivors grieving their losses.

The reality of her losing Glenn to war in the Sandbox and of McCrea losing his whole family to this war they were living had no greater meaning than the sadness that the losses triggered.

"Life is about living," Victoria said. "And it's about dignity. Living with dignity. As shredded as society is, civilization needs to survive. Humanity needs to survive."

Victoria heard McCrea roll over to face her. When he spoke now, she could feel his breath. It was warm and it smelled of coffee.

"I know you're searching for a sign that you're doing the right thing here, Vicky. I know that you're worried about your boys, and that you're worried about all the strays we've picked up. When you start to doubt yourself, remember your own words. Living with dignity. We can do that again. The comforts and conveniences will be slow in coming, I'm sure, but there's no reason why people can't learn to be civil again. But we need leadership. No one is better suited to the job than you."

Victoria closed her eyes as McCrea talked her down. In her private moments—during her flashes of narcissism, perhaps—she knew that McCrea was correct. This was her calling. But why her?

Why doesn't matter.

That was the reality of it, wasn't it? Her heart told her that this was her mission, and apparently, she was persuasive enough to get people to follow her. There was nothing positive or forward thinking about asking why.

As she closed her eyes again, it occurred to her that perhaps the smart move would be to feel thankful that as bad as things were, they weren't worse still.

Primo silenced the breathless message runner with a raised hand. He watched as Spanky Harrison escorted the Emerson kid toward the basement, where they'd hold him until Primo was done with him. As Victoria Emerson's kid, he had usefulness, but Primo hadn't yet put his finger on what it might be.

He handed the kid's shirt and jacket to Wally Dean, one of the observers on the sofa. "Take this outside and find someone you can trust to take it down the mountain to wherever this sainted Emerson bitch is hanging out and deliver the message that I have her spawn and I want to meet here with her tonight. We're going to end this thing."

Roger Parsons had sent him out to establish this outpost as a first line of defense and interdiction for wanderers and lost souls. Similar outposts existed on the other four roads that led directly to the Hilltop Manor. In the very early days after the bombs dropped, and Roger's power was more in his mind than a real thing, the Manorites, as they called themselves—those who lived in the Manor—needed weapons to solidify their hold on panicked people's hearts and minds. They also needed food to feed themselves. The foraging parties started early, and the primary goal was to disarm the rabble and distribute their weapons among the Manorites.

They had woefully underestimated the sheer volume of refugees who were wandering through the wilderness. Now, these weeks later, the Manorites had more weapons and ammunition than they knew what to do with, yet the confiscation had to continue. How could it ever stop? Armed rabble were a hell of a lot more dangerous than unarmed rabble.

More refugees in turn required more manpower to herd them and watch over them. In return for a share of the spoils, more than a few of the wanderers were more than happy to step up to be enforcers. As the camps grew, so did the need for maintenance and basic sanitation. Thus, the need for a worker class, committed to performing the work that no one wanted to do.

Those were the most dangerous, Primo thought, because they had no loyalty. Many felt they were being kept against their will. With Roger's permission, Primo instigated the two-for-one program. If one person tried to get away, they would be shot. If they succeeded in getting away, two people would be executed as retribution. The program seemed brutal when he talked about it—and it was brutal on the few times they'd had to follow through—but the severity of it focused the workers on self-governance. If someone tried to escape, their fellow workers would make sure that the plot was foiled.

Roger worried that the Emerson bitch might try a power grab and move aggressively against Hilltop Manor, but Primo had never taken that threat seriously. It didn't make sense to him. Why rock a steady boat?

By the same logic, Primo had lobbied Roger against mounting an attack against Eden because it would risk everything. Life was unsettled enough without inviting additional violence.

Now, he wondered if Roger wasn't right to be concerned.

They all knew that Emerson was on her way up to the Hilltop Manor in hopes of presiding over the trials of the architects of this god-awful war. Yesterday, Roger thought it was a fine idea, but as of a few hours ago, Primo had gotten word that Emerson was to be stopped. Something about the president escaping from custody.

Primo thought initially that it would be as easy as turning her around without incident. Then, if what Luke Emerson said was true, Buster had gone way too far and hurt people that needn't have been hurt. That triggered the retribution cycle, and now this thing was completely out of control.

A fight was coming. He couldn't see any other result. Why would Emerson have sent her own son on a recon operation if it wasn't to attack? And if it came to that, how well could Primo count on his own soldiers not to run away? Or, worse yet, could he count on them not to switch sides?

That most certainly was what Roger was expecting. He'd sent a runner from the Hilltop Manor telling Primo to expect reinforcements from the resort. The message he'd read in the moments before Luke Emerson was caught in the woods read, "We will make a stand there at your encampment. I'm sending you ten more Manorites, all of them loyal. The destruction of the Emersonians is to be complete and total. No one breathing. The fight will undoubtedly come in the morning."

Since then, as far as he knew, none of those reinforcements had arrived.

For all Primo knew, the force from Eden might be just a few people. Primo's crew had the advantage of cover and shelter. Throw in a long driveway, down which any attackers must walk if they were to reach the house, and this place was pretty damned defendable.

But the real key to success turned out to be the appearance of the kid. His mom might be many things, some good and some bad, but the one thing Primo knew her to be was a *mom*. Soon, she would know that Primo had her kid in custody, and whatever war plans she thought she'd hatched would be shoved to the back burner.

She'd be contrite, and she'd want to negotiate. For his part, Primo wouldn't hesitate for a moment to kill her and make all the inconvenience go away.

Primo turned his attention to the commotion at the front door. People were clumped in the opening, chattering and pointing. Whatever was happening, it was exciting stuff. Primo rose from his chair and walked that way.

"Okay, everyone," he said. "Make a hole. What the hell is going on?"

Two men seemed to be in custody. One looked fairly old, and Primo recognized the other, younger one to be Jason Herringer, formerly one of Roger's most trusted deputies.

"Okay, everybody, step back," Primo said.

The gunmen who had the men in their grasp brought them to a stop, their faces lit up with identical grins.

The older prisoner looked only vaguely like the images Primo had seen of him on the Sunday talk shows back when the world still worked. "I'll be damned," Primo said. "It's Penn Glendale himself."

"That's Mr. President to you."

"Ah, defiant to the end. Good for you. I've heard that you've had an interesting twelve hours or so."

"Go to hell," Glendale said. "Do what you need to do and get on with it."

"Fair enough," Primo said. "I do have standing orders, after all." As he drew his pistol from its holster, he said, "Everybody take a step back from them."

Nobody dawdled. They moved away like ripples in a pond, leaving the two prisoners standing side by side.

From a distance of four feet, Primo raised the pistol, thumbed off the safety and leveled the muzzle at Glendale's forehead. To the politician's credit, he didn't duck and he didn't beg. He just stared back, eye-to-eye.

"Do it," Glendale said.

"Okay." With startling speed, Primo shifted his aim to the right and launched a .45 slug through the bridge of Jason Herringer's nose. The traitor dropped straight down.

Glendale's mouth hung open as he viewed what had happened. Within seconds he regained his composure and stood tall again.

"Take this one down with the kid," Primo said. "Let 'em shiver together."

CHAPTER NINETEEN

"M RS. EMERSON! MRS. EMERSON, WAKE UP!"

She hadn't realized that she'd fallen asleep.

"Mrs. Emerson! Which tent are you in?"

"Over here," she said. She heard the sleepiness in her voice and cleared her throat.

"Want me to take it?" McCrea asked.

"Wouldn't mind if you came with me," she replied.

They slept fully clothed these days, in part for the extra warmth, but mostly because wake-ups without warning were becoming more of a norm. Victoria took her rifle with her as she crawled out of the nylon shelter first, keenly aware that there was no dignified way to crawl on hands and knees. She grunted as she stood, then stepped aside to give McCrea room to join her.

As she stretched her back, she scanned the field for the man who was calling her out. All but two of the campfires had burned to orange coals, and the moon had already set for the night, leaving the whole area dyed black.

"Who's calling for me?" she shouted at less than full voice. She saw no need to awaken all these people.

"Over here! On the roadway!"

Victoria's night vision was as good as it could be under the circumstances. More than half of the refugees who had joined their caravan didn't bother with shelter. They merely lay on the ground to sleep, doing their best to keep warm with whatever clothing or cover they could find. With the grass as tall as it was, she feared stepping on them.

McCrea and Victoria had pitched their tent at the base of a sprawling oak tree so that they would be able to find it in the dark—a trick she'd learned from years of camping in the wild. Whenever you wander from your campsite, make sure you have a way to recognize it on the return. Back when times were normal, she would hang a glow stick from the center post.

Victoria and McCrea held hands as they navigated their way to the silhouette that was waving his hands over his head in the distance.

"Any idea what time it is?" McCrea asked her.

"Not a clue. Too late for this, that's for sure."

As they closed to within a few yards, the silhouette said, "I'm Alex Kramer."

"What's up?" Victoria asked.

"I was standing sentry up the road," Alex said. "Someone approached carrying a white flag on a pole. He said he didn't want any trouble, then he handed me this shirt and coat. He said that this should serve as proof that they have your son, Luke, and that you need to go with him and talk."

McCrea produced a flashlight from his trousers pocket and clicked it to life. The yellow beam revealed a bloodstained flannel shirt. "That could belong to anybody," he said.

"No, it's Luke's," Victoria said. A feeling of doom closed in on her. "Look at the burn marks in the fabric. Those are from the blacksmith." To Alex, she said, "Who are the *they* who want to see me?"

"I didn't ask. The guy who brought them is still here. He's waiting to escort you back. Do you want to talk with him?"

Victoria ran the scenarios through her head. She had to believe that whoever *they* were had taken Luke into custody. Given the events of earlier in the day, his kidnappers would have every reason to kill him out of anger, but she didn't think that was the case here. If *they* wanted her to think that Luke was dead, they'd have sent something more ... *dramatic*, wouldn't they? Or they'd have said that he was dead.

So, if he was still alive, what would *they* want? What was their plan?

"Do you want me to ask the courier to come and talk to you?" Alex asked.

"No," she said. "Invite him to spend the night with us and tell him I'll come in the morning. If he doesn't want to stay, let him go and I'll find them tomorrow."

"Is the man armed?" McCrea asked.

"He's got a rifle," Alex said. "Just like everybody else."

"Okay."

Victoria said, "Thank you, Alex."

"Wait. Aren't you going to do something?" Alex asked. "I mean, it's your son—"

"Thank you, Alex," Victoria repeated. She turned

her back and started walking the other way down the road.

She knew that the footsteps she heard behind her were McCrea's. Launching silent prayers that he not speak to her yet, she wandered into the darkness until she thought she'd gone far enough, but stopped before she'd reached the other sentry point. She allowed her legs to fold under her as she sat down on the pavement.

Fear and sadness rushed up on her and broke like a wave over her soul. A sob escaped her throat before she could stop it. *Oh, my God. Ohmygodohmygodohmygod . . .*

As the emotion poured out, a sound she didn't recognize poured from her throat. It was a keening sound, and it was out of her control.

Had she dispatched her boys to their deaths? Two in the same day? All because of her *mission* to save the world? The images of them as babies, of them playing with their dad, and of learning to hunt and fish flooded her head. She closed her eyes against them.

She had to bring this outburst under control. She took a huge breath and held it. By controlling her breath, she could settle her sobs. She needed to get past the emotion and bring her focus back to where it belonged.

There was a smart move to make here, and there were countless stupid ones. Problem was, at the moment, she didn't know how to separate one from the other.

After two more heavy breaths, she thought she had a handle on it.

"I'm here if you need me," McCrea said. He was

very close, and she hadn't realized that he'd been sitting next to her.

Victoria nodded—a stupid move in the dark, but she didn't quite trust her voice yet.

After a minute passed—maybe two—she said, "I didn't go with the courier because I thought it was a bad idea to go walking into the unknown at night."

"I agree one hundred percent."

"I just have to ignore the fact that they might be torturing him. What do you think they want from us?" Victoria asked.

"Hard to know. The best case is that they just want to use the fact of Luke's presence as a poker chip to keep us from breaking up their operation."

"I can't pay ransom for him." As Victoria spoke the words, she realized how awful they sounded. "We can't bargain for his release."

McCrea put an arm around her. "Let's not get too far out over our skis yet."

"We've got the wagon. We just killed people to protect that wagon. I can't just give it up because Luke is in jeopardy."

"You've got to be kidding," McCrea said. "He's your son. Everybody would understand."

"No, they wouldn't. And they shouldn't. They might say they did, but the truth would be different."

"Do you really think that your leadership is that fragile? For God's sake, Vicky. People aren't going to think—"

"I don't care what they think," she said. "Seriously? Is my leadership *fragile*? I don't give a shit about how I'm perceived, Joe. You must know that by now."

He was quiet for a few seconds. "I confess that I'm lost in the conversation," he said, finally.

She put her hand on his, where it rested on her shoulder. How was she going to make this point? "Perception is irrelevant to what is right and what is wrong," she explained. "Thievery is wrong. Hard stop. It's just wrong. When people try to steal, they need to be stopped. Heavens, that's the number one rule in Ortho, right? In a world of finite resources, there's no way to recover from theft."

She shifted her butt on the street so she was looking straight at McCrea's silhouette. Even in the dark, she could see the flash of his eyes. "I think the odds are solid that these people who took Luke hostage are another element of the gang that shot Adam. That makes them rapists, murderers and thieves. If I look the other way simply because my son is in danger—as opposed to all the other sons and daughters who have been terrorized—I tell them that all of that lawlessness is okay. I become part of the problem."

"But he's your *son*, Vicky. Your little boy."

"Yes, he is. And so are Adam and Caleb, both of whom have taken bullets to preserve the principle of right over wrong."

"But, Vicky—"

"Please stop, Joe. This is not a point of negotiation. We're going to head up the mountain to meet with Luke's kidnappers, but we're going to do it on my timeline. They are going to be expecting us. I don't know what their intentions are, but if past is precedent, they intend to be who they are. That means violent encounter. We need to embrace this discussion as a tactical situation."

In the thirty seconds of silence that followed, Victoria knew that McCrea wanted to pursue the old argument, and she appreciated that he ultimately chose not to. "Tactical solutions are difficult when you have zero intel on what we're going in to find. We don't even know how far away they are."

In that moment, Victoria knew what she had to do. "I think we need to speak with that courier after all," she said.

"He rode away," Alex said. "I told him he could stay, but he said that was a nonstarter. Those were his words. He said it was a nonstarter and that he needed to get back to his camp."

"His camp?" Victoria asked. "Were those his words?"

"Yes, ma'am. I thought you said it was okay for him to leave."

"I did," Victoria said. "Now, I've changed my mind. Was he on horseback?"

"Yes, ma'am. He probably hasn't been gone more than five minutes. Maybe seven."

"Think we can catch him?" Victoria asked McCrea.

"We can certainly try," he said.

Eight minutes later, they had saddles on their horses, and they were ready to go. In the weeks since Hell Day, Victoria had spent a good deal of time astride a horse, and she'd gotten pretty good at it. She still had to hang on to the horn during a trot, but at a walk or a gallop, her butt stayed glued to the saddle.

They started at a walk until they cleared the campsite and were certain not to step on the people who were sleeping or pretending to. Once they were on the road, though, they increased to a canter. They didn't want the sound of the horses' hooves to spook the visitor from the other camp, but they also didn't want to be dragged by him into unfriendly territory before they knew what they were getting into.

Once the road flattened and opened up into wider fields, they veered off the roadway entirely and went through the farm fields. That made less noise, but it also increased the likelihood of their mounts misstepping and throwing them. Everything was a risk. Everything a calculation.

After twenty minutes, they slowed to a walk every few minutes to check if they could hear the other horse on the pavement. On the fourth try, they scored. A line of trees separated them from the roadway, but the *clip-clop* of hooves was undeniable.

"He sounds close," McCrea whispered.

"And going slow," Victoria whispered back. "Let's see if we can get ahead of him." Better to form a roadblock than to trigger a chase through the night.

Victoria was betting that the noise they made through the field would be drowned out by the louder clicks of the other horse's hooves on the hard pavement. If it wouldn't work, it wouldn't work, but she thought it was worth a try. Worst case, they'd have to chase him.

They continued to parallel the other rider's route for about three minutes after they'd passed him, and then they reined their horses through the tree line and onto the road surface. Victoria held her rifle across her knees, chambered with the safety on. Her horse snorted and pawed the ground as they waited for the rider to appear through the gloom.

McCrea sat in his saddle to her right.

"Who is that?" the other rider shouted through the night.

McCrea lit him up with the beam of his flashlight.

"It's Victoria Emerson," she said. "We need—"

The other rider was having none of it. He reined hard and galloped through the trees through which Victoria had just emerged and took off across the field.

"Well, shit," Victoria said.

They took off after him.

The other rider was at a dead run, laid out full tilt as he sailed through the night.

"We can't follow at that pace," Victoria said.

"He's going to kill himself and the horse," McCrea agreed.

As if on cue, there was a cry in the near distance followed by a thump and a scream. In the dark, it was hard to tell if the scream came from the human or the horse.

"That sounds bad," Victoria said.

"Approach carefully," McCrea warned. "He's armed. His motivations aren't clear."

"We should split up," Victoria said. "Come at him from two angles."

"Look at you, thinking like a tactician."

Victoria veered left while McCrea moved to the right.

Triangulating on the site of the fall was not difficult. The cry was definitely human, and whoever the guy was, he was in a lot of pain.

Victoria arrived first. The horse was standing still while his saddle tilted to the right. The rider dangled upside down, his foot still tangled in the stirrup, his leg very much broken below the knee. His foot was facing exactly backward, and the angulation at the fracture site turned Victoria's stomach.

As Victoria approached, the rider's horse spooked and hopped a few steps.

"Oh, God! Jesus! Help me!"

Victoria trained her muzzle on the figure on the ground and tried to see where his hands were. "Where is your weapon?" she asked.

"I don't know," he said. "Please help me."

Victoria heard McCrea's approach at the same instant that the rider was lit up by the bright white halo of light from his flashlight.

The horse spooked and jumped again.

"Stop! Oh, God!" The rider looked young, probably not more than twenty-two years old. As he yelled, his voice cracked.

"I don't see a gun," McCrea said. "Oh, there it is. He dropped it when he fell."

Victoria dismounted and slung her rifle across her back. "I'm going to try to help," she said.

"Please don't spook him again."

"I wasn't trying to spook him the first time," Victoria assured. The ground here was uneven, as if recently plowed. It was no wonder the kid's horse stumbled. Or, maybe it just stopped and decided that the trip was over.

Victoria had a flashlight in a loop on her belt but decided not to use it for fear of frightening the horse again. From what she could tell, the mount was not injured. It had to be uncomfortable, though, to have a saddle and rider hanging off your right side.

"Shh," she hissed as she approached the horse on its

left side. She patted his face. "Easy, boy. I know, I know. It's been a scary night. You want to be a good boy." She made a soothing, clicking sound with her tongue as she grabbed the bridle at the horse's chin. "Okay, I've got the horse."

She watched as McCrea's shadow dismounted and moved to the injured young man. "This is going to hurt," McCrea said.

The young man howled as McCrea unthreaded the broken bones from the stirrup and harness.

"I'm sorry," McCrea said. "I'm not doing it on purpose. I swear. You'll be free in just . . . There you go."

Apparently, being on the ground was only slightly less painful than hanging from the stirrup. It took the kid a good minute to get himself under control. In the meantime, Victoria and McCrea searched his pockets. They found nothing beyond a ball of crusty bread, which Victoria returned to the pocket where she'd found it.

"Oh, God, my leg hurts."

"What were you thinking, galloping at that speed across a field at night?" Victoria scolded. "It looks like a bad break. Tell me about my son."

The question startled the rider.

"Huh? What?"

"You brought me his clothes and told our sentry that I needed to come to your camp. I want to know how my son is."

"Last I saw him, he was fine. Primo's pretty pissed, though."

"Who's Primo?"

The guy fell silent. McCrea lit up his face with the light.

"Hey! Get that out of my eyes."

"Answer our questions," McCrea said.

Victoria asked, "Is Primo the person in charge?"

"Yes."

"Man or woman?"

"Man."

"And what's your name?"

"Tommy Pedigrew."

"What did you do before the war?" Victoria felt McCrea's confusion, his disapproval for going conversational instead of confrontational, but it was her experience that more was accomplished by making people feel comfortable than by frightening them.

"I was a student. I was going to become a barber. Maybe when all this shit settles out, I can get back on track for that."

"I don't think we have a barber down in Ortho," Victoria said.

"Are you really Victoria Emerson? The mayor of Eden?"

"Sure." Why fight the rumor? She'd grown tired of correcting the record. "Am I that famous?"

"Pretty famous, yeah." A jolt of pain made him gasp.

"This is Major McCrea," Victoria explained. "Now that we all know each other, let's get to why I'm here. Where is my son being kept?"

"At the camp."

"Where is the camp?"

"About an hour that way." He pointed down the road.

"Where is he within the camp?"

"And what does the camp look like?" McCrea added.

"It's a farm with a farmhouse and a barn and a couple of other outbuildings. I assume that your son is in the main house. That's where they took him to ask questions, but I wasn't there for that."

"How did he get captured?" Victoria asked.

"I wasn't there for that, either. There was some shooting, but not a real gunfight. There was something about finding someone hiding in the woods, and then there was some shooting, and then they brought a kid across the street to the main house. I presume that was your son, Luke."

"Was he hurt?"

"He didn't look to be, but I don't know. Do you have anything for this pain?"

Victoria ignored his question. "Tell me about the camp. How many people are there?"

"I don't know. I never counted."

"More than twenty?"

"Probably."

McCrea asked, "What percentage of them arc armed?"

"Only the foragers."

"Who are the foragers?" Victoria asked.

"They're the ones who go out for food and stuff. Not everybody does that."

"Do you?"

"No. I'm too new. Roger and Primo don't trust me."

Victoria felt a chill. "You mean Roger Parsons? At the Hilltop Manor?"

Another wave of pain hit Pedigrew. "Ah, shit, that hurts. Damn."

Victoria didn't care. "When you say—"

"Yes. Roger Parsons. He's the main guy in charge."

"But you know what this foraging actually means, right?" McCrea asked. "It means terrorizing people."

"Primo calls it surviving. My leg—"

"It's as broken as any limb I've ever seen," McCrea said.

"Can't you splint it or something?"

"Ask me again after we've finished talking," Mc Crea said.

Pedigrew thumped the ground with his fist. "Look, I know what they do to people out on the roads. Everybody in the camp knows. That's how we all got there in the first place."

"So, this Primo guy mugged you and took your stuff?" Victoria asked.

"Exactly."

"Then why did you stay? I'd think you'd want to run away from that."

"They wouldn't let me. They said they'd shoot me if I tried to leave, and that if I did manage to get away, they would kill two other people."

"That's not what I've heard," Victoria said. "In fact, several people in our group were brutalized and then sent on their way."

"That's how it works," Pedigrew said. "I don't know what their formula is, but it's like they have a number in their mind of how many people need to be at the camp. If you're sick, you're out. If you're too old or too young, you're out. When people die or get killed, they're replaced."

"Are you saying that people there want to leave?" Victoria asked.

"Some do, sure. But nobody wants to get other people killed. Okay, some don't mind, and they disappear anyway."

"Do Primo and his gang make good on their threat to kill?"

"Every time," Pedigrew said. "Two for one. One lady left her husband to be killed by them."

"So, those are the bodies you burn?"

"They're among the bodies we burn, yeah. I mean, when someone dies, that's how we get rid of the corpse."

"What do you do with the ashes?" McCrea asked.

"We leave them in the pit. It's a big pit. Can you put a splint or something on my leg? I mean, it's killing me."

"What kind of defenses does the camp have around it?" Victoria asked.

"Defenses?"

"Protection against attack," McCrea clarified.

"They put out roadblocks. When people approach, they get stopped."

"And they're terrorized?" McCrea said.

"They're searched. If they have weapons, they're taken away. If they've got food, that gets taken, too. We've never had to *defend* anything. Everybody just kind of rolls over."

"Where do Primo and his cohorts hang out?" Victoria asked.

"In the main house, mostly. He goes out sometimes, too."

"Why was Mrs. Emerson summoned for tonight?"

"I don't know. I swear to God I don't. All I know is what I told your guard. Primo wants to meet with you."

"Is Luke still alive?" Victoria asked. The strength of her voice while asking the question surprised her.

"Ma'am, I just don't know. Last I saw him, he was being paraded into the farmhouse. After that, one of Primo's toadies handed me that shirt and coat and told me to go and find you."

"How did you know where to look for us?" McCrea asked.

"Where else could you be? There's only one main road. I mean, I guess you could have been down one of the side roads, but what would be the sense of that?"

"Are they planning to do harm to Mrs. Emerson?"

"Probably. I'm sorry that sounded really blunt, but why else would he send for you? I think he saw an opportunity."

"Why come at us, though?" Victoria asked.

"Aren't you coming at him?" Pedigrew fired back.

"All we want is to pass through," McCrea said.

"Because you want to take a fight to Roger? That's what people are saying."

"What people?" Victoria asked.

"Everybody. Word was out that you were coming to Hilltop to try to restore the government. That's right, isn't it?"

Pedigrew's tone was hard to read. Was he hoping that would be the case?

"What do people think about that?" Victoria asked.

"Is it true?"

"Answer my question."

"It's not like people spend a lot of time talking about it," Pedigrew said, "but I think people would be excited. We've heard the stories about what's been happening in Eden, and I think we'd all like a bit of that."

Victoria started to speak, but Pedigrew wasn't done.

"When people leave here, I think that's where they want to go. I think that Primo and Roger are scared of you and your people. We've heard the stories about people who cross you getting executed. That's scary, but we all know that some assholes need to be executed."

"Where are we likely to encounter the roadblock?" McCrea asked.

"About an hour from here. There'll probably be more than one."

Victoria saw Pedigrew's head pivot to face her. "And, ma'am, if they hear shooting, I don't think it will go good for your son."

CHAPTER TWENTY

LUKE'S ESCORT—WAS HE REALLY NAMED SPANKY?—pushed him through the two or three people who had gathered in the kitchen and out the back door. Clearly, something interesting was happening out front, but Luke was so focused on not falling or getting burned with a candle that he didn't bother to check what the source of excitement might be.

Access to the cellar required a trip outside a few yards away from the house to what appeared to be a concrete box in the ground topped by the kind of slanted wooden panels that Luke had seen only a couple of times, except in movies and television shows. A heavy padlock held the panels together, and when lifted, they exposed a rectangular black hole accessible by steps that looked as if they'd been honed out of bedrock.

"Welcome home," his escort said. He carried one of those old-fashioned kerosene lanterns with a glass globe and a carrying handle on top. From what Luke could see, he and Spanky were the only people back here, though there could have been others lurking in the shadows.

"Please don't make me go in there," Luke said. He had already allowed himself to be caught and tied up. If he allowed himself to be locked into a cellar, he'd have no options left. Plus, it was freezing.

"Sorry, dude," Spanky said. "I got no choice." He carried his Ruger 10/22 unslung, just balanced in the hand that was not burdened by the lantern. A snubby revolver sat in a holster on his right hip.

"Sure, you do," Luke said. "You can just let me go. You can say I overpowered you and ran away."

"No chance. Primo would skin me alive. He's not a man you—"

Luke moved fast. He launched one step forward, grabbed Spanky by the lapels of his jacket and twisted at the hip. The hip throw was one of the first martial arts skills that Luke learned, way back in elementary school. Done efficiently and quickly, there was almost no defense against it.

Spanky's legs cartwheeled through the air as his lamp dropped and his rifle went sailing. The angles being what they were, Spanky dropped through the opening to the cellar without touching a door. The impact happened in the darkness beyond Luke's sight lines, but it involved a loud crash of whatever was stored down there and was punctuated by a heavy, wet thud that Luke imagined to be bone against rock.

Luke moved quickly to gather the lamp and the rifle. No way was Spanky going anywhere after a fall like that. The lantern had fallen in the grass, and the glass globe seemed to be intact.

Luke had no idea what he should do next. Staying here seemed like exactly the wrong thing, but getting spotted running away would bring a quick end to the adventure.

The first step was to relieve Spanky of his coat and search his pockets for anything worthwhile—like extra ammunition. Leading with the lamp, he climbed down the five steep steps to the exposed rock floor. Spanky lay still at the bottom, a trench across his eyes indicating the spot where his head met with the edge of the bottom step. If he wasn't already dead, he soon would be.

"Sorry, dude," he whispered. "That's not what I meant to do."

His lantern launched a swirling kaleidoscope of shadows against the stone walls. The place smelled of mildew and was stacked with old furniture, some Christmas decorations and a half dozen bound stacks of *National Geographic* magazines.

Luke stooped next to the body. First, he pulled the pistol from its holster and shoved it into the pocket of his jeans. He patted Spanky's thighs and rifled through his jacket pockets, hoping to find more ammunition, but came up empty. He did find a folding knife clipped to his pocket, but it was dull as a butter knife. He took it anyway. Finally, he wrestled the corpse's arms out of his lined denim jacket and put it on. It was actually a little tight in the chest, but it was better than bare skin.

He needed to get out of here. If someone came by and closed the doors, he'd be screwed.

Spanky had dropped the padlock on the stairs as he fell, but all it would really take to lock him forever in the cellar would be to slide a stout stick between the handles of the doors. No, that was not going to happen.

Taking care to avoid Spanky's blood, Luke snatched the lock into his left fist and scrabbled up the stairs on his hands and toes.

The night shook with the sound of a gunshot.

"Shit!" He whisper-shouted it aloud and ducked back into the stairwell. He drew the pistol from his pocket, but then stopped.

They're not shooting at you. How could they be? He was in a stone room with only one exit. Given that he was still alive and scared shitless told him that he still had time.

Just not a lot of it.

Decision made. He was going to risk making a run for it. He figured that to be his best chance.

He twisted the knob on the lamp to make the flame extinguish, and then he placed the lamp itself back onto the top step. Then he finished his climb and stepped back up into the night.

The first task was to find the rifle that Spanky had flung during his fall. That was easy. Now, he needed to close the cellar doors. Maybe if everyone thought Luke was safely imprisoned, no one would check on him and realize he was gone.

He lifted first the right-hand door and laid it into its jamb and then, as he was lifting the left-hand door to close it, he sensed movement to his left. Someone with a flashlight was approaching the back of the house from the side.

Shit. Shit-shit-shit.

He didn't have time to run. He was too exposed even to try.

Time to play a bluff. These people didn't seem to know each other very well. Primo wasn't even sure what Spanky's name was.

Luke lifted the left door through its arc, let it drop into place and slipped the hasp through the loop and clicked the padlock closed.

"No!" the guy with the light shouted. "I've got another one. Open it up again."

Luke kept his head down and his eyes shielded from the light. "Dude, you're blinding me," he said.

The light shifted away from him. "Sorry. Open it up again. We've got another one. You ain't gonna believe who it is." He shined the light into the prisoner's face, and Luke recognized him right away. Penn Glendale had eaten at their house a thousand times.

"Who is he?" Luke asked.

"This is the Big Kahuna, dude. This is Penn Glendale."

"Who's Penn Glendale?"

"What an idiot," the captor said. "Open the door back up."

Luke's stomach tensed. He hadn't thought it through this far. Christ, he didn't even have the key. That was probably still in Spanky's pocket.

"Oh, shit," Luke said. He patted his pockets, then brought his palm to his forehead, maybe overselling things a bit. "I left the key down there. The Emerson kid has it."

"How did he get the key?"

"Well, it's not like I gave it to him. I guess it dropped out of my pocket? Shit, Primo is going to kill me."

"Maybe literally," the captor said. "Go back to Primo and tell him. Maybe he has another key."

"Hell no," Luke said. "No way. He's already pissed at me today. Can't you do it? I'll take care of this guy." He hefted the rifle. "I've got this. Little bitty bullet might not kill him, but it'll sure slow him down."

"Ah, shit. I'll take him back with me, then."

"He might get away," Luke argued. "At least here, he's stable and we've got him at gunpoint." He made a point of taking a step back and leveling the rifle at Penn Glendale's head. "If he moves, I'll shoot him."

"Oh, Jesus, don't kill him. I think Primo wants him for something."

"I promise I won't give you cause to shoot me," Penn said.

The president's voice sounded just like . . . well, just like his voice.

The other captor raised his own rifle at Glendale. "Sit on the ground," he commanded.

With some effort, it seemed, Penn Glendale lowered himself to the grass.

"Now, stay there," the captor said.

The president crossed his heart with a finger, then held his hand in the air. "Scout's honor. I assure you that I truly am in no hurry to get shot, whether with a little bullet or a big one."

The captor hesitated. He didn't know what to do.

"Please?" Luke said. "Primo already thinks I'm a dickhead. This isn't going to make anything better."

"If he gets away, it's on me," the captor said.

"How could it be on you?" Luke asked. "And how could he get away? He can't outrun a bullet, and he's too old to move very fast."

"Look, boys," Penn said. "Excuse me—young men. I am wiped out. I don't care who guards me or who runs back to get the spare key. I'm not going anywhere. In fact, I look forward to finally being able to relax in what I'm sure will be a very damp, cold and uncomfortable basement."

His escort still wasn't sure. Then, finally, he said, "Fine. I'll do it."

"I'll trade you rifles," Luke said. "Just until you get back." The other guy was carrying some form of AR15 variant.

"No, I'm fine."

"You got me thinking about the smaller caliber," Luke said. "You've still got a pistol, so I thought—"

"Not gonna happen. Now, I'm gonna go before I change my mind." He turned and took two steps before turning back around. "What's your name, anyway? In case Primo wants to know."

"Oh, he'll know it. My name is George, but everyone calls me Spanky." He threw in the part about George because he thought it made the story sound more natural. "What's yours?"

"None of your business." He headed back toward the way he'd come.

As soon as Noneofyourbusiness was out of sight, Luke bent and grabbed Penn Glendale under his right arm. "Mr. Speaker, we need to get out of here."

Glendale didn't look up. "I've already said I'm not going anywhere tonight."

"Mr. Speaker—"

"It's Mr. President."

"For shit's sake, who cares? I'm Luke Emerson. Victoria Emerson's son."

That got his attention. "What are you—"

"That really doesn't matter, sir. I'm walking very,

very quickly toward those woods over there. If you'd like to come with me, that would be great. I'll tell you this, though. When they come back and open those doors, they're going to find the real Spanky dead and ugly. I wouldn't want to be here for that."

He didn't wait for an answer. He didn't know why or how the president of the United States ended up at the same farmhouse as he did, but none of it mattered. For the moment, Luke was going to take care of Luke. If President Glendale decided to come along, he was welcome to. Otherwise, he was welcome to stay. Either way, Luke was making tracks.

Here in the back of the house, the thinning tree line gave them cover, but they were moving away from the road. Luke didn't know how problematic that would be, necessarily, but it felt bad.

Balancing that was the fact that in just a minute or two, they were going to discover the truth of who was and was not in the cellar, and life would then get very ugly very quickly.

"They're going to be everywhere in a few minutes," Glendale said. "We should hunker down and hide."

"Tried that once," Luke said. "Not doing it again. Once we're in the woods, we're going to move as fast as we can, as far as we can. At least that's what I'm going to do."

"I'll try to keep up," the president said.

Wow, now *this* was an interesting development. The leader of the Free World following a fourteen-year-old in hopes of staying alive.

"Make sure you stay with me," Luke said. "There are some course corrections coming. And if there's shooting, get down and stay down until I tell you it's safe."

Luke stayed as low as he could without crawling until he got to the tree line, and then he picked up the pace. He zipped his stolen jacket closer to his chin to help ward off the cold.

After what felt like five minutes without an alarm going out, Luke decided that it was time to change course and shift to the left to head back toward the road. Mountain Road was the only landmark he knew out here, and while he'd taken a map with him, Primo and his gang had taken it away from him. They'd taken his compass, too. Given all the switchbacks and steep cliffs, it could be difficult to get back to that landmark if they wandered too far.

Five minutes after that, the distance got noisy. People were yelling, though it was too far away, and Luke was moving too quickly to make out any specific words.

"Howya doing, Mr. President?"

"I can talk or I can run. I can't do both."

"Yes, sir, I understand." Luke couldn't help but grin at the sound of exhaustion in Penn Glendale's voice. The old guy probably never got much exercise in the first place, but after all those weeks in a bunker, he was lucky to have any stamina at all.

"How far do we have to go?" the president huffed.

"You don't want to know," Luke said. "A little over three hours on horseback."

"You're right. I didn't want to know."

And the horse was the problem, Luke realized as soon as he mentioned it. With the detour and everything, he had no idea where he was relative to Rover, or if his horse was even there anymore. Surely, the Primo gang would have found him and made him their own. Soon, he figured, the road would be packed with searchers on horseback, so maybe it was a blessing that they didn't have one. The smart money said that Pennington Glendale had no idea how to ride a horse, and if he had, he would not have been in a saddle since before his bones got old. Oh, and they'd have to be riding together on the same horse.

No, that wasn't going to happen.

He had a new strategy. After they found the road, they'd stay parallel to it, but in the woods. If the search party came down the road, Luke and the president could go to ground and wait them out. If they didn't come that far, then after an hour or so, they could step back out into the roadway and make the going that much easier.

They needed to have as much distance between them and Primo's gang, so Luke's intention was to keep walking through the night. Sooner or later, one of two things would happen: Either they'd arrive at the caravan's campsite, or the caravan would come up to meet them. Either way, he had a good feeling about their chances.

Easy-peasy, as his dad liked to say.

He also liked to say that no plan survives the first exposure to reality.

CHAPTER TWENTY-ONE

PRIMO LISTENED IN DISGUST AS WAVERLY MULLINS told him the story of the lost key. He'd returned to his chair near the fireplace when the young man who'd been Penn Glendale's captor was last seen with a rifle to the prisoner's back. He'd arrived breathless, and led with, "Don't be mad at me, it wasn't my fault."

Something about the story didn't add up for Primo. "A spare key? Why would we have a spare key?"

"That's what Spanky told me to ask for."

"Why isn't he asking me himself?" Primo asked. "Who's guarding Glendale?"

"Spanky is. He told me about the way you two got crosswise and he didn't want to be the one to piss you off."

Oh, this wasn't right at all. "I'm not crosswise with—" *Oh, shit.* "Do you know Spanky?"

"Not before I met him tonight. He said that he just locked somebody named Emerman or something like that down in the cellar."

In an instant, it clarified in Primo's brain. "What does Spanky look like?"

Waverly shrugged noncommittally. "It was dark. Young, maybe fifteen. Pretty fit."

Primo shot to his feet, snagged the rifle that used to belong to Luke Emerson and strode toward the back door. "You're a grade A moron, Waverly. I suppose they're armed now?"

Waverly looked at his feet. "He wanted to take my rifle, but I wouldn't let him."

"Are they armed or not?"

"Well, yes, sir. To guard Glendale."

Primo pushed past the onlookers who had not already jumped out of his way. "Somebody get me a goddamn prybar."

Primo rushed through the kitchen out the door into the backyard. Waverly Mullins stayed with him step for step, though for the life of him, Primo couldn't figure out why. The asshole should have been seeking cover.

As soon as his eyes adjusted, he knew that his fears were correct. No one was there. No Glendale, and, he was willing to bet, no Luke Emerson.

"Who's got the prybar?" Primo demanded.

Though a crowd was forming again, no one stepped forward with a bar.

"Goddammit, this is not a difficult request. Someone open up these damn doors!"

One of the older foragers—Primo thought his name might be Randy—emerged from the gawkers with a flathead ax in his hands. "Hey, Primo. I couldn't find a prybar, but this should work. Here, let me in."

Primo slung his rifle across his back and took the ax from Randy's hands. "Step out of the way. I'll do this."

He braced his foot against the right-hand door at the hinges and lifted the blade high over his head. From there, a full swing downward buried the blade a half inch into the old wooden panel, just next to the hasp. It took some effort to pry the blade free and then he swung again. And a third time. On the fourth swing, the hasp broke away.

Primo dropped the ax onto the ground and shouldered his rifle, pointing the muzzle toward the door. "Open it, and someone hit it with a light."

Waverly took this opportunity to earn back some points. He scooted in front of Primo and worked his hands into the shattered hole in the door panel. "Ready?"

"Open it." *Jesus. Ready? Really?*

Waverly pulled hard, lifting the panel and letting it slam to the ground on the right. As the opening revealed itself, Waverly threw himself to the ground, presumably to open a lane for shooting if it came to that.

"Who's got a light?" Primo demanded.

A flashlight beam appeared from Primo's left and shone down into the hole. One glance told the whole story.

"Waverly!" Primo barked. "Get up." The guy was still trying to find his feet when Primo grabbed him by his collar and dragged him to the opening. "There!" he shouted. "That bloody mess is Spanky. *Was* Spanky. Dammit!"

Primo tugged Waverly upright by his jacket, then

shoved him down the stairs. He tumbled once on the stone steps, turning a full somersault before landing on top of Spanky's corpse. "How could you be so stupid?"

Waverly was clearly hurt. He clutched his back and blood trickled down his face from somewhere behind his hair line. "I'm sorry, Primo," he whined.

"Give your apologies to Spanky when you see him." Primo shot Waverly twice in the chest and the man collapsed, dead.

Primo turned to the man with the ax. "Randy, go down there and get those bodies to the burn pits."

"It's Roland," the man corrected.

Primo felt his rage blooming. "Is that really the conversation you want to have with me right now?"

Roland took a step back. "No, sir. I suppose not."

"You suppose right."

"Should we arrange a search party?" a lady asked.

Primo ignored her. He needed time to think.

"Primo? They can't have gotten far," someone else said.

"Just hush!" Primo said. "Be quiet. Let me think. If y'all want to go wandering out into the night to chase down armed men who are likely not to be anywhere you want them to be, go ahead."

He started to wander back toward the woods line.

"Hey, Primo," someone called from back toward the house. "We've got company."

"They can wait," Primo said without looking.

"But they—"

"I swear to God, if I see anyone near me within the

next five minutes, I'm going to blow their heads off. Am I clear?"

The caller fell silent, so Primo assumed that he'd made his point. He needed to assess what was coming.

While his heart screamed at him to chase down the Emerson kid and Glendale, his head told him that was a bad idea. It was just too friggin' dark. They had a head start of at least five minutes if not more, and they had every compass point to choose from.

On the other hand, they were on foot, and it had been a long day for both of them.

Having heard Penn Glendale interviewed a thousand times back when there was such a thing as television (a medium on which Glendale loved to appear), Primo had no time for the man. He didn't think he was particularly smart, though he didn't think any politicians were particularly smart.

The Emerson kid, on the other hand, impressed him. Primo remembered hearing reports early on about the Emerson family being preppers and being taken to task for it by the opposition media. The narrative wrote itself: In the twenty-first century, how crazy did people have to be to drill their children on survival skills like hunting and trapping? Victoria Emerson allowed her children to have access to guns! She was crazy! The whole family was crazy! What do you expect from hicks from West Virginia?

Primo allowed himself a smile as he tried to imagine how the Harvard-trained economists and lawyers were faring in the aftermath of Armageddon.

The Emerson kid knew how to keep his cool under

pressure, and Primo admired that. He chastised himself for not having taken those skills more seriously when he allowed the boy to be taken to the cellar by only one guard.

There were only a few ways for this to go. The Emerson kid and Glendale would hunker down for the night and start moving again in the morning, or they would continue moving through the night and try to make their way back to wherever his mother and her group were holed up.

The option to stay put was complicated by the cold and the fact that the kid was shirtless. The woods were thick and dark. They were easy to get lost in, even in the middle of the day. At night, they could discover a special breed of lost.

The smart move, Primo thought, would be to put some distance between themselves and Primo's camp, but not go too far until daylight.

And then what?

In the end, Primo decided that it wasn't worth the risk to his own people to track down his escapees. In the worst-case scenario, they would meet back up with Bitch-lady Emerson, and at that point, maybe there'd be no need for her to continue toward his camp and the Hilltop Manor beyond. She'd have rescued Glendale and her kid would be safe. Maybe there'd be no need for confrontation.

"Primo!" someone yelled. It was a different voice than before, but he thought he recognized it. "They tell me that if I interrupt you, you'll kill me. I'd appreciate it if you wouldn't do that."

Primo stared into the darkness, toward the sound of the voice. "Who's there?"

"It's Mason Goode," the voice said. "Roger Parsons sent me to find Penn Glendale, but then I heard I was too late. That you already have him. I'm here to take him back with me."

Primo hadn't known Goode before the war. They'd crossed paths in the Hilltop Manor bar the night before the bombs dropped while Primo was hoping to take a selfie with the Mauler. Goode was the de facto security guard whose job was to keep selfies from happening. Roger had turned out to be in a better mood than usual that night, and the selfie turned into an extended night of drinking and chatting. The Mauler was particularly enthralled that Primo had been to four of his bouts.

Then, when the bombs dropped, and the world had shifted into nightmare mode, Roger was looking for helpers and Primo stepped up. Since then, Primo had enjoyed right-hand-man status.

Something told him that that was about to change.

"Tell you what, Mason," Primo said as he walked toward the voice. "Let's go inside, find something that looks like alcohol, and have a chat."

Victoria and McCrea left Pedigrew where they'd interviewed him, with the promise of coming back for him later. They got back to their camp about the time the sky was beginning to turn pink. They policed up their tent and gear and by the time they were done, it was time to roust the others.

As she munched on a strip of venison jerky, Victoria's mind conjured up the smell of bacon and eggs from the recreational camping trips with her family back in normal times. McCrea had brought coffee on this sojourn, but the way he drank it was strong enough to etch glass.

If the caravan had grown overnight, it hadn't been by much.

"Hey, Joe," she said, "can you do a whistle for me?"

"Happy to." By inserting his pinky fingers in front of his tongue, Joe McCrea could produce a piercing whistle that no one could ignore. He did it three times, just to make sure, and when he was done, Victoria saw a sea of drowsy faces.

She shouted to the crowd, "Good morning, everyone! If you're coming along with my group and me this morning, I need to see you over at the wagon in ten minutes. There are things we need to discuss."

Victoria walked to the other end of the encampment and repeated the message there.

"Do I know what you're going to talk about?" McCrea asked.

"Probably. But you'll have to wait."

She gave people a couple of extra minutes to get their stuff together and then climbed up on the wagon bed to make her speech. The assembly before her was a balanced collection of men and women, plus teen boys and girls. She took time to count heads and came up with twenty-three. More were armed than not.

"Good morning, everyone," she said.

Grumbles in return.

"Good morning!" she repeated.

This time they echoed her enthusiasm.

"I need to state again for the record that if you crave safety and the best chances of not getting hurt, you should not come along with me today. If that's what you want—and there's nothing wrong with being sane— Ortho is that way." She pointed down the mountain.

"Ever since Hell Day, I have promised myself and others that I would always be honest and forthcoming. So, I need to tell you that of my three sons, one of them was shot and critically wounded yesterday, a second went back to Ortho to tend to him, and the third is being held captive by the group we will be engaging sometime this afternoon. I tell you this so you will know and understand that whatever happens today will be very personal for me."

"It's personal for us, too!" yelled someone from the crowd. "You know what they've done to us."

"I also need you to understand the nature of what we're planning to do," Victoria said. "I'll start specifically with what we are *not* planning to do. The violence has to stop. This trip—this mission, I suppose—has nothing to do with vengeance. If that is what is in your heart, then I beg you to stay here, or go to Ortho."

"What about justice?" someone said.

"Justice and vengeance are two different things. Sometimes, one requires the other, but my desire is to resolve everything peacefully."

"They're your kids," said one of the Foster brothers.

"You're exactly right. They're my kids. I don't know if they're all hurt, or how badly. I don't even know where one of them is, exactly. I raised them to be strong and independent, but I did not raise them to become bullies. I will not be a bully myself, nor will I tolerate that behavior from any of you. I need you to understand how strong my commitment is to that principle."

"So, if they shoot at us—"

"We shoot back. If it comes to the conflict I don't want, I have every intention of prevailing. But we will *not* pick the fight. Is that clear to everyone? Does anyone have questions?"

"Oh, there'll be a fight, all right," said a familiar voice from the other side of the wagon.

Victoria turned and beamed as she saw Luke approaching from up the mountain. His shoulders were a little slumped and he had a slight limp, but he was the most beautiful sight she'd seen in a long, long time. "Excuse me," she said to the gathered crowd as she stepped over the edge of the wagon, onto the tire and then down to the ground. As she glided across the grass with her arms splayed wide, Luke came at her with that sideways grin, his hands in his pockets until they were just a few feet away from each other, and then he gave her the hug she'd been craving.

"Oh, sweetie, are you all right?" Victoria closed her eyes tightly against the tears that were coming.

"I'm fine. My legs are sore, and I'm a little chilly, but I'm good."

"Have you been walking all night?"

"All. Friggin'. Night."

"Are you hurt?"

Luke pulled away from the hug and glanced uncomfortably at the onlookers. "Not really. But I did see the belly of the beast. I've got great intel. But first, I don't know if you saw—"

"Penn Glendale. Yes, I did. I do. But let's get to that later."

"You're just going to ignore him?"

"I hope so, yes. For now, anyway." Victoria had come to realize that Penn wasn't really the driver in what she had to do over the course of the next twenty-four to forty-eight hours. She knew that introducing him to the crowd would derail all discussion about their strategy for what lay ahead for them.

Without waiting for Luke to object, she draped her arm around her son's shoulders and turned him back toward the crowd. "Look who I found."

People seemed pleased to see the young man, though Victoria was sure that a few didn't even know who he was.

"Where's your shirt?" someone asked. The tone was a teasing one.

"Long story," Victoria answered on his behalf. "Luke got himself taken prisoner last night. Somehow, he got away." She made a point of addressing Luke directly when she said in a loud voice, "But I believe you have seen today's objective, is that right?"

Luke scowled. "Ye . . . s." He drew the word out over a couple of seconds, showing confusion over what he was supposed to do now.

"Tell us," Victoria said. "Get up on the wagon so everyone can see and hear."

He shot her a look that was equal parts anger and terror. He hated speaking to crowds.

"Go on, climb up."

Luke looked like he'd stepped into a trap as he found his way to the bed of the wagon. "What do you want to know?"

"Everything," Victoria said.

McCrea stepped forward and Luke looked relieved. "Start with how far away they are."

"It was a good three hours on horseback. Probably six for us to walk back."

For the first time, apparently, McCrea recognized who'd been walking with Luke, but he interpreted Victoria's glare for exactly what it meant. *Not yet.*

"How many people?"

Over the course of the next ten minutes, Luke explained that from what he could tell, Primo's place was a kind of outpost for the Hilltop Manor. A kind of security station. The pirates that had harassed the Tyler family and Marney Bates were a foraging party. He talked about the guns he saw, the layout of the farmhouse, and every other detail that people wanted to know.

"They're wired for a fight," Luke concluded. "They know we're coming. They were trying to put me into a storm cellar when I accidentally threw a guy down the stairs and killed him. That's when they brought Speaker Glendale around—"

He stopped and looked frightened. He clearly hadn't meant to reveal the secret, but the fact of it rumbled through the crowd. Victoria heard someone say, "I thought he looked familiar."

And: "Why is he dressed like that?"

Victoria stepped forward. "And now for the big surprise. Penn Glendale, please climb up on the wagon."

With a jerk of her head, she told Luke to climb down. He seemed more than relieved.

As Penn approached, Victoria extended her hand for a professional-level handshake.

"It's nice to see you again, Vicky," he said.

"I'll bet it is. Come and meet your rescuers." She beckoned him to the wagon. Speaking softly so that others couldn't hear, she asked, "Do you need help to climb up on the wagon bed?"

"Why am I doing this?"

"Because I'm asking you to."

"Then, no, I don't need help. At least I hope I don't." He stepped first on the wheel hub, then the top of the wheel and then finally transitioned to the bed.

Victoria followed him, then turned to the crowd. "Ladies and gentlemen," she said, "meet Penn Glendale, former Speaker of the House of Representatives."

"And currently president of the United States," he added. "In case you hadn't heard the news."

"There is no United States anymore," said Alex Kramer from the crowd.

"What the hell happened?" asked one of the Fosters.

"We thought you were under arrest," said someone else.

"I *was* under arrest," Penn said. "But I was able to get away before they could execute me. From what I can tell, a few of you are disappointed that the effort didn't succeed."

Victoria sensed bad things coming, so she raised her hand to draw attention. "Penn, you need to know that these people are all here willingly, and they are all here to try to make sure your trial is fair. They're willing to risk their lives for that."

Penn looked uncomfortable, as if he didn't know what he should say. "Thank you. Thank you all."

"Is it true that you've been hunkered down in a bunker with clean sheets and fresh food while all of us have been starving?" someone asked.

Victoria watched his shoulders sag as he heard the question. "I've been getting that a lot," he said. "There's a nuanced answer that gets into continuation of government and such, but the simple answer is, yes. The surviving members of the House and Senate"—he nodded to Victoria—"present company excluded, did, in fact, live in relative comfort in a bunker in the Hilltop Manor Resort. A few weeks ago, the bunker—we called it the Annex—was overrun by ordinary citizens from outside and they arrested my colleagues and me. Yesterday, following a trial that was anything but a fair one, the members of the House and Senate were all executed."

Chatter rumbled through the crowd.

"Good," Alex said. "Look what they did to us. Look what they did to the world. What *you* did to the world."

Penn started to answer, but Victoria spoke instead. "Your words are angry, Alex."

"Damned straight I'm angry. How many billions of people are dead because of him? Because of them?"

"If you think I'm going to defend the decisions Mr. Glendale and the others made, then you are sorely mistaken." Victoria deliberately avoided the honorific of *the president*. "This devastation is the result of countless stacked decisions all made with the best of intentions."

"All politicians care about is power," said the other

Foster kid. "They've never given a shit about us normal people."

Victoria needed to find a way to tamp down the anger. She felt a momentum building that, if allowed to boil over, could end up with Penn getting torn apart. "I'm sorry," she said to the Foster kid. "Which Foster are you? Kyle or Caine?"

"Caine."

"All right, Caine. We're all angry. We've been angry for a long time—even before the war—because the legacy politicians and the media needed you that way. Angry people vote, and votes bring people to office, myself included. I personally feel no shame because I considered it my job to fundamentally change the barnacle-laden machinery that was Washington. And I wasn't the only one."

"I didn't mean to insult you, Vicky," Caine said.

"And I'm not insulted. I want you to know that I understand where you're coming from with your anger. But you need to understand that if it weren't for that last-minute decision on my part, I would have been in that bunker when the doors closed. If that had been the case, I would have been one of the people executed yesterday."

She let that sink in for a few seconds.

"Many of those who were killed were trying to change things, trying to undo the damage that Penn Glendale and his generation of politicians did to American society. If what Mr. Glendale says is true, a couple hundred people—guilty *and* innocent—are dead because of their job titles. They were not tried by peers and judged through serious deliberation. They were lynched on the theory, I suppose, that it felt good to lash out at someone."

Victoria watched the crowd as they processed the point she was trying to make. Some looked confused, others nodded, but no one appeared angry.

"We're not doing that anymore," Victoria said. "We're no longer running things by the hate-driven rules of Mr. Glendale's generation of politicians. We're going to defend justice and promote liberty. We will hold people accountable, but we will presume innocence."

Victoria glanced at McCrea, and he winked. He thought she was doing a good job.

"Most of you here want to mete out your own vigilante justice against the roadside pirates. I get it, I really do. But that's not how society operates. It can't. The way things are now, people are feeding off each other's weaknesses and fomenting fear and mistrust. We can't enjoy a new day—a societal reset—unless and until we replace armed camps with some kind of cooperative spirit."

She feared that she was rambling, so she paused to gather her thoughts.

"Caine Foster. You came along on this trip by your own choice. Why?"

"Because I didn't want you to have to fend for yourself. That, and because you stopped people from—" He stopped himself.

"Stopped people from what, Caine?" Victoria asked. In her peripheral vision, she could see that both Luke and McCrea were smiling. They saw where she was going.

Caine looked down. "From lynching me."

"Bingo! I didn't save you so much as I talked people out of what?"

"Killing me."

"The entire town thought you and your brother were looters, and no matter how loudly you proclaimed your innocence, they still wanted to see you hang, either literally or figuratively."

Caine and his brother Kyle both blushed and looked at their feet. So identical were the twins that they sulked identically.

"I'm not putting you on the spot," Victoria went on. "And the rest of you who are not from Ortho on Hell Day, you don't know what we're talking about, and that doesn't matter."

"So, are you saying we're still going to Hilltop Manor?" Luke asked. "Even though Speaker Glendale is out of danger?"

"I'm saying that I am still going up there."

"They want to kill you, you know. They're afraid of you. They think you're coming for their little kingdoms."

"I do know that they want to kill me." She felt a little smile grow on her face. "That's why I'm hoping a few of you will come along."

"Why pick a fight you don't need to fight anymore?" Greg Gonzales asked.

"I'm not picking a fight," Victoria said. She scanned the crowd for faces she didn't see. "Where are the Tyler family?"

Simone raised her hand. She was by herself, her kids apparently cleaning up their campsite. Or, just sleeping in.

"Your family suffered worse than most. Imagine that you were still among the population of Buster and his gang. Wouldn't you want someone to give you a way out?"

Simone Tyler raised her head high. "That's why we're here. That's why we're gonna keep coming along."

Luke warned, "I'm telling you, Mom, there's a guy named Primo up there where Speaker Glendale and I got away from. They're not going to go down easily. Neither are the people who are with them."

"If that's what happens, that's what happens. If it comes to violence, may our side win."

"So, what about Glendale?" someone yelled. "He just walks away from all this? There's no accountability?"

Victoria turned back to Penn. "What's fair?"

Penn never looked away from the crowd as he shifted his stance and shoved his hands into his pockets. He watched his feet shuffle on the surface of the wagon bed, and then his shoulders straightened and he spoke in a loud, clear voice.

"I can't tell you what's fair. I know you've suffered differently these past months than I have, but I make no apology for the decisions that I made. Each of you is either wired to understand the need to continue government operations during a crisis, or you're not. Standing here, dressed like Fidel Castro, on the back of a wagon in the middle of nowhere, I won't be able to change anyone's mind, so I won't try."

He shifted his gaze back to Victoria. "But I want you to know that I'm going with you, back to the Hilltop Manor. I didn't like the way I left, and I have every intention of returning to face those who accuse me of crimes I didn't commit."

"You know they'll tear you apart," Luke said. "That's been their plan all along, I bet."

Victoria turned back to the members of the caravan. "I won't ask anyone to commit one way or the other on this. In thirty minutes or so, I will head out, up toward the first outpost encampment. If you choose to come along, fall in with me. If you choose not to, I'll fully understand, and I wish you a good life."

She accepted McCrea's hand to help her down off the wagon. As she passed him, he mumbled, "Here's hoping for more than a few volunteers."

CHAPTER TWENTY-TWO

AS PENN STEPPED FROM THE WHEEL HUB BACK TO THE ground, a man of military bearing grabbed his biceps and squeezed. "Mr. President, we need to talk."

"Get your hands off me," Penn said, and he pulled away. At least he tried to.

"Don't make it a fight, sir."

"Who the hell are you?"

"My name is Joe McCrea, formerly a major in the U.S. Army. We've actually met a couple of times while I was pulling various security details. Now, please don't fight me."

"Where are we going?"

"Into a private corner of the woods," McCrea said.

"Is this where you shoot me?"

"I don't see an immediate need for that, but if it arises, I won't hesitate. Sir."

Penn didn't see malice in the major's eyes, but there was no kindness, either. This guy was all business. "I think I'd rather speak to Vicky."

"She doesn't want to speak with you, sir."

"She said that?"

"Those were her very words." The major made a broad sweeping motion with his hand, indicating a nonspecific place near a tree line. The man was well-armed, with a rifle, a pistol and a knife sheathed to his belt.

"What do you wish to talk about?" Penn asked.

McCrea didn't move. His hand stood frozen in the air, gesturing toward the tree line.

"Lead on," Penn said. "I'll follow."

"No, you lead. I'll tell you when to stop."

As he crossed the field, Penn felt the heat of the glares that were coming his way. He sensed the anger. And the fear. While none of the people in his field of view seemed inclined toward violence, he sensed that they wouldn't mind if violence befell him.

Penn reached the base of a sprawling oak and McCrea said, "That's far enough."

Penn turned, half expecting to be staring down the muzzle of a firearm, but instead saw the major standing calmly before him, his hands resting comfortably on his belt.

"If you're about to challenge me to a fight," Penn said, "I'll tell you right now that you win. I'm too old and too tired to duke it out." He tried to sell it with a smile.

McCrea wasn't buying. "Look, Mr. Glendale."

"Mr. President," Penn corrected.

This seemed to frustrate the major. Maybe even anger him.

"Titles are important, Major."

"Only when they're accurate, sir. What, exactly, do you think you're president of? The United States? There is no United States anymore. There's only a ruined frontier."

"The country still exists, Major. It's just very damaged right now. What's left of the nation needs leadership."

"It already has leadership," McCrea said.

Penn saw where this was going. He laughed. "Vicky Emerson? Look, I appreciate her efforts on my behalf, but she's a junior representative from a state that has only two members in the House. Nobody outside West Virginia has any clue who she is." This was absurd. It was one thing to ring doorbells and cut ribbons at grand openings to get elected by local friends, but to be president was so much more than that.

"Mr. Glendale, can you assure anyone that there *is* a population outside West Virginia? And a very narrow slice of it at that?"

Penn started to talk about the communications they had had with survivors across the country and around the world, though scant and infrequent, but McCrea wasn't finished.

"And what difference does it make to us here if, in fact, enclaves in Iowa are thriving? We couldn't communicate with them even if we knew they existed, and if we could, the best we could share would be gossip. National leadership is useless, sir."

Penn bristled at the notion. He understood that times were tough, but impertinence at this level, from a relatively junior officer in the United States Army, offended him. "You know I am the commander-in-chief, right, Major?"

"I fully expect you to file a report with my commanding general, sir. Give him my regards."

"Do you think this is some kind of joke, Major?"

"No more than you think that this is some kind of ring-knocking costume party, sir. You are free to call yourself anything you want. In fact, if there's anything that these past months have shown us, it's that expressing personal freedom is a survival skill."

Penn didn't have to listen to this. The morning had been preceded by a very long night, which itself had been preceded by a couple of endless weeks. He had neither the time nor the inclination to stand still to be insulted. He started to walk away.

McCrea grabbed his biceps again, more forcefully this time. "You're not going anywhere, sir."

"Get your hands off me, Major."

"Don't make this get ugly, Mr. Glendale. You'll either stand there, or you'll sit there because you won't be able to stand."

"Are you *threatening* me, Major?"

"Absolutely, sir."

The words stunned Penn. Who the hell did this guy—

"Mr. Glendale, you are welcome to stay here when we leave, and you are welcome to walk down the mountain with those who are going to Ortho. You are not returning to the Hilltop Manor with us."

Penn felt heat rising in his ears and behind his eyes. "You cannot order me—"

"I can do anything I want. So can you, I suppose, but I'm younger, more fit, and it wouldn't bother me a bit to break your legs."

"I don't understand this," Penn said. "I thought the

whole purpose of your mission up the mountain was to rescue me. That's what the young man Luke told me."

"No, sir, it was not to *rescue* you. It was to try to grant you a fair trial. It was exactly as you wrote in your letter to Vicky. But given even the fairest trial imaginable, there is no conceivable way for you to escape the executioner if you go back there."

"Then let them execute me."

"No, sir, I won't. Civilization is in a shambles, and rightly or wrongly, you are the symbol for why everything is broken. If you return to stand trial, all that will follow is anger. If you're found guilty, those who hate Roger Parsons will cry foul. If you're found not guilty, those who hate you will go apoplectic. Vicky is doing her best to unify people. You, sir, are strife in a jar, prepackaged to make people fight and die unnecessarily."

"There are worse ways to go than to die for a cause," Penn said. "Preserving the United States of America is the very cause for which you built your career."

"I fought to defend the Constitution and liberty," McCrea said. "The republic existed and thrived because of the equal branches of government. Congress made the laws, the president enacted the laws and the courts kept everybody honest. None of that is there anymore, sir. None of it."

Penn held out his hands as if to say, *Ta-dah!* "I am literally one-third of that equation."

"No, sir, you're not. You're a man with a job that used to matter, but no longer does. All you are now is a burden. You consume resources you didn't create, you pose danger to people who would rather be safe, and you're a roadblock in Vicky's path to unifying the warring factions."

"I can tell you right now that Roger Parsons has no interest in unifying."

"What will be, will be. But with you in the posse, we have zero chance of success. Without you, there's at least a glimmer of hope. Too many people have already suffered for you to make them suffer more."

Penn felt as if he'd been slapped. "I'm not a bad person," he said. "If the people would rather have Victoria Emerson as their leader, that's fine with me. I'll fall right in line."

"I'll believe that if you tell me it's true," McCrea said. "But we both know that the world doesn't work that way. Wherever you go, you will be the man who killed billions of people."

"But I'm *not* that man. That person was Helen Blanton. *She* was president —"

"Come on, sir, don't make this more difficult than it needs to be. Whining and excuse-making aside, yours is the desk where the infamous buck stopped. Now, when the music stops, you're not going to have a chair. Not with us."

Penn's brain wouldn't pull all the details together. Suddenly, he felt dizzy. Betrayal does that, perhaps. "Do you expect me just to wander aimlessly?" He heard the whine in his tone. "I don't know how to hunt and fish. I don't know—"

"What do you think the rest of the world faced, Mr. Glendale? While you and your debating society triggered nuclear war, most of America was sound asleep. I imagine that most evaporated in the blast, but I also imagine that there are millions of others who are dying as they try to teach themselves the very skills that you do not know."

"You're asking me to commit suicide!"

McCrea paused, cocked his head. "I would never *ask* a friend of Vicky's to do such a thing. She means too much to me."

"Let me hear this from her, then," Penn said.

"No."

"But if she's the leader, then she's the one—"

"No."

"Does she know that you're telling me these things?"

"This is the only way."

"Some leader. She doesn't even have the courage to deliver her own bad news."

"I'm not rising to that bait, Mr. Glendale." McCrea dug into his front pocket and withdrew a little pistol, probably a .25, maybe a .22. He pressed a button on the side and the back end of the barrel tilted up. McCrea produced a bullet from his other front pocket, slid it into the open breach and then closed it again. He held it out for Penn. "Just cock it and pull the trigger."

Penn stared at the gun, then shifted his gaze back to McCrea. "What is this for?"

"You speak of courage, sir. Here's your opportunity to show some."

Sadness washed over Penn as he stared at the weapon. He didn't want to touch it.

McCrea moved the pistol closer. It wasn't a threatening gesture, but rather an offer. "Sir, the gun is yours to use as you wish. You can hunt a squirrel that you won't know how to clean and cook, or you can be the patriot you pretend to be."

This couldn't be happening. After all that he'd endured—the political fights before the war, and then the ones within the bunker, his escape and the people who'd died in support of it—this junior officer expected him to—

"Take it, Mr. Glendale. I need to be on my way."

When Penn didn't move to take possession, McCrea grabbed Penn's hand at the wrist, pulled it forward and then slapped the pistol into his palm. Without another word, McCrea spun on his heel and strode back to where the horses and riders were assembling.

"Where's the president?" Victoria asked from her saddle as McCrea mounted his horse. They were separated from the rest of the caravan by thirty feet or so.

"I had a talk with him. He decided to stay behind."

"That doesn't sound like Penn," Victoria said. "Maybe I should go and talk to him."

"Please don't do that," McCrea said.

Victoria felt a rush of ice in her veins. "What did you do?"

"I laid out the facts and I think I convinced him that the time has come for a change in leadership."

Victoria reared back in her saddle. "I won't be a part of a coup, Joe. That's not the way to recover from all this."

"I'm not suggesting otherwise, Vicky. The decision is his, not mine. All I did was make my case that as the man who is perceived as the one who ended the world as we knew it, his presence in the future will be an unending source of division."

"So, what is he supposed to do?"

McCrea smiled. "Funny, that's the same question he asked. I told him he should learn to become a common citizen. I told him he needs to reap what he's sown."

"That's not right, Joe. He's a friend. He was a mentor to me when I first got elected."

McCrea shifted his posture in his saddle, took his time formulating his next statement. "Vicky, you need to embrace who you are and what you mean to all these people who are falling in line to follow you. You are their hope to make life less awful. Penn Glendale may be your friend and your mentor, but he understands that you cannot achieve your goals with him as a focus."

How much could Victoria be expected to lose? How many people could she be expected to hurt?

"Please trust me on this," McCrea said.

"What did he say?"

"Mostly, he listened. Better yet, he heard and understood. When you arrive at Hilltop Manor, you won't have to broker a decision on Penn Glendale. Instead, you'll have an honest shot at unifying warring factions. That is what this is all about, right?"

Of course he was right, Victoria thought. But it shouldn't have to be this way. These were not the choices she'd intended to make. Her job in coming up the mountain was to provide for a fair trial. After that, she figured that she would return to Ortho and go on with her life with her family.

She wasn't about power anymore. There'd been a time when that was what she lived for, what drove her—well, not so much the power, but the ability to effect change. She didn't feel that way anymore. She wanted to hand the reins of leadership over to anyone else who was willing to accept them.

She wanted normality and she wanted peace. She wanted all of her sons to be safe and healthy, and she wanted to one day be warm and dry and comfortable again.

Everybody wanted those things.

Everybody wanted leadership, and for reasons Victoria could begin to understand, they were looking for her to provide it.

Victoria turned in her saddle to peer across the crowd to see if she could find Penn Glendale's face among them.

There he was, back near the oak tree where she and McCrea had pitched their tent the night before. Penn stood with his hands in his pockets, his head held low.

He seemed to sense her gaze, though, because he looked up to catch her looking at him. He gave a little wave, and then tossed her a salute—a real one, not a joke.

And then he turned and walked away, toward the burned-out shell of the farmhouse.

When she turned back, she saw that Luke had joined them, and that the rest of the caravan was mounting their horses, climbing into the wagons or just preparing for a walk, whether up or down the mountain was yet to be seen.

"Okay, Major," Victoria said. "Let's get moving."

CHAPTER TWENTY-THREE

*A*FTER VICTORIA AND HER ENTOURAGE HAD LEFT, Penn watched the much smaller crowd join together and walk the other way, down the mountain toward Ortho. Toward Eden. During those thirty minutes or so, no one yelled epithets his way. No one threatened him. No one spoke to him at all.

No one demanded anything from him, yet no one offered anything, either. The refugees he watched spanned the gamut from young child to his age. More men than women went on to Hilltop Manor, more women than men down the mountain in the other direction.

Then, he was alone.

The morning had bloomed cold, but as the sun climbed above the trees, the air warmed to mid-fifties, though the brightness made it feel warmer.

Penn lay on his back on the mulchy ground on the edge of the tree line. Looking up at the canopy of brightly colored leaves, it occurred to him that he used to look at the trees all the time. As a kid, growing up in southwestern Virginia, he'd been fascinated by the patchwork of light and shadows that were formed as the breeze blew and the foliage played peekaboo with the sky.

It had been a long time since he'd heard this depth of quiet. The birds in the trees weren't as loud as he remembered them, but then his ears were a lot older now. The silence was intoxicating in its own way. It was as if he could actually hear his own thoughts. Gone was the constant hum of chattering people and ringing phones. Even in his solitary cell, where he would go twenty or more hours without hearing a single soul, there'd been the steady thrum of the air handler and the buzz of the fluorescent lights.

There was no hurry in what he knew he had to do. But there was no point in dawdling, either.

He wondered how God will have judged his actions on the day of the war. He prayed that his wife, Lianne, and his daughter, Abby, wouldn't be ashamed of him— either of his actions in life or the means by which he would soon join them.

This was the only reasonable thing to do. Truly, it was an act of patriotism that would do his part to help America to somehow heal her wounds.

The pistol was a little bitty thing. According to the markings on the weapon itself, it was manufactured by the Beretta company. McCrea had left him with only one bullet—no subtle fellow, he.

Penn had handled guns and fired them in the past, but he'd never been a fan of them. He considered them to be instruments of evil. These days, perhaps they were instruments of mercy. The lines there were so close as to be nearly indiscernible.

The hammer pulled back easily. The barrel tasted like iron and smelled like rancid oil. He tried not to touch his tongue and cause himself to gag.

His eyes were opened wide, and he was still admiring the trees when he pressed the trigger with his thumb.

CHAPTER TWENTY-FOUR

LUKE'S HORSE, ROVER, STILL STOOD EXACTLY WHERE he had tethered her. The caravan stopped as the boy hopped out of the wagon and retrieved the animal. He mounted and strolled Rover back to where McCrea and Victoria were waiting.

"I thought for sure they'd find her and take her," Luke said. "Maybe this is a sign of good things ahead."

Victoria wanted to believe that more than she did. "How far is the roadblock from here?"

"Not far at all," Luke said. "Not half a mile."

McCrea beckoned the members of the caravan—he counted nineteen—to gather around and he spoke softly. "First, Luke and Caine, you two step out a hundred yards and hold security for us."

They didn't hesitate.

"Okay, here's the plan. Assuming things haven't changed from what was reported last night, in very short order, we're going to encounter the first line of defense for our objective."

"Our objective is peaceful resolution," Victoria reminded.

"Of course."

She could feel the sarcasm in his deference. No one
here but she thought that there was a chance of a peaceful outcome.

McCrea continued, "If they point weapons, you do
not have to wait to engage."

"But you are all to keep your weapons pointed in a
safe direction until that happens," Victoria said.

"That puts us at a disadvantage," Greg Gonzales
said.

"You can't threaten people into being peaceful,"
Victoria said. "The cycle has to start somewhere, so let
it start with us."

McCrea continued, "Vicky's going to do the talking,
I'm going to be next to her. Y'all spread out in a skirmish line and keep your eyes ahead and your muzzles
down. Concentrate on the target that's most directly in
front of you. At no point should you let the other side
take your flank or get behind you. If that starts, shout
out and let me know."

"If they move to flank us, that in and of itself is not
justification to open fire," Victoria said. "Is that clear?"

The nods she got said yes, but the grumbling told
her that they did not approve.

"Okay, here we go," Victoria said.

Luke and Caine Foster fell in line with Victoria and
McCrea as they walked closer to what lay ahead. The
rest of the caravan spread out across the road and into
the surrounding fields. No one spoke. Or, if they did,
Victoria couldn't hear them.

Six minutes later, Victoria saw the first observer

from Primo's camp. He appeared to be a teenager, and he'd been hiding along the tree line. Had he not jumped out and yelled, "They're coming!" Victoria wasn't sure she'd have seen him.

"Whatever happens is going to happen soon," McCrea said at half breath.

Up ahead, the road had been blocked by all manner of debris and furniture. It was stacked haphazardly, and in places leaned dangerously. The barricade was not designed to provide cover or even to withstand assault. To Victoria's eye, its sole purpose was to slow people down and make them easier targets.

"It didn't look like this last night," Luke said. "I told you they were expecting us."

"Well, let's not give them what they're expecting," Victoria said.

As the refugees from the other side scurried about to arm themselves and take positions, Victoria dismounted her horse and handed the reins to McCrea.

"What are you doing?" McCrea whispered.

"Putting my mouth where my money is," Victoria whispered back. Then, to the crowd facing them, she yelled, "We're not here to fight. If you don't shoot, neither will we!"

Her reply came in the form of a general murmur and a sense of confusion.

"I am Victoria Emerson. This is Major Joseph McCrea, and I believe many of you met my son, Luke, last night. I'm told that someone named Primo wants to speak with me." As she heard her own words, she also heard the quaver of fear in her tone. The only way to prevail here was to show strength. It would help to also feel strong, but she'd have to settle for one of two.

"Where's Glendale?" someone asked.

"Who's speaking?"

A man who looked far too healthy and athletic for the times stepped out from behind what appeared to be a dining table that had been tipped up on its side. "My name doesn't matter."

"It matters to me," Victoria said. "It seems only fair. Tit for tat and all that." As her rifle dangled down her front, she rubbed her right fist with her left palm, hoping to cover the trembling in her hands. "Are you Primo?"

"No, I'm afraid I'm not," the man said through a humorless smile. "Primo suffered an unfortunate accident last night."

"They shot him!" someone yelled from beyond the barricade.

Victoria struggled to keep her features flat as she heard the words. She kept her eyes on the man before her. He seemed to be the person in charge of whatever this was. The next question seemed so obvious that she didn't bother to voice it.

"That's true," the man said. The smile stayed pasted.

"And his name is Mason Goode," yelled the tattler on the far side. "He works for Roger Parsons."

"That's true, too," Goode said.

"Why did you shoot him?" Victoria asked.

"Because he was an idiot. He let Penn Glendale get away." He shifted his gaze to Luke. "I understand your boy had a lot to do with that."

Luke remained passive in his saddle, but Victoria saw his thumb check to make sure the selector switch on his new rifle was set to FIRE.

Victoria raised her voice so the crowd could hear.

"Is this really the life you want?" she asked. "You know, it doesn't have to be this way. Random murders and constant shakedowns don't have to be the rule."

Goode shifted his rifle, bringing the muzzle to low-ready. Behind her, Victoria heard a clatter of weapons from her own team.

"Remember the rules!" she shouted without looking back. "We don't start the fight!" To Goode's crowd, she said, "If you lay your weapons on the ground and step away from them, you'll have no trouble from us."

"You were about to tell me where Penn Glendale is," Goode said. Victoria saw something change behind his eyes. It might have been the first trace of growing fear. It also might have been anger. It was hard to tell the difference.

Victoria ignored him. "Alternatively, if you threaten us, we will open fire and many of you will die. It doesn't have to be that way." She was confident that the people in her caravan—certainly the ones who had traveled with her from Ortho—had locked in on the targets that would be theirs if it came down to fighting.

"It's a choice," Victoria said. "If you like the life you're living here, then that's fine. Put your weapons down, let us pass, and get back to doing what you're doing."

"They said we have to kill you," that lone voice said.

"Also true?" Victoria asked Goode, who answered with a shrug that said *maybe*. "Why would you do that? We're not harming you. We're not threatening you." She hoped that by getting him to express the rationale, he'd discover for himself that there really *was* no sensible rationale for engaging them.

Ahead and to the left, back behind Goode, a young lady in her twenties laid her rifle on the ground and stepped away from it. Another did likewise. Then, a third.

"Get back in your positions!" a man yelled at them.

A fourth gunman put his weapon on the ground.

"Goddammit, I'm not saying it again!" The loud-mouth raised his rifle to shoot, but before he could pull the trigger, someone from his own team shot him dead.

The rest of the fight lasted fewer than ten seconds. At the sound of the gunshot, Goode raised his rifle toward Victoria, but McCrea drilled him through the forehead. When he dropped, he left a pink mist hovering in the air over his body.

By Victoria's count, two other gunmen from the other side raised their weapons to fight and died as a result of their decision.

Then it was quiet. All of the refugees from the Primo and Goode encampment were on the ground, and none were pointing weapons at Victoria and her team.

"Everybody all right?" she called as she pivoted on her axis to assess damage to her team. "Call out if you see someone who's been hurt or hit."

"I think we're good," one of the Fosters said.

Victoria looked past him and got a thumbs-up from Mary Gonzales. "Everybody's fine," she said.

"Perfect," Victoria said. She turned back to the refugees sprawled in the yard of the farmhouse. "You can all get up now," she said. "We're not going to hurt you. You're in no danger from us if you don't pose a threat." As she waded into the crowd, she stooped and helped people rise. "Seriously, this is over. I'm sorry about the violence."

Within thirty seconds, they were all either on their feet or sitting comfortably on the ground.

"The weapons are yours to keep," Victoria said. "The ammo, too, and whatever other supplies you have. You need to be able to hunt and defend yourselves."

As she surveyed the faces in this new crowd, she tried to decode the expressions. There was a lot of fear, but she could talk herself into believing that she saw some appreciation, too. Relief, perhaps.

She turned and started back for her horse and the rest of the caravan, none of whom had moved, or even dismounted. To her own people, she said, "Next stop the Hilltop Manor."

"Wait!" someone hollered from behind her.

Victoria turned. To her ear, it was the same voice as the tattletale.

A man she gauged to be in his early forties stepped forward, stooped to pick up the rifle he'd dropped and halved the distance between them, stopping when he was still fifteen, twenty feet away. "I'm Alphonso Veracruz," he said. "Why are you really here? What are you doing?"

She took thirty seconds to give him the short version of her mission to liberate the Hilltop Manor from its tyrannical leader.

"Why would you do that?" Alphonso asked. "I mean, why you? We heard you had a pretty good gig down in Eden."

"The violence has to stop," Victoria said. "It just has to. The highwaymen and pirates have to stop doing what they're doing. People need to be able to live their lives."

"But what does that have to do with you?" asked the

first girl who'd laid down her rifle. "How is that your problem?"

Victoria considered giving her the speech about civilization and humanity being everyone's problem, but decided instead to sum it up with, "If you have to ask that question, then I'm afraid we don't have much to talk about."

"Can I come along?" Alphonso asked.

It wasn't what Victoria had been expecting.

"You wouldn't mind a bigger army, would you?" Alphonso pressed.

"This is not a mission about vengeance," Victoria said. In fact, she'd grown tired of saying it.

"The mission is about whatever you tell me it is," Alphonso said. "I'm deciding to trust you. I've heard the stories about Eden, and even if they're only fifty percent true, I want to be a part of what you're building."

"I think a lot of us do," said that first lady who'd dropped her weapon. "My name is Aggie, and I want to come along, too."

"Here's the thing," Alphonso said. "Sometimes, you just need to fight for what's right. Where you're going and what you're about to do may or may not be right, but I know that what's been happening around here because of Parsons and his goons is definitely *not* right."

"I think we've all recognized our mistakes from the early days," Aggie said. "We let fear take over and we reacted all wrong. We surrendered when we should have fought. I don't speak for anyone but me, but I don't want to surrender again. I want to feel safe again—at least as safe as anyone can be these days."

"We don't want to be victims anymore," Alphonso said.

A young man who might have been the teenager who'd alerted everyone to Victoria's approach stepped forward and raised his hand. "I'll go, too."

Victoria looked back at McCrea, whose face was a giant smile. He bounced his eyebrows as if to say, *See? I told you so.*

Victoria stepped closer to the crowd that had gathered only minutes before to kill her. "Any and all of you are welcome to come along," she said. "But I will not tolerate this group becoming a mob." She reiterated the points she'd made so many times about peace and forgiveness having to start from one side, asymmetrically. "I am not asking you not to defend yourselves, but I am insisting that you try to sell peace as the first and smartest choice."

In fifteen minutes, the expanded caravan was ready to go. They numbered forty-three now, and thirty-one of them were armed. Victoria estimated the youngest among them to be a boy of about ten, and the oldest was probably the guy pushing sixty. The vast majority of them were on foot, though the wagon remained available for those who needed to ride, if only for a short time.

For the life of her, Victoria did not understand how news of their presence traveled ahead of the caravan, but as they approached the Hilltop Manor, groups of refugees were waiting along the road for them. First, there were clumps of threes and fours, but as they came closer to the resort itself, the groups numbered as many as fifteen—and there were five or six of those groups.

Victoria and McCrea led the caravan, with Luke close behind, followed by the Foster brothers on the wagon, and then by everybody else. She didn't stop to count, but she estimated seventy volunteers.

People mostly hung to the sides of the road as they passed, many falling into the end of the caravan. One filthy young woman, with bruises on her face and tattered clothes that barely hung on her shoulders, stepped forward with two small children under the age of ten and approached Victoria's horse.

McCrea moved to block the approach, but Victoria waved him off. She brought her horse to a stop.

"Is it true?" the lady asked. Her eyes glistened red with tears. "Are you really bringing Eden to the Hilltop Manor?"

Victoria didn't know what to say.

"Bless you," the lady said. "Bless you for my children. Damn them for all they've done." She grasped Victoria's hand and kissed it. "I pray for you. I pray for us all."

Victoria fought the urge to pull her hand away. She didn't understand what she was seeing. She knew that people were desperate, and she knew that they needed relief from the constant terror that their lives had become, but she sensed a larger-than-human perception of her abilities that made her very uncomfortable. She sensed that people were expecting *her* to initiate the changes they wanted, and feared that they did not comprehend that *they themselves* needed to be the instrument of change.

Victoria didn't reply because she had no idea what to say. "These people see us as liberators," she said softly to McCrea, "but we haven't done anything yet."

"I disagree," McCrea said. "You've done exactly what these people needed. You've given them hope. More than that, you've *shown* that their oppressors are not invincible. You've demonstrated that the dragon can be slain, and you've shown them the blueprint of how to do it."

Victoria understood nothing that McCrea had just said. The individual words, yes, but not their meaning after they'd all been stitched together.

"Don't look so confused, Vicky," McCrea said. "Providing hope is the Holy Grail of leadership. You make people believe that they can win. People who fight out of fear of what their leaders will do to them if they *don't* fight are always at a disadvantage when they encounter a force that believes both in their cause and in their ability to prevail."

"You did that, Mom," Luke said. "Dad would be proud of you." Then, after a brief pause, he amended his statement. "I meant to say, Dad *is* proud of you. So am I."

Victoria's throat thickened and her vision blurred at Luke's words. The kid didn't entertain a lot of serious thoughts—didn't express them, anyway—and for him to invoke Glenn's memory in such a kind way made her reel a bit.

She looked over to McCrea, who was with her step

for step, and the smirk was still there. "He's right. All this is on you."

Victoria still was not convinced, but she acknowledged that they were speaking the truth as they understood it. It warmed her heart even as it cranked up the tension in her gut.

She'd never intended to inspire anyone. But now that she had—*if* she had—it was incumbent on her not to screw it up.

CHAPTER TWENTY-FIVE

"CHAMP, I TOLD YOU THAT YOU SHOULD HAVE BEEN the one to go get Glendale," said Stony McGillis as Roger Parsons walked a circle around the dining table in his suite.

"Yes, you did," Parsons said. He ignored his urge to tell Stony to shut up. In the end, he didn't go on the retrieval mission for Penn Glendale and the Emerson kid because he didn't like the idea of wading through the crowd of pissed off refugees. He couldn't tell anyone that, of course, because it would make him look like a coward—especially in light of the fact that he pushed Mason Goode into making the trip instead. The excuse he used had to do with making sure that the operations here in the hotel went the way they were supposed to.

"How sure are you that Mason is dead?" Parsons asked Kenny DeWilde.

The young man looked confused by the question. "I don't know how to answer that. There's *sure* in the sense that that's what I've been told by the people out there, and then there's *sure* in the sense that I've seen it with my own eyes. I don't have that."

"Who told you that Mason was dead?"

"A guy that leaks stuff to me. He called himself Billy, but I don't know if that's his real name. Usually, the stuff he gives me is pretty reliable."

"How does he know that he's dead?" Roger pressed. His anger that someone had been brazen enough to kill one of his inner sanctum staffers was nearly matched by the fear in his gut that they'd been able to do so.

Kenny's voice jumped an octave when he said, "I don't know, Roger. If you don't want to believe it, then don't." His frustration was evident in his tone.

Stony said, "The fact that a big caravan from this Eden place is getting closer—"

"Not you, too, Stony," Parsons moaned. "The name of the town is Ortho."

"Call it whatever you want. But the fact that the caravan got past the outpost tells you something. Or I think it should."

Kenny said, "I'm a hundred percent sure that Primo is dead, though. That came directly from Mr. Goode."

Parsons bristled. That news did not come *directly* from Mason Goode. For that to be the case, Mason would have had to deliver the news himself. Instead, he dispatched a runner to share the news. That was a reliable proxy, but not a *direct* communication. Parsons didn't know why this kind of imprecise language bothered him, but it did. Words have meanings, and those meanings are important. He decided to let it go, though.

"Hey, Champ?" Stony said. "Have you thought that maybe it's time for you to take off?"

The words startled Parsons. "Take off?"

"You know, run for your life," Stony clarified. "It's what we talked about before. This is the nightmare, Champ. The people will be rising up against you."

"Bullshit. We'll alert the Manorites. If we place them—"

Something passed between Kenny and Stony—a brief glance that clearly meant something to them, but that Parsons didn't pick up.

"Don't do that," Parsons said. "If you have something to say, say it."

"Tell him," Stony said to Kenny.

The youngster looked terrified. He shook his head, then turned and headed for the door.

"Kenny!" Stony and Parsons yelled it together.

He didn't stop. Hell, he sped up, moving as if frightened that they were going to chase after him. He pulled the suite door open, squirted out and then slammed it shut behind him.

"What the hell?" Parsons said. "What has him so spooked?"

Stony looked sad but said nothing.

"Stony, talk to me."

"You really need me to say it, Champ?"

"I really do, because I'm lost here."

Stony clearly didn't want to do this. His shoulders sagged, and he shoved his hands into his pockets. It was the same posture he'd assumed when he broke the news that Parsons' future bouts had been cancelled due to his substance issues. It was Stony's tell for impending bad news.

"The Manorites aren't going to fight for you, Champ."

Parsons made a noise that sounded like *piff*. "Of course they will. They're not cowards."

"No, they're not," Stony agreed. "But they're pragmatists. They know that the Emerson bitch is going to win."

"Bullshit. Some Congress babe with a couple of townies can't take this whole place. It's huge."

"It's not about the place, Champ. It's never been about the place. I've been trying to tell you that from the beginning—"

"So, now you're going to pile on with an I-told-you-so?" Parsons snapped. He didn't need a lecture from his closest friend and ally. Stony had always preached weakness. He never—

"This is about people's *loyalty*, Champ. The Manorites—and what a stupid name, by the way—followed you because you offered the *stuff* they wanted. They had two squares a day and a dry place to sleep. In return for that, all they had to do was break a head every now and then."

"You make that sound pretty coldhearted," Parsons said.

"You killed a lawyer in this very room!" Stony yelled. "You blew his brains out because you didn't like what he was telling you."

"Maybe that's a lesson for you to learn, Stony."

"Don't you even. I'm not one of your fan boys, Champ. I'm your friend. I'm the guy who holds your hand when you need comforting, and has an ear tuned for you when you want to bitch or whine. But I have never been your ass-kisser. I have never shied away from the truth with you."

Parsons' brain wasn't working fast enough to process it all. "I don't get what you're trying to tell me."

Stony gave a dismissive wave, as if shooing away an annoying fly. "Yeah, you do. You don't want to, but you get it. You can make people afraid of you, or you can earn people's respect. You can't do both."

"The Manorites—"

"Were scared to death of you," Stony interrupted. "You sensed respect because the price for not showing it was higher than anyone wanted to pay. You were the dictator, and they were the dictated." Stony slammed his palm on the polished surface of the dining table. "God*dammit* I told you to open those freezers."

"The Manorites can't hold that against me. I protected that food for them—so that they wouldn't starve."

"The way you let everybody else starve."

"I'm not having this conversation again, Stony. There wasn't enough for—"

"Yeah, Champ, we *are* having this conversation again. And this time, you'll ignore me at your own peril. You were cruel to those people. Deliberately cruel."

"But not to the Manorites."

"Okay, Champ, you want me to stipulate to that? Fine. I stipulate. You took good care of the Manorites. You made sure that they were fed and bedded. Good for you. What was their alternative?"

"What are you saying, Stony?"

"The Manorites are *gone*, Champ. Gone. Poof. Without them to protect you and whip order into the masses, you've got nothing. You need to get out of here before

Emerson and her team arrive. If you miss your window of opportunity, you're going to end up in the crematory pit. You can only hope that you'll be dead first."

The very thought of being burned alive sent a chill through Parsons' body. "Why now?" he asked. "Why are you panicking now, when for months you've been fine? We've stood up against hundreds of these war rats in the time we've been here. Now, you want me to run from a few."

"These people are armed, for one," Stony said.

"Most of those rubes were armed in the beginning. We disarmed them."

"One at a time, Champ. Maybe three at a time. They were all frightened and we outnumbered them at least two to one."

"If we stay together as a team," Parsons said, "we might still outnumber them. If we reconstitute—"

"No, Champ, there's no reconstituting anything. The Manorites are over. Your army is gone. All of them are either on their way out of here or trying their best to melt in with everybody else and hope that no one remembers their faces. You treat those refugees like rabble, but that rabble will eat you alive if they're given the chance. I'm sorry to be the one who has to tell you, but those are the plain facts."

"What about Asa McDonald? Surely, he's with me."

"Gone."

Parsons couldn't believe it. He'd given McDonald shelter and food and even some ladies to love in the evenings. "Buddy Baker? He was one of the best in the field."

"Gone. Jesus, Champ, there's *nobody* left. As in, nobody. If you try to face down that Emerson bitch, you'll be facing her down alone."

Parsons heard the implication in Stony's voice, but he didn't want to believe that, either. "What about you, Stony? You gonna leave me, too?"

"I'm with you step for step, Champ. Provided your decision is to get out while you can. I'm not committing suicide for you or anyone else. We've had a good run here. Now, it's time to try something else."

Parsons felt the walls closing, the air thinning. The depth and breadth of the ingratitude stunned him. "I've gone way out on a limb for you for a lot of years, Stone-man. I've kept you on the payroll long past your usefulness. You owe this to me."

"I owe you a lot, Champ, I ain't sayin' I don't. But I don't owe you the end of my life."

Parsons strode to the window and pointed through the glass. "Look out there, Stony. There's no insurrection. There's nobody storming the front door. You're making too big a deal out of this."

"God*dammit*, Champ, get your head out of your ass. There's nobody storming the front door because there's nobody to stop them from walking right through. There's no security here anymore."

"Okay, Mr. Bigmouth, what's your plan? Clearly, you're not going to stand and fight with me, so what *are* you going to do?"

Stony looked genuinely sad when he said, "You know, Champ, for the first time ever, I don't feel safe in your presence anymore. I don't feel safe sharing my plans with you." He turned and started for the door.

"Don't you turn your back on me, old man!" Parsons shouted. He found his pistol in his hand before he realized he'd pulled it from its holster. "I asked you a question."

Stony turned, saw the gun and smiled. He held his arms out to his sides. "And there it is. The man with the gun threatening the man without one. Are you really going to shoot me for walking away? Does that improve your options even a little bit?"

"I won't be shown disrespect," Parsons said. "You're here and still alive because of me, Stone-man. I've protected you. I've given you shelter, and I've made sure that you were safe."

"And I'm trying to do the same for you," Stony said. "But you won't listen."

As if on cue, the sounds outside the window changed. A commotion grew. It wasn't a sound of violence to Parsons' ear, but rather one of interest. Intrigue maybe. Stony heard it, too. You could see it in his scowl.

"I think it might be too late," Stony said.

Parsons hurried to the window, pressed his hands against the frame. Trees blocked the money shot, but clearly, people were moving toward the back road, the one past the crematory and toward the hidden bunker entrance—the one that Parsons himself had used to lead the attack on Glendale and his people.

Whatever the attraction was, it started as a curiosity outside. People clearly heard something interesting, and they craned their necks for a clearer look. Then, watchers toward the bottom of the hill started moving toward the source of the interest, and that sparked even more interest from the observers in the back.

"Open the window," Stony said. "Maybe we can hear something."

Parsons spun the lock on the bottom panel of the ancient, double-hung window and pressed upward on the sash. A century of countless coats of paint made it a struggle, but finally the window moved. Cold air rushed into the room, bringing with it the chatter and roar of dozens of excited people.

"I think this is it," Stony said. "I think the Emerson bitch is here."

The encampment where Victoria's caravan had picked up Alphonso and the others was only two hours behind them when she got the first inkling that they were approaching the Hilltop Manor. First, there was an increased concentration of humanity. More and more of the refugees they encountered appeared to be more deeply dug into their locations than the previous ones they'd seen. And as the numbers increased per unit of real estate, the more intense the buzzing and whispers. Three or four times, she swore that she heard her name mentioned.

At first, people made way for them and watched, but then as some more fell in line with the parade, others rushed at them from up ahead.

"I believe the word is out," McCrea said.

"Are you really Victoria Emerson?" someone called, finally vocalizing the thoughts of so many.

The gathering crowd pressed in on them.

"Spread out!" McCrea called to his team.

This was a security nightmare. Victoria had not anticipated this many people, or this kind of reaction. They posed no obvious risk, but the sheer numbers put them in danger.

"Nobody's armed!" Victoria told her people, spinning in her seat. "Do not point weapons at anyone who's not a threat." An errant trigger pull right now could cause a panic that resulted in a bloodbath.

"Are you really going to stop them?" someone asked. "Are you going to stop Roger Parsons?"

Victoria's horse didn't like the sudden pressure of people, and its gait showed it. He wasn't bucking or rearing up, but he'd stopped his steady progress. He wanted to turn around, but Victoria wouldn't let him.

"Please, everybody," Victoria said to the gathering crowd. "Give us a little space. You're making the horses nervous."

"I'm not liking this, Vicky," McCrea said.

"If one of them has a gun, we don't have a chance," Luke said.

"We didn't want to do it," someone else hollered. "They made us do it."

Victoria imagined that the voice was talking about the congressmen and senators they'd executed, but she couldn't know for sure.

Victoria needed to do something. She needed to at least say something. These people were spun up in what appeared to be a good way, but if she frustrated them, she could trigger a stampede. "I'm going to make a speech," she said.

"Now?" McCrea seemed horrified.

"As good a time as any." Victoria reined her horse 180 degrees and squeezed through the crowd to approach the Foster brothers and the supplies wagon.

"What are we doing?" one Foster asked.

"I'm going to say something to these people. You're going to keep the wagon from jolting away from me."

Victoria handed her reins to the driver and dismounted directly onto the floorboard of the wagon. From there, she stepped up onto the bench seat. "Sorry, boys, but I want as many people to see me as possible."

"You're going to make a hell of a target," a Foster said.

"I think this is a bad idea," the other one said.

"Won't be my first bad idea," Victoria said. She used the boys' shoulders to steady herself as she planted her feet on the bench and turned around to see the crowd.

They were still coming. She estimated eighty to a hundred, with still more streaming in. This felt like a fragile moment to her, one that could help to map out the next hours and days and weeks. The old expression, *you only get one chance to make a first impression*, rang in her head like a church bell.

"Major McCrea, would you do me the honor of a whistle?" she asked.

McCrea put his pinkies in his mouth and launched his trademark whistle. The people close to him covered their ears. After two more, the crowd seemed to have settled, and it was Victoria's turn to talk.

"Good afternoon." She spoke in a strong, elevated tone, a projected tone that would carry quite a way, but likely not all the way to the back. "My name is Victoria Emerson."

"The mayor of Eden!"

She was done correcting the mistake. "These people with me are my friends—both old and new—who have traveled here with me to help bring an end to the violence. We don't want a fight, but we will engage in one if we have to."

"You shouldn't be here," said a man in his sixties. "Roger Parsons wants you dead. I heard that from many people."

"Yeah!" said a different voice. "He's scared of you."

A murmur of agreement rumbled through the crowd.

"Well, that's his mistake," Victoria said. "I'm not the one he should be afraid of. You—all of you gathered here—are the ones he should be afraid of. You're the ones who can push him from power."

"He's got an army," someone said.

"No, he doesn't," said another. "He's got a bunch of thugs and henchmen. If we push back, those assholes will fold like wrapping paper." The speaker was a guy in his forties. He looked pale and thin, but his green eyes were sharp and clear. "I've been tellin' them this for weeks, but nobody will listen."

"They've got all the guns, Malcom," said a lady standing close to him. "You want us to go charging into suicide?"

Victoria didn't want to listen to bickering. "A couple of days ago, we set out to come here to see that my former colleagues could get a fair trial."

The crowd's murmur switched to something far less excited than it was before. "But I understand that's now a moot point."

"I told them that was wrong," said the man named Malcom. "That weren't no trial. Them people was lynched."

"That doesn't matter," Victoria said. Those weren't the words she'd planned, but this was a time for pragmatism. If the rumors were correct, many of the people in front of her were parties to the lynching. They were all guilty of murder.

But these days, who among them was not?

"If we're going to move forward, we need to forget about the past. Old insults, old crimes, old offenses cannot dictate what lies ahead. I want no part of retribution. Vengeance doesn't bring back the dead. All it does is perpetuate anger and violence."

"We've been through too much just to forgive," somebody said.

Victoria saw her rhetorical opening, her opportunity. She cupped her hands around her mouth and said even more loudly, "A lady up here tells me that you've been mistreated too badly, *hurt* too badly to ever forgive. I know many of you feel the same way. There's anger and there's hatred and there are dreams of revenge. Am I right?"

General consent rippled through the crowd.

"Well, shame on you!" she shouted. "I mean that literally. Shame. On. You. You could have left, but you chose not to. You could have fought back, but you *chose* not to. Don't waste your emotions with *anger*. Grow as a human by embracing your shame."

"You've got some nerve, lady."

"Damn right I do," Victoria said. "So does everyone who's with me. In the weeks since Hell Day, I have fought more than I've wanted to, I've killed more than I ever dreamed I would, and the result is the place you call Eden, but I call Ortho. The result is a community. It's a place where people who don't know each other care about each other anyway."

Some of the people within her sight looked angry, as if they wanted to argue, but most of them looked uncomfortable. Was it because they were hearing the truth, or was it for some other reason?

"Make no mistake," Victoria went on, "this process is not easy. In fact, it's very damned hard. There will be fights and some of you may get hurt, and here we are in an era when merely getting hurt can have devastating consequences, if only because of the lack of medical care. But I believe I can speak for the others who are with me that the thought of fighting for what is right—even if it is at a terrible cost—is better than cowering before others.

"So, ladies and gentlemen, that is our new mission. But I'm not here to fight your fight for you. Where are the weapons that were taken from you?"

When no one answered, Victoria pointed at Malcom. "You. Where are the weapons?"

"In the hotel, I imagine."

"Then let's go get them," she said. "There are many more of you than there are of them."

"But they already have guns. They'll mow us down."

"We have guns, too," Victoria said. "My team and I will be there to support you. If they shoot, we'll shoot back. If they don't, we won't. This isn't complicated."

A young woman—maybe twenty-five—stepped forward with her toddler. "The children might get hurt."

"Yes, they might. If you're afraid—either for them or for yourself—stay behind. *Choose* to stay behind. That's true for everyone. Me? I'm going to go have a chat with Roger Parsons."

Victoria didn't wait for questions or input. Once again using the Fosters' shoulders for stability, she stepped down from the step and turned to remount her horse.

"That was really good, Vicky. I'm Caine."

She smiled. "Thank you."

"Should we pass out the weapons and ammo?" Kyle asked.

"Not yet. Let's see what they do. I want you to hang back, away from the major and me until we see what we'll need."

Victoria stepped from the wagon's floorboard over to her horse, swinging her leg without touching the stirrup.

"Okay," she said. "Let's go."

Slight pressure on the horse's ribs eased it forward. The crowd parted, as if by magnetic field, to let the caravan through, and then they fell in behind. Victoria thought she might recognize this pathway from the night she drove away with her kids, but it was hard to tell in the daylight with the grass trampled and the trees and shrubs torn up.

Enthusiasm for their arrival grew as they walked closer to the hotel, up the sweeping lawn and across the parking lot packed with vehicles that hadn't moved since Hell Day, many of them serving as makeshift shelters.

To the young man who had been walking at her left stirrup step for step, she asked, "Why aren't people staying in the hotel?"

"Roger won't let anyone in the hotel except for the Manorites."

"You mean minorities?"

"No, ma'am. Manorites. You know, Hilltop Manor? Manorites. Those are Roger's hitmen."

"I've met a couple of those already," Victoria said.

"I hear they're in kind of a panic now that you're on the way. They're afraid you're going to kill them."

"I don't intend to kill anyone," Victoria said. The more she thought about it, the more she wondered how anyone could be held to account after the fact, no matter what they did. Bad blood ran so hot through these refugees that there'd be no way to separate true accounts from baseless accusations.

The lack of resistance here startled her, especially in juxtaposition to what they encountered at the Primo encampment. "Do you think they're just lying in wait for us somewhere, Major? Waiting to ambush us?"

"I don't—"

"No," said the man at her stirrup. "Well, maybe, I guess, but most of the Manorites have taken off."

"They know that killing all those congressmen was wrong," said the lady to his left. Were they married? Related? Victoria decided it didn't matter.

"Where were the executions held?" Victoria asked.

"The hangings were done in the Oak Grove," the man said. "There was only a few of those. Ten, I think."

"Were you in attendance?" Victoria asked.

The man said nothing, which she interpreted to be an invocation of the Fifth Amendment.

"Where are the bodies?"

"I don't know," he said. "Probably in the cremation pit. There's hundreds of skeletons in there."

"The hanged ones are still hanging," the lady said. "Roger wanted people to see them and be afraid."

Victoria felt another lecture blooming, but she choked it down. How could the people who were supposed to be afraid—who clearly *were* afraid—not first be enraged? She couldn't wrap her head around the concept of letting corpses rot in the sun because someone *told* you to do that. Who *were* these people? Was humanity truly that fragile?

She'd dealt with the previous gangs who'd tried to conquer Ortho, but those monsters were the invaders, the ones who were trying to take lives and property. Victoria had assumed that such people were the outliers. But here, these people tolerated tyranny without question. They *participated* in the same tyranny that they decried.

It all made her head hurt.

"You okay, Mom?" Luke asked. "You have your mad face on."

She didn't answer, and Luke seemed to get the point. There were times for lightheartedness, but this was not one of them.

As they turned a corner to the right at the top of the hill, the lawn opened up even more, and there, within two hundred yards, stood the postcard image of the Hilltop Manor Resort, with its towering pillars and gleaming marble steps.

"Wow," Luke said.

The man at Victoria's stirrup said, "This is how I know the Manorites are gone. Normally, there'd be a line of them at the base of those stairs. No one was allowed in without an express invitation from Roger."

"There must be dozens of entrances into a place this size."

"Yeah, but this was the only approved one. If you

got caught inside without a pass—and this is the only entrance that gives passes—you'd be shot on the spot."

"Shot," Victoria said, as if to taste the word. "Just for trespassing?"

"No, ma'am. You'd be shot for stealing. Roger was very clear that every resource inside belongs to him."

"What kind of resources?"

"Everything you can think of that keeps people alive. They've got food frozen in there. I hear they have a hospital wing, too. But none of us were allowed to use any of that."

"You weren't *allowed*." Victoria hated the sound of echoing his words, but she felt that if she didn't *hear* herself articulate the word, she wouldn't believe she'd heard it.

"I'd have done it anyway," Luke said. "Just to piss them off."

"It's not worth dying for a prank," the lady said.

Victoria couldn't take it anymore. She urged her horse forward some more, picking up the pace and leaving those two behind. The whole culture of this place was to surrender and be afraid.

Snap out of it, she told herself. She hadn't led their lives and she hadn't endured what they'd gone through. It was wrong for her to judge them harshly.

But *Jesus*.

As she led the way up the lawn and past still more refugees, her caravan no longer existed as such. It had become a crowd. A well-behaved one, but a crowd, nonetheless.

"Major, please make sure that our team is staying together. We are most certainly at a disadvantage if there's an ambush in our future."

"Can't argue with you there." McCrea spun in his saddle and surveyed their group. "The wagons are farther back than I'd like, but otherwise, I think things are as solid as we can expect under the circumstances."

"What's our next step, Mom? I thought we'd be blasting away by this time."

Luke had a very good point and asked a very good question. The thought had not crossed her mind that this might be a peaceful encounter, despite what she'd said before.

Up ahead, a young man—a teenager, really—burst out the ground level entrance of the hotel and sprinted toward the woods.

"That's one of them!" someone yelled. "That's Kenny DeWilde! Get him!"

The kid's charge was a suicidal one. Apparently, he thought he could skirt the gathered crowd and run around their left flank, but he never had a chance. Seventy-five yards away from Victoria, someone chased him down from behind and grabbed enough of his shirt to make him stumble and slow down, but it was the linebacker rush from his left side that almost broke him in half.

A dozen people were on him in seconds, kicking and pulling at him. His screams for mercy were heartbreaking.

Victoria kicked the horse into a gallop and reined to a stop a few seconds later, spinning off her saddle and wading into the crowd. Behind her, she was vaguely aware that McCrea and Luke were yelling at her.

"Stop that!" she yelled. "Let him up. You're hurting him!"

"Goddamn right I'm hurting him," said the tall man

who'd tackled him. "He's one of Roger Parsons' right-hand men." He cocked his fist back to fire a devastating punch.

Victoria hooked his elbow in hers, ruining the shot. "He's not even a man!" she yelled. "He's a boy!"

"He's one of them. He's one of the Manorites."

Victoria used both hands to push another attacker away from the kid and then dropped her body on top of his. "No! This isn't right."

"Don't make me shoot anyone!" McCrea's voice boomed.

Luke added, "I came here for a gunfight. I don't mind having one." They'd both dismounted and stood ready to shoot.

Victoria rose to her knees, adjusted her rifle so that it would be usable if she needed it, and grabbed a fistful of Kenny DeWilde's shirt. "Stand up," she said.

"Please don't hurt me."

"You never minded hurting us!"

"Your name is Kenny, right?" Victoria asked.

"Listen, lady, move," said the man with the big fist. "We'll handle this our way."

Victoria shoved Kenny to McCrea. "Don't let him get away." Then, she spun on the man with the mouth. "Handle it *your* way? *Your* way is to cower and whine and run away. Is that really how you want to do this?"

Someone said, "Mrs. Emerson, you don't understand. Kenny is one—"

Victoria whirled at the sound of the voice. "Who said that?"

A lady in her midforties timidly raised her hand.

"What's your name?"

"Dana."

"Okay, Dana. And who are you?" she asked the man with the fist.

"Oliver. And you don't want—"

"Let's hear the plan," Victoria said, glaring at each of them in turn. "You're going to beat this young man up, and then what? Are you going to kill him, too? Like you killed my colleagues?"

"We didn't—"

"The hell you didn't! You lynched a couple hundred of my friends and colleagues. If you didn't pull the rope or pull the trigger, you stood there and let it happen. That makes you as guilty as the executioners."

"Now wait a second," someone else said. "I think that's a pretty harsh assessment."

"Goddamn right it's a harsh assessment. But harshness doesn't make it untrue. We're talking about your plans for . . . what's your name?"

"Kenny." Blood flowed from both nostrils and dripped heavily off the point of his chin.

"We were talking about your plans for Kenny. What are they, exactly, Oliver?"

The big man looked uncomfortable.

"What about you, Dana? Is the plan to kill him? Will that make it all better? Whatever pain he caused and damage he did, will bashing his brains out make any of that better? If he killed people—just as each of you has—will killing him bring any of them back to life?"

"He has to pay," Dana said.

"Why?" Victoria asked.

The question seemed to baffle Dana.

"This is what I was talking about before," Victoria said. "If we're going to move into a livable future, we have to move beyond the injuries of the past." She turned to McCrea. "Let him go," she said.

McCrea took his hands off the young man, and Kenny shook himself free.

"Get out," Victoria said to him.

Kenny gaped through his bloody face.

"Leave," she said. "Pick a compass direction and start walking."

"Where am I supposed to go?"

"Do you want to stay *here*?"

"No."

"Then walk. If you're smart, you won't come back. If you're dumb and you do come back, what happens, happens."

The kid looked terrified.

"Out," Victoria said.

Kenny wiped his nose, smearing the bloody skid mark across his cheeks and his forearm. He scanned the faces around him. "I'm sorry if I—"

"I wouldn't dawdle if I were you," Victoria said. "Sounds like you've got a fan club who'd tear you apart if they got the chance. You'd best put as much space as you can between them and you."

Kenny continued to stare, the fear in his eyes almost palpable.

"What are you waiting for?" Victoria asked.

"I really am sorry," he said.

"Nobody cares," Oliver said, apparently speaking for the group. "And the lady's right. If I can still see you in thirty seconds, I don't care what she says. I'm going to kill you."

Kenny didn't seem to be capable of grasping how dire his circumstance was. He moved haltingly, as if unwilling to save his own life.

"I can't protect you," Victoria said. "You need to go."

Finally, Kenny turned and started to jog away toward what looked to be a golf course. He'd taken only a dozen steps when he turned and yelled back, "Roger and Stony are upstairs in the Presidential Suite!"

CHAPTER TWENTY-SIX

*P*ARSONS NEEDED TO SEE FOR HIMSELF WHAT WAS GO-
ing on out there. This view was too restrictive, so he
left through the dining room door and out into the hallway beyond. The Presidential Suite was the entire top
floor of the eastern wing of the hotel—every bit of fifteen thousand square feet—and he wanted to find a
window that would allow him to see what everyone
was swarming to see.

As he stepped out of the door and turned to the left,
he saw that Stony was turning right. "Where you
going, Stone-man?"

Stony didn't turn, didn't bother to answer. He just
raised his hand high and waved good-bye.

"Stony, don't. Please don't."

"Be happy for you to join me," Stony said. "But I'm
getting out while I still can."

Parsons drew his pistol. "Don't make me shoot you,
Stone-man."

"I'll do my best not to, Champ." Still, no eye contact. "It's been a good ride."

Parsons' face felt flushed and his ears rang as he raised the pistol at arm's length and settled the front sight on the space between Stony's shoulder blades.

"If you shoot, please make it clean," Stony said. "I'm not good at suffering."

Parsons' hand trembled, and he wrapped it with his other hand to settle it down. He could do this. He should do this. Of all the betrayals he'd suffered as things collapsed around him, Stony's was the hardest to take. They'd been together since the beginning. How could Stony do this to him?

His finger tightened on the trigger.

When the gun boomed, Parsons jumped. He hadn't really intended to fire. At least he didn't think he had. At the far end of the hallway, Stony sprawled face down onto the blue carpet.

"Oh, Jesus, Stony, I'm sorry." Parsons started down the hall to tend to his old friend when Stony stirred and sat up.

"I'm okay, Champ," Stony said as he rose unsteadily to his feet. This time, he had the courtesy to look at Parsons as he said, "When you're that bad a shot, you really shouldn't have access to a gun." His eyebrows knitted together. "Don't ever pull that shit with me again."

Stony brushed himself off, straightened his shoulders, then walked out through the foyer entrance.

Parsons' stomach churned with fear. In that moment, he realized that he'd rarely been alone. He always had his posse with him—first his training team, and most recently the Manorites. Having people near-by kept the doubts away and the fear at bay. Now that he was alone—even in the first minute of his alone-ness—he felt a sense of panic blossoming.

What the hell was he supposed to do now? There was no dignity in running away. In fact, there was only shame in that. He realized that he was going to die today, either at his own hand or at the hands of others.

The courageous choice would be to blow his own brains out before anyone could lay hands on him. But he didn't think he had that kind of courage.

Perhaps he should grab a rifle and engage his at-tackers, taking as many of them down as he could be-fore they took him down.

That would be mass murder. It would be one thing if the Manorites were still here to shoot them down to protect the hotel and its resources, but in that case, with those numbers, the unarmed masses would stay away. He would win.

Now that he was alone, without any backup re-sources, he would have no chance of winning. Taking all those additional lives made no sense.

He wasn't a serial killer, after all. His mission in his own life was not to take the lives of others.

His options, then, boiled down to only two: He could run like a coward or he could die with dignity on his own terms.

Parsons turned away from the open door and went back to his mission of finding an adequate window. Two doors down from the dining room he'd been using as one of his offices, a bedroom—or maybe it was a drawing room—gave him exactly the view he wanted. No trees obstructed things now.

The crowd had parted to allow people on horseback to ooze through, and then the crowd fell in behind them. The lady in the lead had to be Victoria Emerson, but she had dismounted and seemed to be in the middle of a fight out on the lawn. Two of the others on horseback leapt from their saddles onto the ground and raised their rifles but didn't shoot.

Whatever words were being exchanged seemed angry, and then the Emerson bitch pulled someone up from the ground and tossed him to one of the guys with guns.

Holy shit, that was Kenny DeWilde! His face was a mess. The crowd looked angry, and the body language told him that Emerson was trying to be the peacekeeper, but how long could that last?

Parsons felt that he had just seen his future. And he didn't like it.

Decision made. It was time to bug out.

As Stony said, it had been a good run.

Maybe if he moved fast enough, he could somehow disappear and figure out a way to survive out there. The first thing he'd need was a bigger gun that he could better manage. He hurried back to the dining room/office and snatched up the M4 rifle that he'd propped in the corner. He knew it was loaded and chambered because he'd taken care of that detail himself. In fact every room that he frequently occupied had a rifle similarly staged as insurance against some kind of uprising.

Then, he was ready to go.

The foyer door led to an executive lobby, where no doubt there'd been elaborate receptions back in the before days. The carpet out here was still thick and lush, but it hadn't been vacuumed in weeks, and in that time the Manorites had driven the dirt deep. Beyond the reception area was the sweeping grand staircase that led to a terrace level reception area, and from there down to the executive arrival lobby, where in his mind, Parsons could see limousines lined up nose to tail as they dropped off their celebrity passengers.

That was the wrong door for him. He needed to escape from someplace remote, from a door that wouldn't take him out into the middle of the crowd.

He needed to get to the bunker. None of the people out there had ever seen the inside of the Government Relocation Center—well, except for the Manorites who had betrayed him. They didn't know where any of the blast doors were or where any of the tunnels and passageways led. If he could get there, he'd have at least some chance of ending this adventure alive.

But the bunker was a long way away, in a different wing of the hotel from the Presidential Suite. If he buttonhooked around the corner, he'd pass through the Aquatic and Athletic Centers that would dump him onto the croquet court, where a gate in the massive hedgerow would release him out to the open courtyard. That would be the shortest route from his current wing to the Antebellum Wing where the bunker resided.

With all of the security gone, there was no safe route for him to follow outside. Even inside was risky, but there were so many miles of hallway and so many hundreds of rooms, each with a door, that he could probably stay at large for a long time, just by leapfrogging room to room.

Noise in the hallway from the Athletic Center startled him. A crowd was coming, and it was a large one.

They made no effort to be stealthy. In fact, they might have been making as much intentional noise as they could.

Parsons was halfway down the second flight of stairs, stranded between floors when the noise crescendoed and the crowd broke through into the arrival lobby.

"I know this is the way," a voice said. "I know it for sure. Roger is up there."

Good God Almighty, it was Stony's voice. Stony!

"You need to be careful, though," Stony said. "He's got God knows how many guns up there."

It was too much. This level of betrayal was more than Parsons could process.

He brought his M4 to his shoulder, released the bolt and emptied his magazine through the door that separated him from the masses.

Winston McGillis was as frightened a man as Victoria had ever seen. Given Kenny's news that Parsons was still inside the America Wing, in the Presidential Suite, she'd told her team to dismount and follow her inside to take him into custody. She'd asked the rest of the crowd to stay behind, but that turned out to be as effective as petitioning the ocean to avoid the shore. She had, however, convinced most to stay behind her and her caravan, selling the point that if it came to shooting, it would be better to have the people with the return fire to be out in front.

They'd just climbed the bottom half of the gleaming marble exterior stairs when a disheveled yet well-fed man in his sixties charged out of the door. Upon seeing the approaching mob, the man considered turning and dashing back inside, but abandoned that idea right away. He put his hands up. "Please don't shoot me."

"Who are you?" Victoria asked.

"Winston McGillis. People call me Stony."

"He's with Parsons," someone said.

"I hear your boss is still inside," Victoria said.

Stony shook his head quickly, spasmodically, almost. "Yes. Yes, he's in the Presidential Suite. He doesn't want to give up."

"Take us to him," Victoria ordered.

"If I do, will you let me go?"

"One step at a time. Take us to him, and then ask me again."

"Not the most loyal friends, are they?" Luke quipped.

"We're not friends," Stony said. "Roger Parsons is a cruel man. If he knew—"

"Take us to him," Victoria said.

"He already shot at me once," Stony said.

"How come you're still alive, then?" McCrea asked.

"He's a terrible shot."

"How do we know he's not lying?" McCrea asked. "You know, to give Parsons a chance to get away?"

Victoria thought that was a very good point. But there wasn't time to dispatch people to cover all of the many exits from the hotel.

"We're going to trust him," Victoria said. "Worst case, Parsons gets away, and I'm not sure how bad a case that would be." She grabbed Stony by his biceps and pushed him in front. "Lead."

That had been three or four minutes ago. Now, Stony was leading them past an indoor swimming pool and a dark arcade.

"Are you sure you know where you're going?" Victoria asked.

"I know this is the way," Stony said. "I know it for sure. Roger is up there. He's got God knows how many guns with him."

They were still ten yards back from the big security door when the sound of gunfire shook the walls and the metal door shredded under a sustained onslaught of rapid rifle fire.

Instinctively, reflexively, Victoria dropped to her stomach at the explosions. People around her likewise hit the ground. Less than ten seconds after it started, it was over. Victoria didn't think she'd been hit—at least she didn't feel any pain and a glance over at Luke told her that he was okay as well. On the floor around her, some people stirred and others didn't. She didn't know how many had been hit, but she estimated at least five.

Among the dead lay Stony, who'd been drilled through his right cheek. The exit wound through the back of his head left no doubt that he was dead.

"Joe?" she called. "Joe McCrea?"

"Right here. I'm fine, but that was close."

"Okay," Victoria said. "Come with me. Luke, you stay back there and tend—"

"No way. I've come this far."

The wounded could fend for themselves for a while. Now that Parsons had made this a shooting war, that's the way she was going to play it.

She rose to her feet and rushed for the door, pulling it open and dropping to a knee.

"Vicky, goddammit, don't do that!" McCrea said. "That's not how you open a door under fire."

"Seemed to work okay that time," she said.

Straight ahead, the landing was empty, but a grand staircase swept up and around behind them to the next level.

She knew she'd been stupid to rush that door, and now that she'd survived the mistake, she was well aware of the dangers posed by stairs. The defenders always had the advantage on a stairwell, no matter how great the size.

"Parsons!" she yelled. "Give it up and we'll forget about what just happened. You didn't hit anyone. Stony was right when he said you were a bad shot!"

"Is it really a good idea to provoke him?" McCrea asked.

It probably wasn't, but if she could get him to expose his location, this ordeal would end sooner.

From somewhere above, she heard the sound of a door opening and closing.

Shit. "He's moving."

"Out of the way," Luke said as he darted past them and charged up the steps.

"Luke! No!"

"You guys run slower than I walk," Luke said.

He took the steps two at a time as he barreled up to the next level. Victoria and McCrea reached the three-quarters mark on the stairs when they saw him disappear into the space on the other side.

"Little sucker is fast, isn't he?" McCrea said.

A ripple of gunfire exploded from the other side of the door.

"Luke!"

* * *

Parsons didn't know what came over him when he shot at the sound of Stony's voice. Pure anger, he supposed. But now, any chance for a peaceful solution had evaporated. And he'd already decided that suicide wasn't in his repertoire. So, if he couldn't find a way to escape, there was going to be a gunfight.

At least he had a rifle now, along with sixty additional rounds of ammunition.

The only option he saw was to deploy his cat-and-mouse strategy, where he would hide in a room and wait. If someone searched the room and didn't find him, then he would wait until the searchers moved on to the next room, and everybody would go to sleep alive that night. If they did find him, then things would get far too interesting far too quickly.

After emptying that first magazine into the door, he replaced it with a fresh one and headed upstairs. He was surprised by how little time his pursuers took to get their shit back together.

He'd barely made it to the second floor when he heard the Aquatic Center door slam open. He kicked himself for not just waiting there for a few seconds more and firing on the crowd when he had a clear view.

Once on the second floor, he'd only run five or six rooms down the hall when the stairwell door opened, and someone with a rifle stepped through into the second-floor hallway.

Parsons raised the rifle as if it were a pistol and fired off five quick rounds before he ducked into room 2740, pulled the door shut and spun the deadbolt.

But the bolt didn't engage.

"Dammit." The locks were electric and the hotel didn't have electricity.

How quickly a good idea turns to a shitty idea.

As Victoria dashed into the hallway, she spotted Luke on the carpet, facedown, but rolling to his side. "I'm fine," he said. "I feel stupid, but I'm fine. He went into that room."

"Can you stand?" Victoria asked.

"I told you I'm fine." As if to prove his point, he nearly jumped to his feet as he stood. "This way."

"Stay out of the cone," McCrea warned.

"Gotcha," Victoria and Luke said together. The so-called cone of death was the area immediately in front of a door—the spot where most people stood when knocking—as exposed as a silhouette target on the shooting range. The problem was exacerbated by the fact that hotel room walls were hollow and light. Rifle bullets would pass through them as if the walls were made of paper.

They'd slowed to a purposeful walk as Luke led them to room 2740.

"You're sure this is the one?" Victoria whispered.

Luke gave an emphatic nod just before the world erupted in gunfire again. The door to room 2740 was reduced to shards and the wall across the hall was chewed to bits.

Victoria threw herself to her back, imagined what the room on the other side of the wall looked like, and she fired through it. To her right, Luke and McCrea did the same. The noise was intense, punishing, as the hallway filled with gun smoke, plaster fragments and a century's worth of dust.

When they were done, the air stung Victoria's eyes and irritated her throat.

"Everybody okay?" she asked.

They were.

Victoria dropped her empty magazine from the well and slid in a fresh one. "Ready to go in?"

"Not really," Luke said as he released the bolt to seat the first round of a new magazine.

"I'd pay a hundred dollars for a hand grenade right now," McCrea said.

Behind them, down the hall, the Fosters led a group of Ortho townspeople into the warzone.

Victoria felt stupid standing off to the side against the shredded wall as McCrea opened the demolished door. Luke had fallen to a prone shooter's position in the hallway, facing into the room, in case that was needed.

The door damn near came off its hinges as McCrea pushed it open. Inside, the room had been destroyed by the gunfire. Shattered glass from the mirror and window and picture frames littered everything.

But no one was there.

"This isn't possible," McCrea said. "*Somebody* shot at us through that door."

While McCrea and Luke searched the bathroom and closets and peered under the bed, Victoria walked to the window, where a smear of blood on the sill attracted her attention.

"I think I found him," she said, but as she peered down at the ground to see the body, she learned that there was no ground to see. The peaked roof of a breezeway extended from the floor below across to a different wing of the resort. Somehow, Parsons had managed to drop from the window to the roof without falling. As she watched, he was straddling the peak like a horse, inching his way across the 150-foot length of the copper roof, leaving a crimson streak behind him.

His shirt was wet with blood, and he was listing to his left.

"Parsons!" Victoria yelled. "Roger Parsons! Come back. You need medical attention!"

"Go to hell!" he yelled back, and he extended his middle finger high into the air.

"Are you shot?" she yelled. "You're bleeding badly!"

He raised his finger again, this time pumping it in the air.

"He's got style," Luke said.

"He's a murderer," McCrea admonished.

"He's still got style."

As they watched, Parsons stopped scooting. His shoulders sagged and he inched forward till his belly lay parallel to the ridge of the roof and he lay perfectly still as his blood meandered across the pitted copper and found its way to the rain gutter.

CHAPTER TWENTY-SEVEN

Fifteen Days Later

*A*DAM EMERSON TRIED TO PRETEND THAT HE WAS COMfortable as Emma navigated her ancient and well-shot Ford Bronco up the mountain toward the Hilltop Manor Resort. He sat in the shotgun seat while Caleb bitched from the cargo bed about being beaten to death by the bumps in the road.

Adam understood how lucky he was to still be alive. The bullet that drilled him had traveled through-and-through, making a mess of his lower bowel, but missing his liver, kidneys and spinal column. Though he hated giving Caleb the bragging rights, his little brother's efforts on the side of the road and then later on the wagon ride back to Ortho had kept him from bleeding to death. Doctors Young and Robinson had worked some kind of miracle that left a scar across his belly that made him look more like he'd survived a sword fight than a gun battle.

They wanted him to stay around Ortho for another week or two, but Adam, Emma and Caleb all agreed that it was time to reunite with the family. Even the doctors agreed that he was past the danger zone of sepsis or bleeding to death.

George Simmons had arranged to have enough gasoline pumped out of the underground storage tanks at the ruin of his gas station to fill the Bronco's tank, plus one of their three jerry cans. The other cans would remain in Ortho to serve Mike Underwood's El Camino.

The three of them were armed, but the guns proved to be unneeded. The few encampments they passed all seemed peaceful, though the presence of an actual running automobile drew a lot of attention. Adam had lost track of how many times he'd explained that the Bronco was manufactured before the time when cars had become rolling computers, and therefore was exempted from the effects of an electromagnetic pulse.

Adam knew they were getting close to the Hilltop Manor when they encountered the security checkpoint. It was manned by five people, each armed with rifles and clipboards. "Good afternoon," the guard at Emma's window said after she pulled to a stop. "Welcome to Hilltop. Are you passing through or do you plan to stay?"

A second guard appeared at Adam's window. They weren't overtly threatening, but the message was clear. Adam recognized the training marks left by Major McCrea.

"We're going to stay," Emma said.

"Welcome, then. Nice car, by the way. Lucky you. I need to know your names, and what skills you bring to the community."

"My name is Emma Carson."

The guard wrote it down on his board. "Skills?"

"I guess I'm an okay carpenter."

More writing. "No worries. If you can hold a hammer, we've got lots of work for you to do."

The guard at Emma's window nodded to the guard on Adam's side, who took his turn with the clipboard, "Same questions for you."

"My name is Adam Emerson, and my skill is—"

"Any relation to Vicky Emerson?"

"She's my mother."

"*Our* mother," Caleb corrected from the cargo bed.

"No shit?"

"No shit."

"I've heard a lot about you," the guard said. "I heard you survived getting shot, but you look better than I thought you would."

Adam exchanged smiles with Emma. "Um, thanks?"

"Go on through," the guard said. "Welcome home."

Adam had been expecting a war-torn look surrounding the Hilltop Manor, but the place showed no visible signs of violence. The once grand landscaping had been torn to shit and the lawns weren't really lawns anymore, but overall, the place looked mostly pleasant.

The grand lawn in front of the famous facade was a hive of activity as people hammered away at shelters built of various materials and in various states of completion. The presence of fifty-five-gallon drums filled with water to be used for fire suppression was enough evidence that his mom had been involved in the establishment of a new Shanty Town—a place for newcomers to build a community.

Adam wasn't sure why the hotel wouldn't suffice, but he knew there'd be a good reason.

Emma piloted the Bronco up the sweeping driveway to the base of the marble staircase and parked. "I guess this is legal," she said.

Caleb laughed. "Want me to draw a handicapped sticker and put it on the dash?"

It'd be a while before Adam's range and ease of motion returned to where it was before he was shot, and it was a struggle to get in and out of the vehicle. The old school hook-top cane embarrassed him, and Caleb made sure that the air was filled with old-man jokes at least five times per hour.

He'd just planted his feet on solid ground and found his balance when a familiar voice called, "You look like hammered shit!"

Adam rolled his eyes and smiled as Luke bounded down the marble staircase and folded Adam and Caleb both in a bear hug. "I'm really glad you're not dead," he said.

"Take it easy," Adam said. "You know I've got a hole through me."

"All he does is whine," Caleb said.

Emma came around the front of the Bronco to join the reunion. "Can I get a brotherly hug, too?" she asked.

Adam and Luke held their arms out and added Emma to the group embrace.

"I've been worried about you," Luke said.

"Good," Adam said. "There was a lot to worry about."

"Nah," Caleb said, swiping the idea aside with his hand. "They can try to kill the Emerson brothers, but it'll never work."

"Indestructible, are you?" Emma asked.

"So it would seem," Luke said.

Adam groaned. "Either of you ever heard of karma? You shouldn't say that shit out loud." He turned and looked up the steps. "Where's Mom? Does she know I'm here?"

"Yes, she knows," Luke said. "And she wants you to know she'll see you as soon as she can. Now, care to guess where she is?"

Adam and Caleb said it together: "In a meeting."

Perhaps the world was returning to normal after all.

AFTERWORD

I first pitched the Victoria Emerson thriller series to my agent and publisher in the summer of 2019, at a time when I was neck deep in finishing *Hellfire*, that year's entry in my long-running Jonathan Grave thriller series. By January of 2020, I was ready to plunge into *Crimson Phoenix*, the first Victoria Emerson book.

The one that describes Armageddon.

Then, in March of 2020, a real Armageddon arrived in the form of Covid-19. At the very time when I was imagining the feral nature of humans when they are pushed to the point of panic, every news outlet featured stories of people shooting each other over toilet paper. When hand sanitizer was considered to be a lifesaving product, people hoarded more than they could possibly use in their lifetimes, essentially flipping the bird at their neighbors and fellow citizens.

In the ensuing months, the governmental and public health agencies that were designed to protect the citizenry and help guide them through their fear seemed incapable of presenting a consistent message. Masks

were useless before they were essential, then manda-
tory before they were optional. Daily activities that
were off limits for the rest of us—trips to the beauty
parlor, dining indoors—remained accessible to the
elites of the entertainment and political classes.

After I wrote about roving gangs terrorizing honest
people in *Blue Fire*, a Portland courthouse was torched
by gangs and allowed to burn by politicians. After I
wrote of honest people having to face down lawlessness themselves in the absence of police forces, actual
police forces were vilified, defunded, and encouraged
not to intervene with lawlessness.

After I wrote in *Blue Fire* about an angry citizenry
rising up to oust politicians who seemed to care more
about their own survival than the misery of their constituents and storming the Annex, the events of January 6, 2021 happened.

Intellectually, I understand that there is no causality
in the correlation of my fiction being followed by
closely imitated fact. But there were times in this process when my lonely writer's garret got pretty small
and dark.

When it's over, though, there's a happy ending.

In *White Smoke*, Victoria Emerson brings peace to
warring factions, replaces lawlessness with accountability, and takes the first steps toward healing wounds.
In the final chapters, she says, "If we're going to move
into a livable future, we have to move beyond the injuries of the past." As I write this afterword, I feel that
America is in a dark place. People are angry. Friends
of mine consider differing points of view to be insults
rather than topics for discussion.

I really do hope that we all find a way to move beyond the injuries of the past and rediscover the sense of community that seems so elusive these days.

John Gilstrap
August 9, 2022
Berkeley County, West Virginia

If you've enjoyed this Victoria Emerson thriller,
you won't want to miss John Gilstrap's Jonathan
Grave thriller series!

Keep reading to enjoy an excerpt from the next
Jonathan Grave thriller, *Heat Seeker* . . .

Coming soon from Kensington Publishing Corp.

CHAPTER ONE

*J*oeDog GROWLED.

Jonathan snapped awake. His right hand found the cocked and locked Colt 1911 .45 right where he'd left it—right where it always was—on the edge of the nightstand. His left thumb found the switch for the muzzle light and an 800-lumen disk revealed the entirety of his bedroom.

If there'd been an intruder, said intruder would have been dead now. But the room was empty, save for him and the ever-flatulent 65-pound Labrador retriever that shared his bed tonight.

"What's wrong, girl?"

JoeDog just stood there atop the mattress, her head cocked, staring back at him. She whined.

Over the course of the next few seconds, as his heart rate slowed, Jonathan became aware that the lighting was all wrong. Deflected red, white, and blue strobes flashed through the windows on the Church Street side, painting odd shadows across the ceiling.

"Good eye, JoeDog. What's going on?"

She whined again.

Jonathan returned the pistol to its resting spot and swung his feet to the floor. He hadn't yet stood to his full height when his cell phone rang. The caller I.D. told him it was Venice Alexander. (It's pronounced Ven-EE-chay, and don't ask why.)

Jonathan punched the connect button. "Yeah, Ven. What's going on?"

Her tone was urgent. "Digger, you need to come to RezHouse." Resurrection House was a residential school for children of incarcerated parents. No one paid tuition because Jonathan paid all the bills.

"What's going on?"

"Not on the phone. You need to come up."

"Don't toy with me, Ven. It's late." Actually, he supposed that 02:43 was technically early.

"A student died," Venice said. "Overdose."

Jonathan's stomach flipped. "Ten minutes."

Somehow, JoeDog knew to hang back as Jonathan strode up the hill from the converted firehouse that served as his home and the offices for his business toward the Fisherman's Cove police cruiser that was blocking access to RezHouse. The first floor of the sprawling mansion that once served as Jonathan's childhood home now served as the administrative headquarters for the school, while Venice and her family lived on the upper floors.

A skinny teenager with a badge and a ballistic vest that weighed as much as he did stepped away from the vehicle to block Jonathan's path.

"I'm sorry, sir, but—"

Jonathan slowed but he did not stop. "Out of my way."

The cop winced a little as he prepared to physically intervene.

Jonathan cut him a break and pulled up short. "Officer, do you know who I am?"

"Yes, sir. You're Jonathan Grave, sir. But I have specific instructions to tell you that I can't let you pass."

"And so you did. Well done." He pressed past the kid.

"I'll tase you if I have to."

Jonathan spun on him, causing the young cop to take a step back.

"What's your name, officer?"

"Hoffman, sir. Kurt Hoffman."

"Are you really going to tase me, Officer Hoffman? What's your play after that? Are you going to arrest me and put me in jail? All for trying to help people who are grieving inside that house that I *donated* to the church? How do you think that's going to play?"

Hoffman gaped. He looked like he didn't want to be here anymore.

Jonathan turned away from him and started walking again. "You do whatever you think is the right thing," he said. As he continued up the hill toward the mansion and the dormitories that lay beyond it, he wondered what it was going to feel like when he rode the lightning bolt from Officer Hoffman's Taser.

Ultimately, it wasn't an issue.

Jonathan skirted the mansion and walked straight toward the dormitory farther up the hill, where the presence of an ambulance told him that that was where the action was. He was barely to the halfway mark when he was greeted by a fireplug of a man in a police uniform and gold badge. He was walking quickly, presumably to intercept Jonathan.

"Digger, you need to stop," the approaching cop said. Jonathan recognized him by silhouette alone. He'd known Police Chief Doug Kramer since their shared boyhoods. Kramer held his hands to his sides, cruciform, to block the pathway.

"Officer Hoffman already threatened to shoot me," Jonathan said. "Who the hell do you think you're dealing with?" He stopped when he came nose-to-nose with Kramer.

"I'm the friend who's going to stop you from committing a felony," Kramer said. "You need to calm down."

"I'm not spun up," Jonathan said. "Not yet, anyway, unless you keep pissing me off. Venice said somebody died."

"Yes."

"A student."

"Yes."

"Then get out of my way."

"Please, Dig. Just wait, will you?"

Jonathan took a step back and crossed his arms.

Kramer inhaled noisily and stuffed his thumbs into the top of his Sam Browne belt. "The patient is, indeed, a student. Was. Her name was Magdalena LoCicero, and she was nine years old."

Jonathan's heart sagged. "Nine?"

Kramer nodded.

"How the hell does a nine-year-old overdose in a secure facility?"

"How did you know about the overdose?"

"Venice told me. She left out the part about the age. What happened?"

"We're still—"

Jonathan held up a hand. "It's me, Doug. You're not on the record. Nobody's going to quote you."

Kramer shifted his weight from his right foot to his left. He had something to say that he didn't want to articulate.

"Screw it," Jonathan said. "I'm not doing this." He moved to push past the chief.

Kramer grabbed his biceps.

"Be careful, Doug. We haven't exchanged blows since we were twelve. I've gotten a lot better at it since then."

"You can't go all vigilante on me," Kramer said.

"I don't even know what that means."

The chief took a few seconds to sort his thoughts, then he set his shoulders. "It was fentanyl," he said. "Disguised as candy."

Jonathan felt heat rising in his ears. "So . . . what was her name again?"

"Magdalena LoCicero." Doug spoke to his feet.

"So, Magdalena died for eating what she thought was Pez?"

"I can't know what she was thinking, or what was in her heart."

Jonathan felt the kind of anger building that was never helpful and often harmful. Fentanyl was a profitable product of the Chinese Communist Party. It found unlimited distribution throughout the United States courtesy of President Tony Darmond's mandate to keep the southern borders wide open.

Jonathan knew—yet couldn't yet prove—that Darmond and his family had close financial ties to the cartels that killed tens of thousands of Americans every year.

"Who were Magdalena's parents?" Jonathan asked. The residents of Resurrection House were all products of criminal households where violence was often the rule. Harm to one always posed a threat to all.

"Robert LoCicero will never see freedom again," Kramer said. "Among other crimes, he's serving a life sentence for killing Priscila LoCicero, Magdalena's mother."

"Is Robert connected to the mob?"

"I don't know that yet. Why?"

"There's always a chance that something like this is retribution for something else. It's not just the mob. Happens with gang bangers, too. Where are Mama and Venice?"

Kramer pointed up the hill with his forehead. "In the dorm."

"How are they?"

"About like you'd expect. Distraught."

"I need to go and be with them."

As he moved to pass Kramer, the chief grabbed his biceps again.

"I thought we already had this conversation," Jonathan said.

"Dig, this is a police matter. You need to understand that. You need to *accept* that."

Jonathan cocked his head. "What's the alternative? What are you suggesting?" He had long suspected that Kramer knew more about the clandestine side of Jonathan's business dealings than he had a right to know. Jonathan and his team were not, and had never been, vigilantes. But they did have a history of bringing justice to people who had hurt others. He waited for Kramer to make the rest of his point.

"You know exactly what I'm talking about, Digger. I've seen how you react when violence cuts too close to home. You run a private detective agency and you have more money than any three police forces within a hundred miles. You need to stay out of the way and let us do our jobs."

"Duly noted. Now, either arrest me or let go of my arm."

Kramer released his grip and Jonathan resumed his walk up the hill.

As far as Jonathan was concerned, Kramer had no worries about him getting in the way of the chief's official investigation, which would inevitably drag on at a glacial pace while making sure that the perpetrators' Constitutional rights were carefully protected. Kramer would have no idea when Jonathan and his team would be running high-speed circles around him.

Kramer stayed with Jonathan step for step, but three paces behind. The police officer standing guard at the dorm's main entrance seemed confused by what he saw. As Jonathan approached, the guard's eyes focused on the chief. Whatever transpired in the silence prompted the cop to step aside.

"Thank you, Officer," Jonathan said as he passed. He wouldn't swear to it, but he was pretty sure that this was the same cop he'd seen cowering behind the front wheel well of his cruiser not too long ago as Resurrection House was under fire. The young cop was the personification of what politicians had forced police officers to become—armed eunuchs in uniforms.

The activity in the dormitory's foyer was a study in useless, unfocused meandering. Uniformed cops and plainclothes detectives postured and chatted among themselves as the house mother and the senior students, all in the same issued pale blue pajamas, tried to corral and comfort the younger children and themselves.

Somewhere in the swirl of activity, Jonathan was confident that he would find Father Dom D'Angelo, the pastor of St. Katherine's Catholic Church. In addition to his doctor of divinity diploma, Dom also carried a PhD in psychology, which allowed him to provide counsel and comfort to the traumatized children of RezHouse.

"Where are Venice and Mama?" Jonathan asked the first non-cop he saw.

The woman he presumed to be the house mother pointed to a closed door along the foyer's right-hand wall.

He pushed it open and there they were. When Jonathan saw the distress in their eyes, he found himself transplanted back decades. Jonathan's mother died when he was just a little boy, and Mama Alexander—the family's housekeeper—had stepped in as his chief disciplinarian and soother of wounds. Venice was Mama's daughter. Jonathan had known her as a cranky baby and toddler long before she became one of the most feared hackers to haunt cyberspace.

The ladies stood together from the cramped love

seat they'd been sharing. Mama got to him first and en-
cased him in a massive hug. As soon as they made
physical contact, she started to sob.

"Oh, Jonny, this is awful." Exactly one person in the
world still called him by that name. "I saw her there in
the hallway. So tiny, so young. Lordy, it tore my heart
out."

Jonathan wasn't much of a hugger. He'd hang in
there in a pinch—and this was a pinch—but he'd
rather be putting a fork in his eye. He shot a plaintive
look to Venice, who was only a click and a half more
composed than her mother.

After thirty seconds or so, Jonathan lightened his
embrace and eased Mama away. "We'll get through
this," he said. "*You'll* get through this." He kissed her
forehead and accompanied her back to the sofa and
helped her sit back down. Venice joined her.

Jonathan pulled the Ottoman away from the over-
stuffed chair on the other side of the room so he could
sit directly in front. "Tell me what happened."

Venice recapped what he already knew about the
fentanyl disguised as candy. "There were only a few in
the bag," she finished. Then, her voice caught in her
throat when she added, "Roman nearly took one."

Roman was Venice's fourteen-year-old son, and a
resident of RezHouse, placed there not because of his
parent's indiscretions, but for security concerns.

"Is he all right?" As soon as he asked the question,
he knew it was stupid. If Roman had taken the drug,
that would have been the lede.

"Yes. But he said he had a piece of it in his hand. He
was ready to eat it when he saw Magdalena collapse."

"Thank God he's okay," Jonathan said. "I'll take dumb luck and good timing any day of the week."

Mama reached over and grabbed her daughter's thigh. Gave it a little squeeze. "Go ahead and tell him the rest, Venny."

Jonathan cocked his head. "What's the rest?"

Venice cast her gaze to the floor. "Roman says he knows where the drugs came from."